R. KARL LARGENT

The Master of Sinister Fiction

Critical acclaim for Largent's *Pagoda*:

"In the penultimate (section), a scheme by two spoiled boys against the Mother Superior of their New Mexico school backfires in ways powerfully evocative of the primal childhood fears that Stephen King so successfully exploits. The last chapter undercuts the supernatural aspect of the book while reaffirming in spades its view of human corruption. Largent is a writer to watch."

—*Publishers Weekly*

Other Leisure Books by R. Karl Largent:

BLACK DEATH
THE PROMETHEUS PROJECT
PAGODA

SOMEONE — OR SOMETHING — HAD KILLED THEM

"I've never seen anything like it," I muttered.

"It's a goddamn sicko, that's what it is."

This was the part of it I had never gotten used to. I forced myself to move in closer and made a more careful assessment. Each of the incisions in the boy's chest had been made with uncanny precision. The chest cavity had been pried open and the heart removed, with each artery severed at just the precise location. It appeared as though the youth had just lain back and allowed whatever it was to take his source of life. He had a stupid, almost euphoric look on his face, like he had been viewing the whole proceeding and only when the blood quit pumping to his numbed brain had realized what was happening.

The girl hadn't fared much better. The butcher had obviously been attracted to her eyes. Consequently, she stared back at me with hollow and empty sockets, a futile, pleading look on her young face.

I shuddered and stepped back.

R. KARL LARGENT

ANCIENTS

LEISURE BOOKS ◨ NEW YORK CITY

A LEISURE BOOK®

February 1990

Published by

Dorchester Publishing Co., Inc.
276 Fifth Avenue
New York, NY 10001

Printed in the United States of America.

A NOTE FROM THE AUTHOR:

A wise man I have known for many years clings tenaciously to the belief that it is not the cataclysmic events of history that alter and shape our lives. Rather, he claims, it is the sum total of all those small and seemingly innocuous happenings and decisions that are the most important factors in defining and shaping our destiny.

I tend to agree with him.

It rained that day—not a storm, just a steady, dreary drizzle that blew foul in off the gulf. I had fully intended to journey south of the border and spend the day foolishly squandering hard earned Yankee dollars in an attempt to bolster the sagging Mexican economy, but—I hate to shop in the rain.

I sought refuge instead in a decidedly non-tourista cantina that happily concealed itself on a deserted stretch of beach miles from the teeming masses. The bar was populated by two men; one was the prototypical bartender—bold, massive in girth and the possessor of numerous chins. The other had a thick rust-colored mat of unruly hair and a lush, if tightly cropped, reddish brown beard. The latter's name was Elliott Grant

Wages. He had then, still possesses, grey-green haunting eyes that mirror his multitude of passions. Then, as now, his mind was cluttered with the trash and treasures of virtually dozens of mind-bending escapades into the bizarre, the strange, and yes, even the supernatural.

Beneath that intimidating exterior, I later discovered a sensitive human being with a rapier-like wit, a willingness to laugh at his own frailties, and perhaps most important, an undaunted zest for life—and death.

All too many years have passed since that fateful day, and Elliott and I have become quite good friends. I still marvel at his unending fascination with the dark side of man, his delight in the unexplained and his unbridled lust for things that, quite literally, go bump in the night.

A record of these events has been kept in dusty, half-forgotten journals, journals that make for enchanting, if somewhat terrifying reading. These are the stories he did not write.

On a more recent stormy night, while the wind howled and the snow swirled in kaleidoscopic patterns on the barren landscape, close by a crackling fire and fortified by Elliott's favorite Scotch, I asked the one question I had long hesitated to ask.

Would he allow me to share the contents of his journals with others?

To my utter astonishment, he said "yes."

REFERENCE: INCIDENT 1

Choker Point, Devon Island, 1 Northwest Territories
1943

EXCERPTS FROM THE TESTIMONY OF CAPTAIN LUTHER M. CARTWRIGHT, COMMANDER, HMS PERCIFIELD

"The worst of it was over! Seven days, seven of the longest days of my life. The sea was an angry woman, alright. Most of the ice had cleared the inlet, but we was still maintaining radio silence. We knew the Jerrys was there alright—them sneaky bastards . . ."

"I must remind Captain Cartwright that this is an official inquiry by Her Majesty's maritime review board and that, therefore, he will be required to maintain a decorum befitting and consistent to both his rank as an officer and the dignity and purpose of this panel. No further obscenities, please."

"Sorry, sir."

"Please continue, Captain Cartwright."

"Up until that point we had been in touch with NEAP command. They was advising us about the comings and goings of the U-boats from their base near Sonderstrom. Then when NEAP told us a Jerry was running some sixty to seventy minutes off our stern, I curled the old girl into Lancaster Sound. I figured to lay her in the inlet, hard by Carber shallows at Choker Point."

"Let the record show that Captain Cartwright is referring to the arctic supply barge, HMS Percifield. Go ahead, Captain."

"I was a fightin' her all the way, waves comin' across the bow was a runnin' twenty-two and sometimes nearer thirty foot. Winds was in excess of thirty-seven knots—recorded one peak gust right on fifty. When I got her in the shallows she settled down, but in the shallows we picked up the rains, beastly things, sheets of rain and needles of ice. I ordered the men to lace her up and shut her down."

"Can you fix the time for us, Captain?"

"Aye. The ship's log shows we dropped anchor at 0741 hours on the morning of the twentieth. That would be June, sir, this year."

"Continue, Captain."

"I was takin' my breakfast in my cabin on the morning of the twenty-seventh, when the First Mate—that being Hiram Bellows, sir, the one what testified before me—comes to tell me that the storms was abating. I already had me some indication that that be the case because of the way the old girl was a-temperin' her protests. I grabs me bundle and gear and goes topside with Bellows. Aye, it was somethin' to see, alright. It was a white ice world, hoar frost everywhere and everything coated with ice fog and sea mist. Couldn't see more'n twenty or thirty feet in front of me."

"Then what, Captain?"

"We put ashore. I wanted to find out what was happenin'. We was still under wraps; no radio, no news, no orders. Choker Point was a smoke station."

"Let the record show that Captain Cartwright is referring to a Canadian radio contact point. Smoke signal does mean designated communications point, doesn't it, Captain?"

"Aye, I'd put into Choker a number of times afore the war. That's how I knew about them shallows. It weren't much but a handful of Lutes, a supply depot for fishermen and some Kiska kids."

"Kiska kids?"

"They be Lute orphans, sir, some seven or eight of 'em. All in all, ain't more'n twenty, twenty-five people total at Choker."

"Please continue, Captain Cartwright; tell the panel what you found."

"It was deserted, sir."

"Completely deserted?"

"Aye, sir. Nary a sign of a livin' soul."

"Please tell us what happened."

"Well, we was able to get the dinghy down and the four of us—Frampton, Calderly, Bellows and me—all went ashore. Except for the ice fog, it wasn't all that bad. I'd been there in the summer of '38 and had some recollection of the place. We went to the depot first. The door was standin' open and the fog an' ice an' rains had ruined purt'near everything. We shouted and raised a real ruckus, but we couldn't roust a soul. Then Bellows found the generator—it was all froze up—and he tells me it don't show signs of operatin' for a long time.

"I sends Frampton and Calderly out to look for someone, anyone who could tell us where the depot master was. It was Calderly what found 'em."

"Let the record show that Captain Cartwright had reference to Seaman Second Class Chester Calderly of Peltville, Nova Scotia. Now, Captain, please tell us what Seaman Calderly found."

"Them Kiska kids, Sir."

"You'd better explain, Captain Cartwright."

"Like I said, them Kiska children is Lute orphans. They got an old nun what come up there thirty years ago to teach them heathens the holy book. Whenever she'd find one of them Lute children wanderin' around with nobody to look after 'em, she'd take 'em in.

"Well, Calderly was a hammerin' on the door and tryin' to roust someone, but no one was answerin'—so he let himself in. The place was a mess, especially the galley; he saw what had happened and started screamin' and yellin'. By the time Bellows and me got to him, he was stark ravin' mad, eyes all buggy and poppin' outta his head, spit comin' outta his mouth. He couldn't do nothin' but babble and point."

"Now, very carefully, Captain Cartwright, tell the panel what Seaman Calderly had discovered."

"Bones, sir. Bones and body parts. Them bones was picked clean as a whistle."

"Can you give us a little more detail, Captain?"

"Well, sir, like I said, I ain't no authority on this kinda stuff, but it appeared to Bellows and me that somethin' ate them."

"All right, Captain, this is a question of supposition. From your long experience in the Northwest Territories, would you hazard a guess as to what kind of arctic animal attacked these children?"

"That weren't no animal, sir. Animals don't cook 'em first."

REFERENCE: INCIDENT 2

Frobisher Bay, Baffin Island,
1   North Labrador Sea
1954

**EXTRAPOLATED FROM THE
OFFICIAL UNITED STATES
WEATHER BUREAU, CANADIAN
METEOROLOGICAL EXPE-
DITION WORLDWIDE
GEOPHYSICAL FILE**

My name is Doctor George R. Hastings. I am a clinical psychologist assigned to the Second Weather Wing, Northeastern Air Command, Fifth Weather Group. As a reserve officer in the United States Air Force, I was reactivated for arctic duty during the worldwide geophysical year.

I was the senior investigating officer at the Frobisher Bay incident.

The following is the chronology of events as I recorded them.

The Frobisher Bay weather detachment is a permanent weather observation out-post. It has been staffed, at various times since it was established, by representatives of the Danish, Canadian and American world meteorological agencies.

On June 3, 1954, a full strength phase three occurred at Frobisher Bay and all radio transmissions with this observation site were cut off. Subsequent readings of min and max instrumentation indicated that the detachment personnel experienced an arctic storm of the first magnitude. Despite the date and upper air charts which showed that a warm air mass and very deep low pressure area existed at the time of the phase three, the following conditions were recorded—seven inches of precipitation, mostly in the form of frozen rain, winds in excess of seventy knots, and temperature variations of almost 45 degrees. Frobisher Bay was completely obscured for almost 72 hours.

I arrived at Frobisher at 1830 hours on the night of June seven with a party of three—Captain Paul Gear of Second Weather Wing, Airman 1/C Clancy Bingham of the Goose Bay detachment, and Jules Priestly, an associate from Pennsylvania State University. Unedited copies of these gentlemen's affidavits have been prepared in support of this report.

The outpost, which was staffed by seven permanent party personnel of the Danish Weather Service, included three men and their wives plus their four children, three enlisted men, all single, and a Doctor Jana Ludvigsen of the Danish Bureau. Doctor Ludvigsen, despite her youth (she was 41 at the time of her assignment to Frobisher), was generally considered to be one of the world's foremost authorities on arctic environmental phenomena.

The detachment and its appointment and equipment were in complete disarray. It was obvious to our investigating team that there had been a struggle of significant proportions.

A generator powered walk-in refrigeration unit, serial number USAF-776523-AA, was discovered to be holding the remains of the six men. All six had been butchered and hung by their legs in the unit. They appeared to be, if you will pardon the expression, prepared for consumption. The bodies were hung right beside two frozen beef carcasses. From this, we drew the assumption that there was no shortage of meat at the time of this outrage.

The Frobisher complex includes four tarpaper constructed buildings of the billet type. One was used for married personnel and their families; one was used for single personnel. A third building contained an activities room, a kitchen, the chapel and the medical facilities. The fourth building, of course, contained the weather equipment.

Based on our discovery in the isolated

refrigeration locker, we were prepared for an assault by a force or forces unknown. Our search was then conducted with great caution, building by building.

In the day room of the activities building, we discovered the bodies of two of the three wives and the remains of Doctor Ludvigsen. All three of the women had been brutally assaulted.

In the kitchen unit we found the dismembered parts of the four children. The subsequent attempt at inventory after attempting to reconstruct the bodies, using both the dismembered parts and the clean bones, indicated that several components of those bodies were still missing.

The nature and arrangement of the cooking utensils, the desposits of dried blood and certain entrails, found frozen on the floor of the kitchen unit, indicated a surprisingly sophisticated selection of cannibalized human parts.

It was evident from our preliminary investigation that some attempt was made to save, possibly for future consumption, certain parts of the children. Apparently, this effort was aborted when two crudely fashioned containers containing those parts were found some ten miles from the Frobisher camp.

Despite the extended investigation conducted by my party and subsequent visits by other agencies of the WMO, no further details have been recorded.

We are unable to explain the following:

1. The whereabouts of Mrs. Gunther Erickson, the wife of one of the Danish detachment scientists.
2. The cause or reason for this violation.
3. The whereabouts of the perpetrators.
4. The repeated discovery of a sub-human print, not unlike that normally attributed to a species of prehistoric animal from the Cenozoic era.

REFERENCE: INCIDENT 3

Battle Harbor, Newfoundland 1965

EXCERPTS FROM THE JULY 17 CBC REMOTE COVERAGE OF THE INFAMOUS BATTLE HARBOR, NEWFOUNDLAND, CHILDREN'S MASSACRE

"Authorities today continued the grisly task of searching for more victims in this terrible scene of carnage and wanton disregard for human life. The death toll now stands at six and Pastor T. Emmett Copley, the rector of the Battle Harbor Sanctuary Church, informs me that at least three more children are still missing.

"So far, this is what authorities have been able to reconstruct from this bizarre and puzzling series of events.

"Myron Bell, the church's assistant pastor, was chauffeuring the church's youth group to this remote forest retreat when he encountered mechanical troubles. Authorities speculate that since the bus was discovered only two miles from its destination at the time of the difficulties, Pastor Bell encouraged the children to take only what was necessary and hike on to the retreat area. There is evidence the children left in two groups, one group of six led by thirteen-year-old Jenna Simmons, a church group youth leader. This group, authorities inform us, is the group whose bodies have been located.

"The second group was all boys; fourteen-year-old Donald Capers, fifteen-year-old Gaston Maccar and fifteen-year-old Ronal Breathwaite are still missing. Both Capers and Maccar are residents of the Chinchapah Boy's Home and were employed by the church to assist Pastor Bell at the retreat. Both boys, incidentally, have minor police records and are regarded by both pastors as church rehabilitation projects.

"Let me review the facts as we know them at this time.

"Battle Harbor authorities have thus far found the bodies of six children. All of the children discovered thus far have been dismembered and mutilated. In addition, there is strong evidence to indicate that some parts of the children were surgically removed prior to the mutilation. Authorities also found evidence of extensive cannibalistic activity.

"We're going to speak now to Constable

Jeffrey Hullings of the Battle Harbor investigating team and learn if authorities have developed any new theories on what actually happened here.

"You've heard my report up to this point, Constable. Is there anything additional you can tell our listeners?"

"We are still looking for the three boys. So far we haven't found any trace of them."

"Do authorities have any theories about what happened here?"

"There are two possibilities as we see it. One, that the children fell victim to some sort of cult that eats human flesh, or, second, that the three missing boys are somehow involved with this in some manner."

"What have you been able to learn from Myron Bell, the church's assistant pastor?"

"Very little. It appears that he was unable to repair the bus and that he too ventured on into the retreat area. He either arrived after the fact, or he managed somehow to escape from the perpetrators of the crime; we don't know which. He was discovered two days later wandering around in the woods north of here, completely incoherent and in a daze. He has been taken to the clinic in Chesterfield. So far we haven't been able to talk to him."

"I take it then that the authorities have completely dismissed the possibility that this could have been the work of some sort of animal."

"Yes, sir, the discovery of certain parts of some of the children would indicate that any theory involving an attack by wild animals can be completely dismissed. There is strong evidence to indicate that parts of these children were actually consumed."

"During the press briefing yesterday, there was some discussion about the unusual prints found throughout the area. Would you care to comment on that?"

"It's true that we have uncovered some unusual prints. They were structured such as to give us a strong indication that they weren't human."

"Would you describe these prints for our listeners, Constable Hullings?"

"Well . . . they are actually not unlike that of a man, but the pattern seems to indicate that there are two thumbs and three fingers—with a rather large space between the two sets."

"I see that you are being called by one of your fellow officers, Constable Hullings. Thank you."

"Well, there you have it. Authorities are still quite perplexed by the discovery. The death toll now stands at six. Three youths are still missing, and police are unable to interrogate Pastor Myron Bell about what he saw and heard here at this remote Battle Harbor forest retreat.

"This is Maxwell Rinehart reporting. Now back to our studios."

REFERENCE: INCIDENT 4
Owl's Head, Quebec

1976

THE FINAL DIARY ENTRY IN THE JOURNAL OF SISTER RHONDA RAINDAY

Brother Raymond is convinced we have no alternative. Brother Johnn and Sister Anita May are hopeless as well.

Our biggest concern is the attitude of the authorities. When the storm finally does abate, there is little doubt that they will come, and we are certain they will bring the media with them; they always do. The authorities and the media—like everyone else we come in contact with—are hostile to our effort.

Brother Raymond says it is only because they do not understand what it is we are trying to do—and I concur. I love Brother Raymond. He continues to demonstrate great wisdom. I will bend my soul to his and acquiesce to his judgment.

We were gone a mere 18 hours. It is a difficult journey because we must walk. The rock road had washed out for the second time this year, and the people of Livingston will not allow us to pass through their village. That is such a shame because we could market our wares there if only those people would open their hearts and minds to us.

The shock of the discovery upon our return is beyond all my descriptive powers. Even now it is difficult for me to accept the reality of what has happened.

There were four in all—Gentle, the five-year-old, Sweet Jasmine, his sister, and my own sweet fruits, David and Anna Child. None of them had witnessed more than eight summers.

They were mutilated. Oh, sweetest Jesus, how could anyone do this to the children? How could anyone outrage and violate these most precious vessels of love and innocence?

Brother Johnn found young Gentle. He had been decapitated. Sweet Jasmine had been violated, her woman-child parts eviscerated. David and Anna Child were similarly treated and then dismembered. There is strong evidence—my heart tears at the thought of this unholy desecration—that they were cannibalized.

Sister Paula was the first; may her soul rest in the everlasting light of the Almighty. Brother Johnn accepts her wrenching anguish as sufficient reason for the taking of her own life. After all, young Gentle was her first born.

It is Marry Marry and Dawn that I and the others cannot, as yet, find the inner strength to forgive. They fled. They were older. The children were left in the safety and sanctuary of their love. They abandoned their charge; they have left us with our hopes dashed, our children murdered and our prayers unanswered.

So it has come down to this. Perhaps Brother Raymond is right, perhaps man cannot live in peace. Perhaps there is no hope for that gentle faction of sweet Jesus's people who would live without war and hunger and inhumanity.

I will do as Brother Raymond bids me. I will drink because I am as one with my universe. I will drink this because it will free my tortured soul to renew its quest for all that is good and just and right and peaceful. . . .

Researcher's note:
A crudely penciled notation was found at the bottom of the last page of the original copy of this diary:

"This journal was discovered at the mass suicide site of the members of the Owl's Head commune known around these parts as the Coalition. The evidence indicates these sick bastards

disembowled and ate their own kids before they killed themselves. Sick as it is, maybe it's all for the better. We don't need their kind around these parts anyway."

PART 1

Cosmo shoved the stack of papers back at me, went through the ritual of stoking and relighting his pipe, then puffed and exhaled softly. I knew he was stalling. Cosmo always stalled; he hates to commit himself. If he committed himself, he was fixed with that commitment in time and space, a position Cosmo Leach found intolerable, a position he wished devoutly to avoid.

"Well," I grunted, "what do you think?"

"Intriguing," he granted, hiding behind another puff.

"Is that all you have to say?" It was Cosmo's game and I had to let him play it out. I had been doing so for years.

"Tell me, Elliott." (Cosmo always calls me

Elliott when he's about to torpedo me.) "Where did you come up with this shit? It reads like something out of one of those supermarket rags."

This time I had him. "Does the name Brenda Cashman mean anything to you?"

He rolled his faded blue eyes and curled a few strands of his bushy white beard around his index finger while he referenced the name. "Sounds familiar. Why? Do I know her?"

"She was your graduate research assistant three years ago. You gave her excellent academic references when she applied to the University of Michigan for their doctoral program."

"Oh, yes, now I remember," he lied. In 30 years of banter, both serious and light-hearted, I have never known Cosmo to admit being wrong or forgetful. His ego just won't permit it. But the ravages of time were coming down on him and occasionally it showed. "What's all this have to do with her?" he grunted.

I leaned back, riffled through the stack of papers and asked myself how much further I wanted to push this whole affair. "Brenda Cashman sent me these documents. She said she was doing some research and ran across the first incident, the report from Choker Point. She said she poked around some, but she wasn't able to uncover anything else on it."

"We were fighting a war," Cosmo reminded me. "We were too damn busy to tie nice tidy little bows around lots of things."

I ignored the old man's caustic remarks and continued. "It's all here in her letter. A couple of months later, she uncovered the Baffin Island incident. She thought she saw some similarity in the two events and sent them to me."

"Why you?"

"Damn it, Cosmo, because I write about stuff like this," I snapped back at him. "Just once, step out of your role as resident curmudgeon and help me sort through all of this."

Having a mentor like Cosmo Leach is never easy, but then, we don't always have the luxury of selecting our mentors; sometimes it just happens. You wake up one morning and there they are, warts on their nose and all. Such was the case with me, Elliott Grant Wages, and one Doctor Cosmo Lorimar Leach. The world famous anthropologist and social psychologist was nothing more than a "required attendance" date on my lecture series calendar during my senior year in college, and since that was the year of Gibby Marshall and lots of all night parties, I was sweating out a passing grade in Cultural Anthropology. At any rate, I went—and I was fascinated by the old fart. Maybe enchanted is a better word. At any rate, I hung around the podium until the lecture hall had cleared and did something I had never done before. I informed the grizzled old codger that I enjoyed what he had to say.

In what I've come to learn as the typical Cosmo Leach acerbic manner of fielding compliments, he informed me that he appreciated my kind remarks but that he was equally convinced that a good 80 percent of what he had to say went over my head.

Surprisingly enough, that was the beginning of our relationship.

Cosmo is somewhere in his seventies and does not fall into the category of lovable old man. His red and wrinkled face emerges above a fleecy white beard like a cloudy sunrise. He has a bulbous nose and mean little green-blue eyes which are hard to read. That's because they are usually hidden behind quarter-inch-thick, tinted lenses encased in an outlandish pair of black and blue striped plastic frames. His mouth is hidden by the aforementioned beard, and long strands of stringy white hair flare out from his partially bald head to conceal too large ears. He is ornery, chauvinistic, vitriolic, brilliant and bullheaded. And, as you can plainly see, I treasure the old fart. No man studies another unless there is something there that he admires, and I've been studying Cosmo Leach for a long, long time.

"So, where did the other two events come from?" he harumphed.

"I stumbled across them."

"That's the kind of research I'd expect out of you," he bristled. "What makes you think they're related?"

"What would you think?" Answer a question with a question; it's an irritating little trick I learned from Gibby Marshall, and professors hate it.

"I think you're beginning to believe this dark fantasy crap you write about, Elliott."

"I hate to be obvious, Cosmo, but all you have to do is look at the evidence. Each time the focus of the incident is on children. Can't you see the pattern?"

"Pattern?"

"Sure." I hastily sketched out a map loosely resembling the cluttered mass of islands and waterways that represented the vast Northwest Territories. "Now, trace it—from Devon Island, down and over to Baffin Island. Then you go down the coast to Newfoundland and finally over to Quebec. If a person were following the coastline, they're damn near equidistant from each other. And surely you can't help but notice that these events have all happened exactly eleven years apart."

Cosmo was back to sucking on his pipe, but this time it was different. Now he was listening, and despite the glower, I could tell he was intrigued. "I suppose you've already developed some half-ass theory to support your pathetic little fistful of what you call research?"

"I have," I admitted, "and if I'm right, we're about to get another visit from these whatever they are. In fact, the way I have it figured, it could happen any day now. All four of the previous attacks happened in the summer, and that, my crusty old friend, is exactly what we're smack dab in the middle of—the summer of '87."

Cosmo harumphed. "Could be," he acknowledged.

Despite the somewhat questionable nature of my literary efforts, I have been the "writer-in-residence" at good old Saint Francis for over four years now. There is little doubt that the august little institution would prefer to have someone of more significant literary fame, but it is a small Catholic college, and we all know that small Catholic colleges can't afford to pay much.

Still, the affiliation has its advantages. The campus is a delight with lovely jewel-like little lakes, tall stately trees and the true aura of academia. It is endowed with a magnificent library which rivals that of some of our larger state institutions, and the environment is conducive to writing. Lastly, the good order of Sisters is both lenient and flexible when it comes to my lecture schedule.

So, after leaving Cosmo in his upstate New York retreat, I hustled back to Saint Francis and began systematically plugging all my facts, assumptions and out-and-out wild-ass guesses into my hypothesis. The once laborious chore was made a whole lot easier by virtue of the fact that most of the data could be formatted and plugged into my computer. It's an Apple and, as the high tech world of electronics goes, a somewhat outdated piece of gear. Nevertheless, it has become such an integral part of my life that I consider it, in order of importance, right along with the other items in the E.G. Wages never-go-anywhere-without-it survival kit.

It's virtually impossible to read every item about every bizarre incident that goes on in our old world on any given day. So, pushing my theory a little, I confined myself to two geographical areas. I did this on the assumption that the "things" (because I don't know what to call them at this point in time) would pop up somewhere similar to the areas in which the previous events had been recorded. I plotted two possible locations, equidistant from the site of the incident at the Coalition commune.

Admittedly, these were arbitrary locations at best, but they seemed logical to me. One of the locations would be Camptown, Maine—but that would require the "things" to cross water. So far there wasn't any evidence to support the fact that they could accomplish such a feat unless, of course, the waterway was frozen. The other point dovetailed even better into my theory and was even closer to my profile of the first four—somewhere in the vicinity of Chambers Bay, a relatively remote section of Ontario on Lake Superior.

For the next several days, I relegated myself to a steady diet of satellite news transmissions from television stations emanating from the Detroit-Toronto-Thunder Bay triangle. Under most circumstances, this would have been an awesome assignment, but it's not too bad when you can hire two destitute and money-grubbing graduate students to assist in the project. When they weren't watching television and taking notes, I had them monitoring the wire services. My premise was simple—if a bunch of "things" started eating people, the press services would hop on the story like a free lunch.

On day five, I struck pay dirt. Lucy, one of my graduate groupies, was pounding on the door of my condo at a little past seven in the morning. I didn't even have an opportunity to offer her coffee before she blurted out her news. She had located the Reverend Myron Bell, former Associate Pastor of the Battle Harbor Sanctuary Church. He was, she reported, institutionalized more or less in a church-sponsored nursing home in Saint Anthony in New-foundland. And there, she informed me with a grin, the housekeeper reported he had long periods of lucidity.

I knew that any investigation of any event, especially one that occurred more than 20 years ago, hinges in large part on the integrity of the records that were kept on that event. The best we can hope for when we're searching back through the records is that someone took the time to thorough-ly document the component parts of that incident without bias. By the same token, an investigation is equally dependent on the determination of the individual. He has to dig and dig and dig, be willing to play a hunch or two, and now and then follow a long shot. Tenacity is the key. And as any researcher knows, be resilient. There are a helluva lot of dead-end roads out there. The discovery of the whereabouts of Myron Bell was a real plus. Now I wasn't totally de-pendent on records. I was going to be able to talk to someone who had actually lived through one of these incidents. I didn't know which I could put the most faith in— the records, or the often fallible human memory.

Armed with Lucy's welcome input, some telephone numbers, an overnight bag and my survival kit, I booked Air Canada to Saint John's, a provincial shuttle to Deer Lake, and rented a car for the long journey to Saint Anthony.

The nursing home itself sat high atop a craggy bluff overlooking a small inlet on the Strait of Belle Isle. My arrival was greeted by shrill winds, high seas and chilling temperatures that were destined to hold the tourist traffic to an absolute minimum. Saint Anthony itself—and particularly Dormain House where Myron Bell reportedly spent his tortured hours and endless days—was an austere and somber and un-inviting world.

If the setting of Dormain House was intimidating, Mrs. Lancaster was just the opposite. She was a warm, round, white-haired lady of uncertain vintage who was quick to seat me in the parlor and offer me tea and crumb cake.

"You've come a long way, Mr. Wages," she said smiling. I had the distinct impression Mrs. Lancaster had very few opportunities to display her hospitality.

My previous contact with the woman had been confined to a brief telephone conversation that had in fact confirmed Myron Bell's residency and that I would be able to talk to him if I made the journey. Outside of that, I had no assurances that I was going to learn anything over and above what was contained in the text of the CBC transcript. Consequently, I was anxious to get on with it. "How is Reverend Bell?"

"You are fortunate," she assured me. "He

seems quite at peace these days. He has been intensely devoted to his scripture over these past several weeks."

"Does he have bad times?"

The woman's pleasant smile faded, and she nodded dourly.

"When may I see him?"

Mrs. Lancaster finished her tea, stood up and motioned for me to follow. We left the warmth of the parlor and walked down an austere corridor with a series of varnished hardwood doors. She stopped at the last one on the left and knocked quietly.

Myron Bell's door isn't the first door I've passed through only to be astonished. Perhaps that's because my mind paints elaborate mental images of things as I expect them to be under a set of given circumstances. At any rate, I was expecting the worst—after all, Myron Bell had been through the worst—but there he sat, a cherub of a man with a round soft face, beaming broadly. A massive, gilt-edged volume of the Bible was perched precariously on his robed lap. For some reason, he was younger than I had anticipated—late forties to early fifties—and he was confined to a rickety old wheelchair.

"This is the man I told you about, Reverend Bell, the American. Won't you say hello to Mr. Wages?"

The reverend extended a pudgy, too white, too soft hand in greeting. All traces of masculinity had vanished. "How do you do, Mr. Wages." His greeting was soft, almost musical. "Am I correct in assuming that you're here to talk about Battle Harbor?"

The question surprised me. Obviously I wasn't the first one to follow this path. "How did you know?"

The man sighed, laid his book aside and wheeled his chair over to the window overlooking the churning waters of the strait. "Because that's the way of things; it's my destiny. You see, Mr. Wages, I hope I don't offend you, but every so often, someone, usually a writer, uncovers that sordid little piece of provincial history. That discovery is usually followed by a visit to Saint Anthony to see what else they can learn."

My ego had been abruptly deflated.

"You see, Mr. Wages, it's really quite a shame that I'm remembered for being a part of one of our darker hours, because the truth is, I have so much more to offer. I'm really a quite knowledgeable Biblical scholar. I have had a great deal of time to study the holy word. There is much I could tell you of things far more important than the tragedy at Battle Harbor."

I was disarmed. Hostility or senility I was prepared for and could have handled, but I wasn't prepared for this lucid, gentle soul that had survived a tragedy and was forced to relive it each time someone paging through history discovered it. I glanced over at Mrs. Lancaster; she understood and smiled compassionately.

"Tell me, Mr. Wages, what is it you want to know about Battle Harbor?"

"I have the transcript of the remote coverage of the CBC and a few newspaper clippings. Outside of that I must admit that I don't know a great deal."

The little man didn't look at me. His gaze was still fixed on the watery panorama spread out before him. "It was a terrible thing," he whispered, "all those sweet, lovely children with their innocent bodies mutilated. Do you understand that they were budding temples of our Savior, and they were desecrated and defiled?"

"I don't want you to relive that part of it, Reverend Bell. I'm more concerned with what you felt, what you observed, the experiencing of it."

The reverend was still not looking at me. Instead he seemed to be reflecting back on that day. His soft, unlined and peaceful face was a deception, hiding the real torture that lived in his mind. "I went back, you know. I went back several times. Then the holy mother church decided I should come here to Dormain to study."

I was doing all I could to keep my own voice on an even keel without stress or anxiety. "What were your impressions?"

"It was very strange, Mr. Wages. There

was more to it than just the mutilation of those lovely children. There was something else, something very ominous. You could feel it and see evidence of it—the way the bark was stripped off the trees, the way things were smashed. It was a scene of total devastation. Everything was dead—trees, animals, even the flowers." His voice trailed off, and he began to sob.

"I take it from what you've just said that the three boys had nothing to do with the murder of those children?"

"Oh, no, Mr. Wages. The authorities had nothing else to go on. For a while they were inclined to suspect young Capers and Maccar had enticed the Breathwaite boy to join them in the despicable act, but I personally never supported that theory."

"Were the boys ever found?"

Bell sighed and shook his head. "Not to my knowledge," he said sleepily. His eyes were beginning to drift shut, and his head nodded. Mrs. Lancaster discreetly cleared her throat, a signal that, for the moment at least, my conversation with the Right Reverend Myron Bell was at an end. Despite her bulk, she gracefully maneuvered us out of the room without disturbing the slumbering man.

Writing fiction, for the most part, is a crawl-off-in-some-dark-corner and do-your-duty kind of thing. Most of the writers I know write because they have no choice; it's what my friend Cosmo Leach would call obsessive-compulsive behavior. Writing, I have discovered, since I became addicted to it at a very early age, is very much like being hooked on anything. I have known both men and women who were addicted to sex; some of them would screw anything, anywhere, anytime, for any reason. Others get hooked on alcohol, drugs, even their careers. It doesn't seem to matter much; if they're hooked, they're hooked. I'll admit to being hooked on telling a story.

The problem with this view is that it is a far too narrow perspective of the phenomenon known as an addiction, and it is an unbecoming assessment of a perfectly acceptable way of making a living. There is the rewarding side of being a writer—and that is, of course, the good story. And the session with Myron Bell only served to convince me that I was onto one.

I worked my way back to Saint John's, my tape machine in one hand and one eye on the often spectacular scenery. I stopped in the port city just long enough to exchange pleasantries with an old college chum and then crawled onto a flight for New York. Somewhere during the course of all of this, I made a mental note to call Brenda Cashman to see if she had come up with anything new on her project and another note to sic one of the graduate students on digging up more information on the Coalition commune in Owl's Head. Based on what I knew so far, the two girls who deserted their charge and fled the commune, the three boys from Battle Harbor and the wife of Gunther Erickson had just disappeared. Were they dead? I had no way of knowing. But if they were alive and if they could be located (two very big "ifs"), they would certainly be able to shed some light on what happened in each of the incidents. Like I said, every now and then you've got to be willing to follow a hunch and chase a long shot.

During my New York layover I had lunch with my agent, Elaine Goldman. Elaine is the mother of two, a self-confessed workaholic and one of the few people willing to try to peddle my wares in the unfriendly canyons of the Big Apple. I told her what I was working on and received my customary lecture on going home and writing instead of flitting around the countryside chasing the ghosts of kid eaters. The lecture, as usual, was delivered over a seafood salad at the noisy bar at Squints in the Village. Ten minutes later I was standing on the curb waving goodbye as Elaine hopped into a taxi and roared off in pursuit of an unwary publisher. Brief as they are, these touchstone visits with Elaine are vital to my self-esteem; she is the validation of the fact that I write for a living. I feel even more validated when she sells something.

The transition from New York to the campus of Saint Francis is a great deal like plunging head first into a time warp. It was dark by the time I pulled up in front of the condo complex. I stumbled up to the second floor, dragging my survival kit and the overnight bag, plunked them down in the foyer and went directly to the answering machine. There were three messages.

The first one was from the "call lady" (we had a lengthy discussion one time on why she shouldn't call herself the "call girl") of our local writers group informing me that the monthly meeting was postponed. The second was from Brenda Cashman, and the third from a growling Cosmo Leach who was more than mildly irritated that I wasn't there to snap up the phone and hang breathlessly on his every word. It was after nine o'clock, which meant that Cosmo had already retired to his study for the evening and wouldn't answer the phone even if I returned his call. Ergo, I called Brenda. To my surprise, it was a local number, and she answered on the third ring.

"I came to see you," she said in a voice surprisingly husky for a woman I had pictured as sounding much younger.

"You're lucky you caught me. I've been out of town."

"It was a long shot," she admitted. "Did you get the clippings I sent you, and did you find them interesting?"

"Yes to both of your questions."

"Were they interesting enough that you'd like to know more?"

"Interesting enough that I invested several hundred bucks in airline tickets, rental cars and motel bills to spend a few minutes with what's left of Myron Bell."

"And?" she pushed. Brenda Cashman was fast establishing her reputation with E.G. Wages as one very aggressive female. Already she was interrogating me, and I hadn't even met the woman. "So what did you learn?"

"Nothing! Something! I don't know yet. I'm still thinking about it."

Her next question was right out of left field. "What do you drink, Mr. Wages?"

Questions like that have a tendency to leave me speechless. Over the years, my bachelor lifestyle has allowed me to become a pretty private sort of person; most folks sense that and keep their distance. Still, when a question is asked, I feel obliged to respond. "Scotch. Why?"

"Me, too. I'm a Scotch drinker. Haul out a bottle of your best 'cause I'm on my way over. I've got something to tell you."

There was a time when I would have been absolutely enchanted and perhaps even salivated at such a proposal, but that was another time and another place—and I think even another world. The truth is, after a day of battling New York traffic and United Airlines, a hot soapy tub, four ounces of my trusty Black and White splashed over an equal amount of shaved ice and some peace and quiet sounded decidedly more appealing. Besides, I needed the opportunity to review all those brilliant observations I had so cleverly poured into my little recorder. On balance, all of the above far outweighed exchanging whatever with someone called Brenda Cashman.

"I have a better idea," I countered, albeit a little weakly.

"I'm open to suggestions."

"There's a terrific little breakfast restaurant on High Street, two blocks down from Elmore—world class biscuits and gravy. I'll meet you there at eight o'clock tomorrow morning. I'll be the one who looks like his beard is rusty."

"I know what you look like, Mr. Wages." She giggled, hung up and left me with that irritating buzz that goes hand in hand with an empty line.

Later, while soaking in my tub and sipping my Scotch, I paused to wonder what I had passed up.

Brenda Cashman was one of those wispy, moon-child-looking females you see in perfume advertisements for fragrances with masculine names. She had soft, shoulder-length auburn hair and deep, liquid lime-green eyes that could penetrate granite. She was willow thin and wore a chic one piece olive-colored jumpsuit that concealed every female feature.

She demolished her plate of sausage gravy, then started on what I couldn't finish.

The exchange of pleasantries was unusually brief, and within a matter of minutes she vaulted headlong into the personal aspects of her life. She was 29 years old (I would have guessed younger), a doctoral candidate at Ann Arbor in the field of anthropology, never married, twice engaged, and flat broke. Along the way she avoided any mention of her family, her hometown and any other references to a life prior to her association with Cosmo Leach. She'd arrived on time (a plus with E.G. Wages) with a battered rust-colored portfolio that she carefully guarded on the seat beside her.

Only once did she fumble. She began a slavish proclamation that she had read everything I had ever written, and that if such things could be measured, she was in fact probably one of my biggest fans.

The great Cosmo Leach once endowed me with a great one-liner for such occasions, and it seemed appropriate to haul it out. "Miss Cashman, you're full of bullshit." Having demonstrated my Leachonian vocabulary, I continued. "If we're going to have an adult, semi-intelligent conversation, let's start with the premise that we're going to be honest with each other. Okay?"

Score one for E.G. She winced, blushed, intensified her fragile smile and sagged back in the booth; she looked a little more relaxed. "I wanted you to like me. The truth is, I do like the stuff you write—and the truth is, I haven't read everything simply because I didn't discover you till I ran into our mutual old grump, Cosmo. He's the one that told me about you."

I reached across the table in a gesture of conciliation. We shook hands and settled down to the business of talking about our mutual interest.

"So tell me, Brenda Cashman, how did you develop this bizarre little theory of yours?"

"Research," she said cryptically. "I was fascinated with the social structure of some of the nomadic cultures of the Northwest Territories. My thesis advisor suggested that some of the military and maritime records were untapped sources of unbiased information. I was focusing on the Lutes when I ran across the Baffin Island incident. I don't know why it occurred to me to send those two pieces of information to you, but I got curious when I couldn't get through to you on the phone and ended up contacting the only other person that knew us both."

"Good old Cosmo."

"Precisely! He said you talked to him and that you had come up with some additional information, all of which only served to make me more curious."

"I can guess the rest, but I have to ask, why me?"

"Cosmo Leach, serendipity—I don't know. Maybe it's because Doctor Leach spent one whole lecture on you. I just happened to be reading your *The Terror of Teacup* at the same time he dumped that lecture on us. Knowing Cosmo, he probably never told you, but he's quite a fan of yours, too."

I ingored Brenda's assessment of Cosmo's opinion. I knew the old fart well enough to know that his opinion could change with nothing more than a little gas on the stomach. "Let's vault right into your conclusion. You discovered some pretty weird stuff in some dusty old books. How convinced are you that there is anything to all of this?"

"There's something to it, all right. I can feel it."

I took a sip of coffee and agreed with her. "You're right. There's something going on here, but I just don't know what yet. What I do have to ask you is, why share it? Why not track it down yourself?"

"Money," she said simply. "I'm broke. I can't even afford to pay attention."

"So you want me to follow up on this?"

"Precisely, but only if you think it's worth the time and effort."

I started to laugh. Brenda Cashman was a cagey one; she knew I was hooked. It was simply a case of reeling in the line, and I was all too aware that she had already started. Still I had to ask. "I'm missing something here. Suppose I do follow up on this, and it turns out to be one helluva story. What do you get out of it?"

The Cashman smile had gone from manufactured to genuine; I was talking her language. "Two things," she admitted. "You follow up, and if this leads where I think it leads, you've got yourself one spine-tingling, dark fantasy in the making. Then, while your publisher is doing his thing, I use the same data to write my obscure, albeit sensational thesis and complete the requirements for my doctorate."

"Intriguing bit of chicanery," I admitted. In truth, it's a little tough to negotiate nose to nose with someone who's broke and struggling to get their credentials. Only a prick would chip away at an offer like hers, and I wasn't feeling prickish on this particular morning. "So, let's see what it is that triggered your trip to Saint Francis."

She hauled out the bulky, oversized portfolio and reached into a side pocket, emerging with two pieces of paper. She unfolded them and slid them across the table.

The first was datelined Chambers Bay, Ontario. Just the location of the report triggered a couple of extra beats in my old pulse rate. Actually it was nothing more than a filler item, the kind the layout folks use to balance out the copy on a page of newsprint. The brief paragraph detailed how a local lad in the vicinity of Chambers Bay had discovered two of his prize sheep, mutilated and half-eaten, amidst a scene of extensive destruction in the woods adjacent to his father's farm. I reread the item twice and handed it back to her. It was a long way from being conclusive evidence in support of anything.

The second item had more substance to it. Only this time it was a horse and, according to the article, a big horse. The article indicated the big animal had been killed and eaten on the spot. Again there was the mention of extensive damage to the surrounding countryside, but there was a kicker in this report. Authorities reported finding unusual animal prints over the entire area. The prints were described as being quite large, almost 14 inches in span and yet quite similar to that of a human—except that there were three fingers and two thumbs.

Brenda was reading the article right along with me. "Ta da," she said musically when I came to the punch line. "Harken back ye skeptics to the Battle Harbor CBC report . . . 'two thumbs, three fingers with a rather large space between the two sets'."

It was my turn to slump back in the seat. From there I stared at her over the breakfast clutter. In my mind it was no longer a loose set of somewhat similar incidents. We suddenly had a tie-in. "What kind of animal has two thumbs and three fingers?" I muttered.

Brenda went back to her battered case and fished out a Xerox copy of an article from *National Geographic*; the subject was Australia, and it featured the koala bear. "They do," she said triumphantly.

"A koala bear? Come on, koalas are cuddly little things."

"I didn't say it was a koala bear. I simply said there is such an animal—one that has two thumbs and three fingers."

The E.G. Wages penchant for trivia was emerging. I was reaching back into one of those dark convolutions of my cluttered mind, trying to remember what I knew about koala bears. As I recalled, koalas aren't really bears. They're marsupials, and they have some sort of strange ability in their digestive systems to convert toxic substances to food value. Koalas. My mind was spinning.

"Well, Mr. Wages, have we got something here, or have we got something here?" There was a definite smirk on her face.

"It's two weeks till the fall semester

starts. I suppose I could take a little jaunt up to Chambers Bay and poke around."

"When do we leave?"

"Whoa! Wait a minute! I don't recall . . ."

"No, you wait a minute, Elliott Grant Wages; it's my research, my idea, my theory. There's no way you can shut me out now."

"But I . . ."

Again she cut me off. "Go back to the beginning. I said I wanted two things. You get your book, and I get my thesis—that's one. Number two is—I go with you." With that she made one final swipe of her plate with the bottom half of her biscuit, jammed it in her mouth and gave me a contrived smile. "I'm ready when you are."

PART 2

There are two ways to get to Chambers Bay. You can fly into Thunder Bay and backtrack—or commit to 17 long hours behind the wheel over the Mackinac and take the southern leg of the Transcan. The population gets pretty sparse north of the Sault and thinner still after you put Wawa behind you. It's not exactly what you would call primitive country, but full-fledged city folks might well find it a tad intimidating.

Brenda, who admitted to a fair amount of cross-country wandering in her earlier days, seemed quite at ease with a landscape dotted by jewel-like lakes laced together by pine forests as far as the eye could see. At Turpin we turned south off of the main road and followed the lake shore road to a small motel that obviously catered to fishermen. The late August sun was just beginning to dip behind two craggy outcroppings off of Tacker Point when we finally stopped.

The young man behind the desk was tall and too slender, with long wavy red-brown hair parted down the middle. He had haunting, deep-set brown eyes that peered out from their hiding place under a prominent ridge that traversed the width of his forehead. He was the possessor of a full, sensuous mouth that seemed somehow to be curved into a permanent pout, and his unusual clothes hung straight down much like they would from a wire hanger. On balance, and I hate to use this word in describing a man, he was "beautiful." He eyed Brenda with a peculiar kind of envy.

"Any rooms left in the inn?" I chirped.

The young man nodded without uttering a word and pushed an old-fashioned desk ledger across the surface at me.

"I'll need two rooms," I announced, louder than necessary. I had no intention of giving anybody an excuse to call me a lecher. Actually, I've known a lot of couples with a greater age disparity than my traveling companion and yours truly—but that was their problem, not mine.

Our silent and sullen desk clerk produced two keys, laid them on the registration desk and promptly disappeared behind a draped doorway behind the desk. He had accomplished the whole sign-in process without speaking or, for that matter, without changing his expression.

Brenda, to my amazement, hadn't said anything either. Somehow, I had the feeling she was holding back.

I managed to get our luggage out of the crammed little Z and carry it down the row of dingy doors badly in need of a good coat of paint. The room numbers were designated by shiny little black plastic numerals, the kind that could be purchased in any dime store. I gave Brenda the key to number seven, and I took number eight. We were inside before I realized that the two rooms were connected, again by a draped doorway. The young woman must have detected a look of consternation. "Don't worry," she flipped, "I promise not to peek."

My instructions were simple; do whatever it is you have to do to freshen up, and we'll crawl back in the car and search out something to eat. I didn't tell Brenda, but I wasn't holding out much hope that we would find some unknown culinary wizard practicing his cooking magic in some undiscovered hideaway on the bay. The truth is, I was going to be more than grateful for any warm food, a hot shower and a good night's sleep.

Three-quarters of an hour later, darkness had arrived, and we had cased out the

village of Chambers Bay. It consisted of one
stop light, three churches, five taverns, a
public pier, a combination constable's office
and volunteer fire department, four stores
(one bait, one hardware, one variety and one
drug), two gas stations and three restau-
rants (two of which were closed).

Our only choice was a diner about a
quarter of a mile from the motel. Inside we
found a booth that looked out over the
darkened bay. The waitress, as it turned
out, was one notch above the sullen young
clerk back at the motel; she didn't smile, but
at least she could talk.

From the series of lighted signs and advertisements littering the grubby walls, I
easily determined that the house specialty
was Moosehead and that there was no limit
to the variety of ways they could serve it.
Considering it a challenge, I taxed the
scowling barmaid with an order for two
bottles, chilled, opened and poured in
glasses. I'm sure the woman did her best,
but the Moosehead was no better than lukewarm. Brenda didn't seem to mind, so I let
the matter rest.

"Somehow I had it pictured a little
different from this," she admitted.

I gave her the stock E.G. Wages quizzical
look.

"Oh, you know, successful author, cock-
tail parties, the beautiful people hanging on
your every word." She looked around the

dingy room, and her pretty mouth curled into a portrait of disappointment. "This place is the pits!"

"This is where we think the story is, remember?"

Before she could respond, the room was suddenly filled with a barrel-chested mountain of a man with several chins, squinty blue eyes and a mop of unruly dishwater blond hair. He towered six foot four or five and strained his faded chambray shirt to the maximum. He didn't need an invitation. He headed straight for our booth, leaned over and extended a grizzly-sized paw in greeting. I wouldn't have been a bit surprised if the ham-sized appendage had sported two thumbs and three fingers.

"Howdy, folks. I'm Constable Madden, but everyone calls me Jake." With that opening volley he was already leading two to nothing. Jake Madden was a Chambers Bay marvel—he could both smile and talk.

"Evening, Constable." My own response sounded inordinately stuffy compared to Brenda's.

She was gushing. "Hi, Jake." She hauled out her dewy-eyed smile, shifted slightly in the booth and batted her eyes. Big Jake promptly forgot about me.

"You folks just passin' through or plannin' to stick around a couple of days and do a little fishin'?"

"May do a little fishing," I acknowledged.

"Just passing through," Brenda informed him. The answers came out almost simultaneously.

Madden laughed. "Funny," he countered, still smiling, "I got the impression you two were traveling together." With that he lowered himself into the booth next to Brenda and signaled the waitress for another round. With three fresh ones sitting in front of us, he eased back, shoved his hat back and sighed expectantly.

Over the years, I've developed a lot of habits—some good, most bad. Generally speaking, I'm somewhat cynical and almost always skeptical about people I meet, but Jake Madden had an entirely different effect on me. It was instant like; there was something about the man. I knew this when I heard myself actually blurting out our reason for being there. "I do research and Miss Cashman here is similarly occupied."

"What kind of research?" Jake grunted.

"Local lore . . . Canadian stuff . . . off-the-main-highway stories," Brenda informed him.

Jake leaned forward with an air of confidentially and lowered his voice. "It ain't that I'm snoopin', you understand. Fact is, most folks drivin' through here don't give us much more than a polite nod. But things is a little different these days with all this weird shit that's been goin' on." The words had no more than escaped big Jake's ample mouth when his face began to color. "Sorry," he muttered, "I usually don't get sloppy with my talk when I'm around ladies."

"What kind of weird shit are you referring to?" nda smiled. In one fell swoop she put the big man back at ease.

Madden lowered his voice again. I'm not sure why, since we were the only ones in the place besides the waitress, who was listening to the radio. "To tell the truth, when I walked in here and saw you two, I figured you might be reporters. If you was, though, you'd be the first ones that stayed overnight."

"Reporters?" Brenda was working him over. Now it was the wide-eyed, innocent question routine. I wondered if Jake Madden had any idea what kind of buzz saw he was seated next to.

"Well," Jake confided, "seems like a couple of 'em have been showin' up just about every day. They ask a few questions, go down to the drugstore, talk to Percy Kramer, ask me if they can go out to the Carson farm to see where it happened and by nightfall, they've hightailed it outta' town."

"See what?" Honest to God, she was actually fluttering her eyes at him.

"Surely you heard about it," Jake wheezed. "It's been in all the newspapers and was even on television over at Thunder

Bay."

"We haven't heard much news. We've been on the road the last couple of days."

"We got somethin' weird goin' on. The RCMP thinks we got some kinda marauder type animal runnin' around these parts, killin' other animals and eatin' 'em. There's been hell to pay the past couple of days. People are pretty nervous."

Brenda emitted an appropriate "echh" sound, and Big Jake smiled knowingly. I knew exactly what he was thinking; as far as he was concerned, the little lady was having trouble handling the big man's sordid story of the real life in the wilds of the Canadian woods. How wrong could one man be? Brenda had him right where she wanted him.

It was time for me to jump in. "What kind of animal?"

Jake Madden shook his head, grunted, checked his watch, looked at the starry-eyed Brenda and decided he'd better earn his keep. "Well, I can tell you one thing—we'll get the critter. It's just a matter of time." He crawled out of the booth and extended his hand again. "You folks have a good time while you're here."

He lumbered across the room, patted our sullen waitress on her ample behind, muttered something in her ear and disappeared out the door.

Jake had been gone for several minutes

before I asked, "Well, what do you think?"

Brenda batted her green-blue eyes, snapped up the menu, and began to scour it. "I think I'm hungry," she said, smiling.

Back at the motel, we found ourselves a couple of old metal lawn chairs, propped them up so that we had a view of the motel parking lot and, for the most part, escaped into a world of our own private thoughts. Whatever she was thinking caused her to frown. I, on the other hand, was replaying the conversation with the Chambers Bay Constable. So the RCMP thought it was some kind of animal; that seemed logical in view of the fact that only animals had fallen victim to whatever it was so far. The hand-paw prints were throwing them off as well. At this point, I was reasonably certain no one had tied it in to the four previous incidents—if in fact there was a tie-in. I had to keep reminding myself that the whole thing could be a wild goose chase.

Whatever thoughts or fantasies Brenda was entertaining, it was weighing heavily on her mind. She had reassumed her fragile moon child personna, and the delicate smile that normally went with that had deteriorated into a semi-pout. She stirred a couple of times and finally broke the silence.

"What the hell is this all about, E.G.?"

"These things never turn out the way I've got them figured," I admitted.

B.C. wasn't looking at me. Instead she was content to stare out across the dusty, gravel surface of the parking lot past the road at the trees. There was an ominous stillness, like the calm before the storm. There was no moon, and the barriers created by the dense pine forests that came right up to the side of the small motel created the illusion of being in the one small space allocated for the use of humans.

As far as I could tell, the motel had two or three other guests besides us. Several doors down, a new Buick with Kansas license plates hovered in front of a darkened unit. Beyond that, at the far end of the motel, a red pickup truck with Manitoba plates and a boat trailer was parked.

A layer of haze, the kind you get in the muggy stillness on a hot summer evening, hovered over everything. Chambers Bay was the kind of place 99 percent of the human race never sees, never wants to see and doesn't even know exists. After three hours' exposure to its decidedly limited charms, I had about decided you could fold me right in with the 99 percent.

Again it was Brenda who broke the solitude. "You've read everything I've read and had a chance to think about it—what's this all about? Everytime I try to reason through it all, I run right back up against that same old brick wall. It can't be an animal—but then how do you explain those strange prints?" Her voice trailed off again. It was plain to see she didn't know where to go with her line of logic. "Damn it," she grumbled, "why can't I make some sense out of this?"

"I've got it all figured out," I assured her. "It has something to do with giant koala bears purchased by the Russians, airlifted up from Australia, and dumped in the Canadian wilderness. Their whole purpose is to screw up the Canadian lumber industry so that the Russians can sell some of their low quality Siberian timber at higher prices in the world market."

My feeble attempt at light-hearted banter didn't even elicit a groan. Brenda gave me her version of the moon child cold stare riddled with contempt and announced that she was turning in.

When the door clicked behind her, I got up and headed for the office. My fascination with the no-talk, no-smile motel clerk had to be checked out. By the time I got there, I realized that the lights had been dimmed, and the young man was nowhere in sight.

There are very few times when a closed door will stop me, and this wasn't one of them. When I tried the knob, it turned, and I let myself in. The office was an austere affair—two cracked vinyl chairs, a worn, patterned linoleum floor covering and a battle-scarred cashier's desk complete with a montage of cigarette burns. An antique Emerson fan struggled valiantly to circulate the stale air. Outside of the hum of the fan, you could have heard a pin drop. One thing for sure, sullen boy was nowhere in sight.

The whole setting was an invitation for a little exploring. I slipped behind the counter, pulled back the makeshift drape from the doorway and peered into the darkness. It revealed nothing more than another dingy corridor lined with a series of doors, all closed. At the far end of the hallway, a single 40-watt bulb was charged with an impossible mission. It hung right next to a faded, crudely lettered sign that informed the occupants that this was the exit. I tried to picture the tiny hall, full of choking smoke, and some poor soul trying to find the obligatory exit sign. If they were dependent on that sign, they were doomed.

I worked my way down the dimly lit hallway and inched the back door open. The small, tree-sheltered parking lot behind the motel was unlit. The only activity was confined to a dark car parked on a small strip of land jutting out from an adjacent drive into the shallows of the bay. A young couple were entertaining themselves with a journey into the ugly world of crack. The bittersweet smell of their little experiment had drifted all the way up to the back door of the motel. With nothing else to record,

I turned to go back.

"Are you looking for something?"

The almost freakish, broken quality of the voice startled me, throwing me off guard. I couldn't tell whether it was the fact that he was there or whether it was the quality of his voice. Nevertheless, there he was; the immobile, too pretty face with the hooded brown-black eyes staring back at me. Even in the darkness there was something disturbing, something intensely evil about the way he looked at me.

"Hey, you're just the guy I was looking for," I quickly said.

"Do you need something?" he managed. All the while I was trying to piece together the voice; it was too hoarse, too raspy, barely a whisper, wholly inconsistent with his almost unreal, unblemished countenance.

"Matter of fact, I do. I can't find the ice machine. It's hotter than hell in my room. I think I should report it to the manager, er . . . what's your name?" I was pulling out all the stops.

"Kelto, sir."

"Kelto," I repeated. "What the hell nationality is that?" Everybody has heard of the ugly American; well, I was giving the kid my version.

"Kelto is a Lute name, sir."

"Lute?" I repeated. I made it sound like a question.

"My people come from the vast North-west Territories—the outlands." He was all too content to let it drop at that. Nothing about him correlated with the vision of Lutes as I knew them—squat, dark and swarthy people one step removed from their Mongol heritage. Kelto was the antithesis of everything Lute. "I'll get you some ice, sir," he said and disappeared back through the same door I had used.

I listened briefly to the howls of unbridled laughter emanating from the darkened car out on the point and followed Kelto back into the hallway.

Five minutes later I had my bucket of ice and returned to my room. Brenda had left the flimsy drape between the two rooms partially open, and I wondered if it was an invitation or evidence of the same tendency that allowed her to walk around all day with a gaping hole in the right knee of her faded jeans.

Deciding it was the latter, I poured the ice in the toilet, pulled back the smoke-stained chenille bedspread and crashed.

Some people sleep well in motels. Others manage a good night's sleep only when they're bedded down in the womb-like security of their own bedroom. Me, I've never been able to sleep anywhere. That's not to say I don't nap—those quick cobwebby, not quite enough trips into a hazy, half-satisfying never-never land. That I can do, and I can do it anywhere. Unfortunately, I can do it on a plane, in a car and even in a meeting with my publisher. Consequently, I've spent most of my life viewing the world through splotchy red orbs that make me look like my eyes were painted in by a half-crazed surrealist.

At any rate, there I was, five o'clock in the morning, wide awake, peering out of blood-shot eyes at a hint of the dawn and wishing I could go back to sleep.

Nevertheless, I hauled my aging frame out of the rack and staggered to the window for the ritualistic early morning appraisal of the new day. Something had happened during the course of the night. The new dawn was gray and brooding and somber; the bay was angry and busy with whitecaps. The sky was painted with streaks of polluted orange laced with slate gray streaks of clouds trailing back to the still dark western horizon. Fracto stratus, I mumbled to myself—and even though those weather bureau days were some 25 years in my checkered past, the definition of the clouds was still a portend of rain.

Nothing would delight me more than to paint you a bright, cheery portrait of one Elliott Grant Wages that bounced out of bed, smiled at the world, slipped into a pair of designer sweats and jocked it up for 30 minutes before sitting down to a bowl of

Grape Nuts. Such, sadly, is not the case. After 50 troubled summers on this old planet, the only thing that can force this worn old transmission into gear is a couple of shots; one is nicotine, the other caffeine. It's true that I'm holding it under one pack a day, but that first one in the morning is critical to all systems go.

With no more lofty purpose in mind other than finding a cup of steaming black coffee and a chance to suck on a Camel, I searched around for my crusty old Reeboks, tugged on a pair of blue shorts and a tee shirt, and ran a curry comb through the crop of thick red-brown hair my father had once likened to the fur on a rat's nuts.

I paused just long enough to sneak a peek into Cashman's inner sanctum, taking note of the fact that she was even sloppier than me. Garments ranging from the aforementioned well-worn Levis to an unexcitingly small bra were strewn haphazardly about the room. In addition to everything else, she snored. I made a mental note; Brenda Cashman had just turned up with two big negatives on her scorecard. She snored, and she had small boobs.

It was even more ominous outside than I had anticipated. A grumbling, still distant storm was approaching from the west, and the temperature had plunged a good 30 degrees since our arrival. I headed straight for the small diner where Brenda and I had dinner the previous evening, a distance of not more than a quarter of a mile up the road. I even felt smug because I jogged.

The parking lot was jammed and so was the diner. Most of the early morning customers were sitting at the counter slurping coffee out of heavy green china mugs with spoons still in them. Unlike the small town I grew up in, there was no light banter. Instead, the assemblage had their heads down, tending to their own business, postured in somber melancholy.

The locals had the seats at the counter filled, so I was shuttled off into what had to be the tourist area next to a middle-aged couple with two of the ugliest kids I've ever seen. The pimply, thickly lensed progeny were complaining about soggy french fries which they had buried under the remnants of two half bottles of runny ketchup. The combination of whining kids and the smell of french fries at a little past six in the morning was more than my constitution could handle. I ordered my coffee to go and decided to find a quiet place where I could stare at the water and destroy my health in solitude.

I picked my way down a narrow path in back of the diner, found myself a spot on a stretch of sandy, rock-studded beach and assessed the situation. There was a lot to think about—Madden's definition of the problem, the role of Brenda Cashman in all of this, and the sullen Kelto. I took several sips of coffee and lit my Camel; suddenly the day looked a little brighter.

Ten minutes later I had finished my communion with mother nature and started back to the motel, wondering if that lump under the covers in the room adjacent to mine was up and about, celebrating the new day. Approaching from the west, I could see the Constable's car sitting on the drive near the back of the motel. Jake Madden was standing beside the dusty dark green Pontiac, engrossed in a conversation with two other men. The old E.G. Wage's antenna went up and started spinning.

I waited until that conversation broke up, stuck another cigarette in my mouth and casually sauntered back in the big man's direction. For all intents and purposes, I was nothing more than a tourist out for his morning stroll. Halfway down the drive, I got a new reading on the situation. There was a whole lot more going on than I had anticipated. The dirty old Chevrolet was still parked right where it had been the night before, but now it had a yellow strip of plastic tape around it, cordoning it off from the rest of the world. In typical E.G. Wage fashion, I immediately assumed the young couple had gotten themselves caught with their cache and that I was approaching the scene of a Chambers Bay version of a drug bust. By the time I managed to maneuver closer to the scene, I was aware the situation was considerably more serious.

Madden looked up, then away, then back again. The affibility was gone. The Constable looked worn and haggard.

"Morning," I tried.

Big Jake reached through the window and laid his clipboard on the seat of his car. He started toward me in that peculiar gait of his, frowning. "You're that research fella I met over at the diner last night, right?"

"Elliott Wages," I reminded him. "You look like you've had a hard night." The closer he got to me the harder the night looked.

"Been a long one," he acknowledged. "I knew we was gonna have a damned nightmare around here when they found Ruby Carson's old draft horse half-eaten and the rest of the parts all sorted out and hangin' from trees."

The all too graphic description of the Carson event sent a shudder across my shoulders and down my spine. "More trouble last night?"

Jake nodded and looked like he needed someone to commiserate with him. "I knew it wasn't no animal when I saw what had been done to that old mare, but the local folk are as superstitious as hell. They heard about them unusual prints and right away they're ready to start claimin' we got us a modern day Big Foot thumpin' around this neck of the woods."

"How do you know you don't?" I shot back at him. Playing the role of the devil's advocate comes easy to me.

Madden signed and turned his back on the old Chevy. "Come on over here, Researcher."

I followed him to the edge of the blacktop, stepped over the elevated yellow tape barrier and followed him out on the craggy strip jutting out into the shallows. He kept talking along the way, but the wind carried away his words. He threw open the car door, and my stomach did a somersault. For a moment I had to close my eyes.

The boy probably wasn't much more than 18 years old, and the girl looked as though she could be a year or two younger. What was left of the lad was slumped in the far corner of the front seat. The remains of the young woman were unceremoniously sprawled, arms and legs akimbo on the back seat. Each of them rested in crimson black pools of their own congealed blood. My stomach did another flip-flop and yawed back and forth a couple of times. I gulped, trying to get my equalibrium. The "holy shit" just slipped out, but it was appropriate. Someone or something had worked them over with a knife.

I looked up at Madden. His face was bone white. "I've never seen anything like it," I muttered.

"It's a goddamn sicko, that's what it is."

This was the part of it I had never gotten used to. I forced myself to move in closer and made a more careful assessment. Each of the incisions in the boy's chest had been made with uncanny precision. The chest cavity had been pried open and the heart removed, with each artery severed at just the precise location. It appeared as though the youth had just laid back and allowed whatever it was to take his source of life. He had a stupid, almost euphoric look on his face, like he had been viewing the whole proceeding and only when the blood quit pumping to his numbed brain had realized what was happening. It had been, in the final analysis, one very bad trip indeed.

The girl hadn't fared much better. The butcher had obviously been attracted to her eyes. Consequently, she stared back at me with hollow and empty sockets, a futile, pleading look on her young face.

I shuddered and stepped back.

Madden gave me a long critical appraisal, folded his huge arms over his massive chest and leaned back against the car. "I know you'd be disappointed if I didn't ask you where you were last night."

The question surprised me, and yet it didn't. "I suppose you have to ask everybody," I admitted, "but, for the record, I was right there in the motel, room number eight."

"I suppose Miss Cashman can verify that?" The question had a double edge and I knew it. No answer was going to be entirely satisfactory in this case. Something told me that Madden didn't like the idea of a crusty, rusty-bearded old man sleeping with the young woman. But if Brenda couldn't verify my whereabouts, who could?

"Matter of fact, Miss Cashman can't verify anything; we have separate rooms." The revelation did something for his eyes. It was almost imperceptible, but it was there. "At this stage, I imagine everyone is a suspect."

"Chambers Bay ain't much more than a grease spot in the road," Madden scoffed, "and most of the folks around these parts have known each other since the day they was born. That means they know each other pretty well. If I got me any suspects, they'll be outsiders; them's the ones you can't trust."

There was no malice in the big man's manner. I knew exactly where he was coming from. I also knew he had a deteriorating situation on his hands that he had no idea how to solve. He began to amble away from the scene of the atrocity down toward the water's edge. When he turned back to face me, his eyes were a giveaway. "I ain't much of a Constable, ain't had much train-in', and it's times like this that make me realize that."

I had a hunch Jake Madden, for reasons known only to him, had already written me off his suspect list. I nodded my head back toward the car containing the two bodies. "So, what happens now?"

Madden shrugged. "The Mounties take over. I handle little stuff; this is big stuff." He paused, looked out at the troubled water, then back at me again. "I know one thing for certain," he sighed. "This time they won't be writin' off the whole thing as some sort of animal attack. Ain't no damn animal I ever heard of that could take a scalpel and cut out a man's heart."

PART 3

I stayed with Madden till the Mounties arrived and watched in childlike fascination as their slick investigative team swarmed over the scene. They took my name despite Madden's assurances that I was above suspicion and gave me the standard "don't stray too far from here" admonition. Finally I shook free and went back to the motel to see if B.C. had crawled out of the sack yet. I glanced at my watch; it was only eight-thirty. At the present rate, it was going to be one helluva day.

Brenda was up. In fact, she had already showered (her hair was still damp) and had managed to get dressed. That is to say, she was wearing the same old pair of blue jeans with the hole in the knee and Reeboks that looked even saltier than mine. The blouse was different; this one looked like a military issue of some sort, and she had it knotted at the midriff. I didn't tell her, but I thought she looked more than just passingly appealing.

"Good morning," she chimed.

"Did you know you snore?" I asked flatly. I wasn't about to let her forget that I was a protege of the infamous Cosmo Leach. With those kinds of slammers for openers, she never would.

She gave me an easy smile, flipped her hair and leaned back on her bed. "How do you know? You weren't peeking, were you?" She knew she had me, but she was quick to let me off the hook. "Had your breakfast yet?"

"Been waiting for you," I admitted. I had already made up my mind not to say anything about the gory scene that was still unfolding behind the motel. That wasn't the sort of thing you hit someone with before they've had breakfast. "Are you ready?"

She bounced off the bed and fell into step beside me as we headed back for the diner. By the time we got there, the spoon-in-the-cup gang had departed. I suspected the word was out by now that Madden had something worse than a couple of crudely slaughtered animals on his hand.

With the exception of a lone trucker, we

had the place to ourselves. The same waitress led us to the same table we had occupied the previous evening, and again Brenda took time to assess the mood of the bay. It was still choppy and gray, the same color as the sky, only now there was no way to distinguish between the two. They had become one, a somber, slate-gray brooding landscape. What earlier hope there had been for sunshine was continuing to diminish as the day wore on. "Doesn't look very friendly, does it?" she mused.

I had to agree with her. The winds were aggravating the pines, the waves were running a good six to eight feet, and the day was holding out damn little promise. B.C. shuddered, hunched her shoulders forward and seemed to withdraw into herself. I wondered if now was the time to tell her—and decided again to wait.

The mood prevailed right on into breakfast itself. Halfway through, she slumped back in the booth with both hands wrapped around her coffee cup. She had barely touched her food. "I'm not sure I'm ready to begin yet," she muttered.

"Begin what?"

"The research, or whatever it is that writers do when they go somewhere and start digging into things. I don't know. You tell me, you're the writer."

"It's already begun," I informed her. The time was now, I reasoned.

She gave me that quizzical moon child look which I interpreted as meaning, "Tell me more."

"I hope you're ready for this. Last night, while we were sleeping, all of our suspicions were confirmed. We're definitely on the right track; our 'thing' struck again."

"Another animal?"

"I'm afraid not, not this time. Our whatever-it-is calmly carved up a teenage couple that was parked out on the point behind the motel."

The color slowly drained out of Brenda's face as she set her cup down. Her hands were shaking.

"Oh, my God," she managed, "what happened?"

I told her everything, starting from the point when she retired for the night, through the brief encounter with Kelto, and finally describing the scene on the rocky strip of land jutting out from the motel. Along the way I gave her my impressions of the sullen young motel clerk and the somewhat different perspective I now had of Jake Madden. Brenda was stone-faced through it all. I concluded with a list of things that I thought needed to be checked out. She listened as if in a coma. Finally I stopped. "Are you all right?"

The intense blue-green eyes blinked a couple of times, and she finally nodded. "Yeah, I guess so." The favorable assessment was obviously hesitant. "It's one thing to go to the library and read about something like this in a bunch of dusty old archives, but it's something else altogether to be caught up in the middle of it."

I reached into my pocket and took out a stack of three by five file cards (another old trick borrowed from Cosmo), filled with the hastily jotted notes made after my early morning encounter with Madden. He had mentioned that the reporters seemed to gravitate to Percy Kramer's drugstore, and I figured there had to be a reason. Maybe the old boy was a real talker and just maybe Brenda could learn something more than Jake had volunteered. I also figured that the old boy might be more inclined to spend his time with a pretty young lady than a bearded old coot like me—so Brenda got that assignment.

I had two things on my list. First, I wanted to call Lucy, who had access to the main computer in the school's research library. I wanted her to search for the similarities between the locations of the four previous incidents and Chambers Bay. Secondly, I wanted to have a second go-around with young Mister Kelto. In theory at least, he was the night clerk and should have been on duty when the young couple was killed. What had he seen? What had he heard? Was there anything at all unusual? The list went on.

With the typical E.G. Wages propensity for overestimating what could be accomplished within a certain time frame, I glanced at my watch and decided we could have everything done by lunchtime. After we walked back to the motel, I put Brenda in the tired old Z with the warning to keep her eyes open. As she pulled out onto the main road, I wondered which one was the real Brenda Cashman—street-smart or innocent; whichever it was, it was submerged for the moment under a heavy blanket of good old-fashioned anxiety. I had to hope she would keep her wits about her.

I went back to my room and called my office at the college. No one answered so I left a message on the recorder. The instructions were simple enough—profile the locations of the four previous attacks, looking for anything that might remotely tie the events together. Lucy was a bright gal and would know exactly what to do with one of my typical open-ended assignments. With that little chore completed, I set out in search of the sullen young man who called himself Kelto.

The Chamber Bay Motel was a 12-unit, white clapboard affair with ten units on one side of the office and two on the other. There was a time, I suppose, 30 or maybe 40 years ago, when the pace of our pell-mell society was a little slower and life was a little less complicated, that it held a certain appeal for travelers. But now, with the advent of ultramodern resort motels on every corner of every major highway, places like the timeworn Chambers Bay struggled just to hold their heads above water.

On balance, it was clean, comfortable and reasonably well kept, but it was evident that the ravages of time were exacting their inevitable toll. Next to the entrance was an old-fashioned, carefully lettered welcoming sign complete with cuddling bluebirds that proudly proclaimed Bert and Polly Johnson to be the owners since 1957.

Kelto wasn't behind the desk. Instead I was confronted by a smiling, open-faced man with large horn-rimmed glasses and friendly brown eyes. For the most part he was bald. He had a grease smear on one cheek and busied himself trying to repair an old mechanical calculator. He looked up at me expectantly. "Can I help you?"

"You can if you can spare a moment or two."

"Need a room?" he asked hopefully.

"Nope. I'm already registered. The name is Wages, E.G. Wages. My partner and I checked in last night."

The man wiped his hands on an oily rag and reached across the desk to shake my hand. "My name's Bert Johnson. Me and my wife Polly own this place."

"Nice place. We like it." Some white lies are good for the soul.

"Appreciate that, Mr. Wages. Polly and me work real hard to keep it up. Chambers Bay ain't exactly what you'd call a resort town and we know our little place ain't a Holiday Inn, but it's our home and we like it."

"Well, since my partner and I are going to be sticking around here for a few days, we'll have some spare time on our hands. I was wondering if you could direct me to some of the local points of interest."

"There's a little bit of everything," he said proudly. "Caleb Hall has a real nice charter fishin' boat. He moors her down at the public pier right near the center of town." It was obvious that Bert was pleased with his suggestion; it was equally obvious he was having a difficult time thinking of anything else. Finally, he reached around, pulled back the curtain and shouted down the hall. "Polly, I got me a fella out here that wants to know what he and his friend can find to do around Chambers Bay."

There was the sudden unmistakable sound of a creaking, protesting mechanism. As the noise grew louder, Polly emerged from the shadowed hall in an old motorized wheelchair. Her smile was even broader and brighter than Bert's.

"Mr. Wages here is our guest," he explained.

Polly had laughing, rich hazel eyes, closely cropped brown and gray hair and a body twisted by arthritis. Even the most subtle of movements brought on a wave of pain. Still, she looked up at me and intensified her smile. "Bert has never been very good at letting people know about our fair community, Mr. Wages. You see, Bert's mind begins and ends with Caleb Hall's fishing boat. When Bert gets to thinking about going fishing, nothing else much matters. If you know where to go fishing, you know everything you need to know."

There was no way of knowing how Polly Johnson had ended up in Chambers Bay, because her voice betrayed a deep Southern heritage. I figured Bert Johnson must have been a helluva man in his day—that, or one helluva salesman.

"Like I was telling your husband, my partner and I are going to be here for a couple of days, and we'd like to take in the local sights when we get some spare time. What do you suggest?"

Polly suddenly looked a little sad. "Most of the time I'd encourage you to spend some time in our lovely provincial forest—we have some seven hundred thousand acres of it—but I don't know how safe it is what with all the strange things that have been going on around these parts the last few days." She paused as though she was reflecting on the string of events, and I wondered how much she knew and whether or not Bert had spared her some of the ugly details. "We have some lovely waterfalls, miles and miles of trails for hiking or biking and even some rather intriguing caves."

"Do ya like caves?" Bert inquired.

"Not particularly. Seems to me they're always dark and damp and cold—not my cup of tea."

Bert's shoulders sagged. He had finally come up with something other than Caleb Hall's fishing boat, and I had rejected it outright.

"Maybe that young fellow that works for you has some ideas," I tried.

The proprietors of the Chambers Bay Motel exchanged a quick glance, and Bert went back to fidgeting with his adding machine. Polly cleared her throat. "You must mean Kelto."

"Kelto, that's it, a young fella, working the desk when we arrived last night. Nice-looking young man," I added.

Bert laid his tools down and leaned forward on the counter. "You mean a *weird*-lookin' young man, don't you, Mr. Wages?"

Polly made a disapproving clucking sound and reached out to pat her husband on the hand. "Bert and I agree on just about everything, Mr. Wages, but we don't see eye to eye on Kelto."

"I think the kid is weird," Bert protested. "I don't like the way he never smiles or the way he sneaks around this place. It ain't natural for a boy his age to not have no friends and be that quiet and off to himself all the time."

"Help is hard to come by," Polly said defensively, "and he is very dependable." I had a hunch there weren't too many people that Polly didn't like.

"He came draggin' in here one day, carryin' that damn back pack, sweat runnin' down his face, askin' us if there was anything he could do to earn a meal. Said he hadn't had anything to eat in days. I put him to paintin' gutters and the kinda stuff I never seem to get to. Now we can't get rid of him."

Polly shook her head at Bert's intolerance. "Just having him around has been a godsend," she said quietly. "It gives Bert and me a few hours to ourselves, and we haven't had many of those since we bought this old place."

"Have any idea where I could get in touch with him?"

"He stays in unit number ten," Bert groused. "It was Polly's idea, not mine. Hell, Polly feels sorry for everybody."

I had more questions about young Kelto, but it didn't seem to be the time or place to ask them. Where had he come from? What was his background? Had anybody checked his references or tried to learn anything about him? For that matter, was Kelto his first or last name? Maybe Polly had the right idea—give a guy a chance and let him stand or fall on his own merits. "Suppose he's there?" I asked.

"Don't rightly know," Bert snarled. "Polly gave him today and tomorrow off. He found out about what went on out there behind the motel last night and said he needed some time off."

"I don't imagine you'll find him in his room, Mr. Wages. I saw him packing his back pack; he seems to want to spend every spare moment in the woods. Goes there every chance he gets." Polly was doing her best to defuse Bert's agitation. She turned her wheelchair around and smiled at him. I had the feeling that Bert was either going to come around to her way of thinking or he was going to get his attitude readjusted. Polly may have been working with a handicap, but all signs indicated she could handle the situation.

Polly was right. I knocked three different times but there wasn't any response. Kelto was either out or unconscious; I assumed it was the former. I went back to my own room, lit up a cigarette (number four for the day), whipped out my three by fives and started scribbling notes. I had lots of questions and an equal amount of observations, and I didn't want any of them to get away from me.

The weather had continued to deteriorate. By noon the clouds were hanging low over the area like a choking blanket of wet, slate gray smoke. With a steady drizzle settling in, it was destined to be one of those afternoons that men like to think would be perfect for spending under a blanket with some love-starved sex kitten. I probably would have dwelled on that rather intriguing thought, but when the phone rang, the images were whisked away by reality.

"Didn't think I'd be lucky enough to catch you on the first try," Lucy chimed.

"Just hangin' around the motel, watching it rain," I offered laconically.

"Before we get into the meat of this conversation, the scuttlebutt back here has it that you've got a girl with you."

Let me fix Lucy in time and space for you. Lucy Martin may very well be the world's longest running, never finishing anything, graduate assistant. My esteemed fellow academians back at good old Saint Francis inform me that Lucy, the perpetual student, has been there long enough to have tenure. She has achieved this distinction by changing her major several times, and at the rate of one class a semester, she may very well journey into senility without a degree. She embraces her questionable goal orientation by virtue of the fact that her father is stinking rich and endorses her "I'm interested in everything" philosophy. Still, Lucy has proven to be a valuable resource; I can trust her.

For the record, Lucy is a pint-sized, button-nosed, overly animated, pleasantly plump little blonde who has appointed herself guardian of my office, career and morals. Now she was giving me the needle about my female traveling companion.

"Just for the record, little Miss Snoopy, her name is Brenda Cashman and she's a graduate student at the University of Michigan, one of Cosmo Leach's whiz kids."

I could tell Lucy wasn't impressed. She allowed the silence to stretch on. It was a level-one reprimand.

"I take it you called me for a reason," I reminded her.

"Similarities," she repeated flatly. "You wanted similarities, so here's what the trusty computer came up with. It seems that all four of the incidents in the file happened in some very remote, almost inaccessible location. All had low population density profiles. . . ."

I was scribbling notes frantically. "Got it. What else?"

"I suppose you've already taken note of the fact that each of these events took place on some sort of coastal terrain?"

I had. "What else?"

"Chambers Bay has the same topographical features as the sites in those reports."

"Like?"

"Rock composition, heavy forestation at the last three sites, and of course, the coastal caves."

I underlined the word "caves." "What kind of caves?"

"Oh, you know, the typical ones, a hole in the ground." She started to giggle. Her efforts at humor were few and far between, and I was never prepared for them.

I grunted to let her know that, as feeble as I considered the effort to be, I still acknowledged it. "Is that it?"

"Well," Lucy drawled, dwelling on the obvious, "should I even bother to mention that all of the incidents have been within the Canadian border?"

The last one was a cheap shot. She was still laughing when I hung up. Again I checked to make sure I had a complete set of notes; the stack of file cards was growing rapidly. So far there were no surprises; if anything, my hypothesis was holding a little more water than before. The one thing that still didn't make any sense was the two completely different kinds of crimes. On one hand there was more than ample evidence of some kind of cold, calculating and skilled pathological killer who deftly carved up his victims with the skill of a surgeon. On the other, there was evidence of an almost barbaric killing machine, mutilating and in some cases devouring his victims. Needless to say, the two didn't go hand in hand. It was like having the pieces of two different yet similar puzzles in the same box. I lit up another cigarette. I was past the halfway mark and still had more than a half a pack to go.

Half an hour later I heard the sound of gravel crunching in the driveway. There was no mistaking the sound of the out-of-tune Z. The door slammed, and I heard footsteps darting through the rain to the shelter of the overhang in front of the unit. The door flew open, and B.C. stood in the middle of the doorway glaring at me. She was soaked to the bone. Her face was flushed, and her hair hung straight down like strands of wet rope. "This ain't what I had in mind when I volunteered for this damn mission," she fumed.

Given the opportunity, I probably would have hauled out my gallant act and offered the wet lady a drink. That opportunity never materialized, because Brenda Cashman marched defiantly past me and straight to the dresser. She grabbed the bottle of Black and White, an empty glass, combined the two and plunked down on the edge of the bed. She took two quick jolts, and within less than 30 seconds she had peeled out of her wet clothes and sat shivering in her bra and panties.

"What the hell happened?" I managed.

"I'll talk about it when I get out of the damn shower," she snapped.

With that she discarded what was left of her limited wardrobe and disappeared into the bathroom. Fifteen minutes and one steamy shower later, she re-emerged wrapped in two towels, one around her body and the other around her hair. She grabbed the glass again, took two more healthy gulps and refocused her glare.

"Do you mind telling me what happened?"

"Any further dialogue with one Percy Kramer is going to be conducted by one Elliott Grant Wages. I will have nothing further to do with that lecherous little bastard."

"So, druggist Percy has a thing for flat-chested girls, huh?"

B.C. gave me the iciest stare in her repertoire, pulled the towel up tighter around her and took two more monumental swigs of my patented firewater.

"Okay, I'm sorry. Now let's start at the beginning. What the hell happened?"

The moon child had fled the scene, and the street-smart side of my fellow investigator was still fuming. I could tell that at the moment she didn't know whether to cuss or cry. She took a deep breath, measured herself and began. "I did exactly what you told me to do. I went in and introduced myself. I told him I was a freelance reporter working on the whole series of bizarre goings-on that had been happening around Chambers Bay. Plus, I put a little icing on the cake by telling him that Jake

Madden had even suggested that I talk to him. The old bastard couldn't have been nicer at that point. He took me back to his soda fountain at the back of the store, fixed me a vanilla coke and started telling me all kinds of stuff about this place." B.C. paused, took another stiff jolt of Scotch, wiped off her mouth and continued. "Then he started telling me about what he knew about Carson's horse and offered to drive me out and show me where it happened. I believed him."

"Look, Brenda, I don't want to sound like a broken record, but you still haven't told me what happened. This sure as hell isn't the first time some guy paid you some unwanted attention, is it?"

B.C. was more angry than hurt. She was also calmer. I think the repeated blitzes of Scotland's finest were beginning to have an effect on her. "Percy has a pickup truck," she said haltingly, "and we crawled in it to drive out to the Carson place. We drove out there, turned off the highway and went back down this long lane. He started pointing out where this whatever it is that we're chasing tore up everything. Actually I couldn't see much except for a few broken branches, a place where a couple of very small trees had been knocked down and a few gouges in the earth. You know how I tease. Well, I told him, 'I'm disappointed if this is all there is.' "

"Let's get to the part that upset you," I reminded her.

Brenda sighed. "Well, there we are. It's damp, and the place is really grungy. I'm poking around looking for some sign of those two thumb, three finger prints we've heard about when all of a sudden it really starts to rain. Percy baby throws down the tailgate and crawls up under the shelter of the cap. Within minutes it's pouring, and I crawl up there with him. All of a sudden, Percy, the fat little druggist, is Percy, the fat little sex maniac. He's clawing, biting, breathing heavy, tearing at my clothes. The little bastard tried to rape me. So I cold-cocked him, a fistful of Brenda Cashman knuckles right to his fat chops. I never hit a man that hard before. He went down like a sack of rocks." There was the look of universal woman triumphant in her snapping eyes.

"Let me guess the rest. You crawled out in the rain, back in the cab of the truck, drove him back to town and left him in front of his store with no apology, right?"

"Wrong. I couldn't find the damn keys. Finally I got desperate, walked out and left him there."

"You walked all the way back into town?"

Brenda nodded. "That's how I got soaked to the bone."

Outside of the fact that Percy had come unglued and tried to put the make on

97

Brenda, my new partner had come up with some solid information. In the long run, it could be more valuable info than I had been able to put together in my efforts. When I was certain I wouldn't break out laughing at the slightly bizarre picture of the woman sitting on my bed, I started filling her in on what I had learned. When I came to the part about caves, she perked up.

"Kramer said there were caves all around this area. In fact, he showed me where one was located."

"Think you could find it?"

"I could if I ever went back there again— which I'm not willing to do." There was the definite tinge of offended female belligerence in her voice.

I stood looking out the window at the dismal gray day. For the moment, it had quit raining. I measured my voice and started slowly. "We've got to go out there. I don't want to raise any more flags about what we're really interested in and the fact that you know where the Carson incident took place is a big plus." I paused for effect. "So what do you say? Let's go out and take another look at it."

The pep talk was greeted with stony silence. I continued to stare out the window and prepared to renew my plea. Finally I turned around. B.C. had curled herself up in a fetal position in the middle of my bed and was sound asleep.

ANCIENTS

* * *

By late afternoon, Brenda was up again and had somehow managed to locate and pour herself into dry clothes. I coaxed her into the Z and conned her into showing me the Carson place. We drove through town, past Percy's drugstore and out to the western edge of the village. There we turned left toward the lakefront and drove about 500 yards back down a narrow lane to a small unbridged stream. I did a little estimating of ground clearance and decided we had better go the rest of the way on foot. Brenda was apprehensive about it, but she pulled the slicker up tighter around her throat and trudged on. I heard only one small, and for her, insignificant grouse. "Why the hell couldn't we have waited till the weather was better?"

We crossed the shallow rockbed stream, worked our way up the slope of the bank, rounded the curve in the lane and headed for the clearing at the water's edge. The clearing was supposedly the place where the thing had decimated Carson's horse and Brenda had decimated good old Percy. Suddenly she let out a shriek and pointed to the far side of the clearing; Percy's truck was still there.

"Oh," she moaned, "don't tell me I did more to him than just punch out his lights."

"Hell, he probably came to and couldn't find his keys either." I laughed, but the laugh, was half-hearted at best and pretty much stripped of sincerity. I was concerned. I checked my watch and worked the time backwards. Percy had been there far too long for somebody who had taken a simple shot to the chops, especially from no more than a 110-pounder.

My mind was doing a flip-flop on me. I suppose she could have hurt him—that had to be a possibility—but I reasoned that was damned unlikely. More than likely, since his truck was still there, he was trying to cope with his wounded ego and construct some kind of face-saving story to tell the boys back at the drugstore.

I told Brenda to stay where she was and went over to the truck to check it out. I had a vision of a half-pissed, very nervous little man leaping out of the back of his pickup, tire iron in hand, swinging wildly. I didn't want Brenda to get in the way if I had to beat a hasty retreat.

I did a double take when I discovered the truck was empty.

While I carefully formulated any number of plausible, rational and completely logical reasons for Percy to have left his truck behind, I wasn't sure I would have bought any of them. In truth, in the glaring light of a sunny, no nonsense day, all of my current hypothetical reasons for the man's absence would have sounded pretty idiotic. On the other hand, it probably didn't matter much.

It was obvious Brenda wouldn't buy any of them anyway.

The setting was straight out of a low budget horror film. The rain had stopped for the moment, but a raw wind was whipping in off the bay and the temperature had dropped several degrees since we had left the motel. Despite the wind, the cloud deck had dropped another couple of hundred feet, and I had the uneasy feeling that the clouds were low enough for me to reach up and wring the moisture out of them.

B.C.'s description had been fairly accurate. Several small trees had been uprooted, and there were some decidedly nasty gouges in the earth as though some rather large creature had tried to claw holes in the surface. For an area of about 50 feet in diameter, the ground appeared to be charred. I couldn't find a single surviving blade of grass.

The area where Carson's mare had been killed was actually a small hollow with rock-studded hills swelling up on three sides and the fourth sloping away to the rocky beach of the bay. Further west, I would estimate no more than a quarter of a mile, there were a number of jagged outcroppings, columnar rock formations that jutted some 40 or 50 feet in the air. The bases of the formations were guarded by dense clusters of rock pine and white birch. In the gray shadows of the rainy late afternoon, it was impossible to make out any detail.

Over the course of the years, I've been witness to and part of any number of bizarre situations, so I consider myself adaptable, but I was really becoming uncomfortable with this one. The Z was a couple of hundred yards back up the trail and headed the wrong way. If we had to beat a hasty retreat, I didn't have the slightest idea how I would get it turned around and headed in the other direction. On balance, any escape effort was reduced to running like hell, and I didn't know how fast our so-called creature could run either.

Brenda, at this point, wasn't much help. She had worked her way over to Percy's truck to verify my disquieting news. Her shoulders were hunched forward, and she was shivering.

"I know you're in no mood to answer questions, but did Percy show you where any of the caves were actually located?"

She managed to get one hand out from under the slicker and gesture toward the rock formation to the west. "Up there," she mumbled. I had the feeling she wasn't all that certain. The shiver was too much in evidence; she wasn't thinking clearly.

I had about decided to save any further investigation for future periods of broad daylight. A little less chill wind, a little less grayness and a whole lot more sunshine would do a great deal to defuse my suddenly overactive imagination. Common sense was telling me that I had better get B.C. back to the car. Percy Kramer and his pickup truck were on their own. I had already begun to rationalize alternative courses of action—and hunting up Jake Madden to tell him where Percy and his truck were made the most sense to me.

On balance, I will admit to having handled the whole thing rather sloppily. So far, this wasn't what I like to think of as a typical E.G. Wages performance. Allowing Brenda Cashman to come along had been my first mistake, and bringing her back out to the site of the Percy Kramer affair had been an even bigger one. To top it off, I had ignored Cosmo's advice, and instead of carrying my survival kit with me everywhere I went, I had opted to leave it in the Z. Here I was, practically defenseless, at the site of an all too recent unsolved atrocity. The closest thing I had to a weapon was a small butane cigarette lighter. Not vintage E.G. Wages.

I had uttered the magic words, and it was just what Brenda wanted to hear. Immediately, a look of relief captured her finely sculptured face, and she quit shaking. She slipped her hand into mine and leaned forward with her head on my chest. "I'm sorry, E.G.," she managed, "but I'm worried about him. What could have happened to him?"

"Probably the same thing that happened

to you. I figure he came to, realized what happened, couldn't find his keys and did the same thing you did—stumbled out of here."

"Where did he go?"

"Probably home. Remember, he's embarrassed. Getting yourself zonked out by the lady of your choice when you're trying to put the moves on her is a little tough to explain. I'll give you two to one odds he falls all over you with apologies the next time he sees you."

Brenda looked up at me, smiled and squeezed my hand. Before she could get the words out, a shrill, piercing scream raced up and around the words already forming in her throat. The sound erupted into the twilight grayness. She fell back, pointing, her face twisted in terror.

I spun around.

There he was. Percy Kramer hadn't stumbled out of his embarrassing situation after all. Instead, he was hanging by his feet from the gnarled limb of a dead rock pine. His throat had been slit.

B.C. was hysterical. "Oh, my God, E.G., look at him. What have they done to him?"

It was all too obvious. Percy Kramer had been intentionally hung upside down to drain the blood. Percy Kramer, Chambers Bay druggist and erstwhile Brenda swain, was somebody or something's intended food supply.

PART 4

Jake Madden's office was a drafty, inadequately lighted, two-room citadel of chaos tucked away at the rear of the same building that housed the Chambers Bay volunteer fire department. One room contained Jake's somewhat limited official needs—a battered old oak desk, a couple of nondescript chairs, circa sometime in the twenties, two three-drawer gray metal file cabinets, and an arsenal. The desk was cluttered with papers, a tarnished brass gooseneck lamp, a telephone and two empty Coke bottles.

The room adjacent to his office was somewhat larger, just as poorly illuminated and equally uninviting. The room's main feature was an old yellow formica dinette table that served as the center of the village council meetings. At other times the room was employed as the big man's holding pen, an interrogation room, and just about anything else he wanted it to be. There was an overhead light sheltered by a dirty, military green, metal lampshade. The walls, once papered, now defied description.

I had the distinct feeling that the old room existed primarily in these more modern times for the swapping of stories, guns and telephone numbers, all-night poker games, and the painful passing of all too many long, snowy Canadian nights.

Jake was there along with a man he had introduced as Harlan Gorman, a string bean of a man, bereft of hair and minus a few teeth as well. Harlan was the chief of the volunteer fire department. Those two, along with Caleb Hall, the charter boat captain and elected head of the village council, who now sat at the far end of the table, constituted the "officialdom" of Chambers Bay.

Jake had summoned them when I reported the discovery of Percy Kramer's body.

Jake was an artful juggler. He had somehow managed to round up his cohorts, organize this meeting and, at the same time, supervise the discreet delivery of Percy's remains to the closest undertaker in the village of Kemper, a wide spot in the road some 17 miles west of Chambers Bay. He had accomplished this rather impressive list in the short span of two and one-half hours, amidst a now driving rain which the locals were calling a lake squall.

Brenda had tried valiantly, but the day, the hour and the ordeal had taken their toll. She had repeated her story for each of them, and now she was exhausted. At the moment, she sat in the far corner of the room next to the potbellied wood-burning stove with an old woolen blanket wrapped around her shoulders. She had a cup of coffee tightly clenched between her hands, and she had slipped off into her own world.

"You say you're a writer?" Caleb asked. He was a white-haired, hawk-nosed man with cracked and weathered skin and a musky voice that sounded like it was coming at you through damp speakers.

"I checked him out," Madden confirmed. "He's a writer, all right; had the boys at the RCMP post down at Waverly punch him up on their computer." Then he turned and looked at me. "They tell me you're a professor, too, right?"

It didn't particularly seem like the time or place to get into a long dissertation on the subtle differences between a professor and a writer-in-residence, so I let Jake's explanation stand, confirming it with a nod.

Harlan Gorman was the silent type. For the past hour he hadn't said more than a couple of words. Again, I had the distinct feeling that old Harlan would have given just about anything to be anywhere else other than here, sorting through what was fast becoming the fifth in the series of incidents. That's the way both Jake and Caleb were referring to it now that I had paraded them step by step through the sequence of similar attacks.

"Every eleven years, huh?" Harlan repeated.

I nodded. "So far that's the pattern we think we see."

"But it ain't the same thing, Harlan," Jake insisted. "Like Wages here was sayin', we got two different things goin' on. Them kids we discovered out back of the motel this mornin'—that's a different thing than old Percy. Them kids was carved up slick as a whistle; those parts was taken out just like a surgeon had done it."

"You mean we got us two killers on the loose?" Harlan gulped.

"To be honest, I don't know how many there are," I admitted.

"You're tellin' us that them kids this mornin' are just as different from Percy Kramer as old Percy was from those animals we found earlier this week," Caleb parroted. He looked over at me for confirmation of his assessment.

Brenda looked up from her cup just long enough to insist that all of the incidents were somehow related.

"She's right," I confirmed, "but that's the second thing we don't know. We don't know how all these incidents are related."

For the last several minutes, Madden had been in the pacing mode. He was walking around the room, checking on the progress of the storm, checking on Brenda, pouring more coffee. Finally he lowered his bulk in the chair next to mine. "Weird thing about this is I ain't seen anything different goin' on around here. I haven't noticed anyone or anything."

"Me neither," Caleb confessed, "but then I'm pretty well tied up all day down at the slip. By the time I get home of an evenin', the old village is pretty well buttoned up for the night. Outside of a couple of fishermen that've been hangin' around for the past week or so, there ain't nobody new in town."

"What about the Austin woman?" Harlan grunted.

Jake looked up. "What about her?"

"Weird old gal," Harlan assessed. "I see her comin' and goin' at all hours of the day and night. Seems awful busy for a widow lady."

Jake slumped back in his chair, neither frowning nor smiling. He looked at me as though the Austin woman needed some sort of explanation. "Chambers Bay is small enough that everybody knows what everybody else is doin'. The old lady Harlan is talkin' about is a widow woman. Gotta be close to seventy from the looks of her. I kinda figure she ain't all there." Jake gestured to his head to make the point.

"Maybe we oughta check her out," Harlan persisted.

Madden suddenly looked exasperated. "Hell's fire, this ain't no witch hunt. Use your head, Harlan. No old lady is goin' around eatin' goats and horses, cuttin' up kids and butcherin' the local druggist."

"Well, I been here less than two days, and I can think of a newcomer to these parts."

Harlan looked at me open-mouthed. "Who?"

"What about this kid Kelto that works for Bert and Polly Johnson down at the motel?"

Jake looked at me out of the corner of his eye. It was one of those "why the hell didn't I think of that" kind of looks. "Now, there's one for you," he muttered.

"Jake," I interrupted, "how did you learn about those two kids that were found down behind the motel this morning?"

"Couple of fishermen that have been stayin' at the motel reported it. They went out about midnight, came in about dawn, saw that the car was still sittin' there and that the kids were still in it."

"I was out behind that motel last night," I admitted. "After we left you at the diner, we went back to the motel, sat out in front for a while, and when Brenda went in to go to bed, I went to the office, walked through the motel, out the back door and saw the car with the couple in it sitting out on the point. That's when this Kelto kid shows up."

Jake wearily took the notebook out of his shirt pocket, wet his pencil with the tip of his tongue and scribbled a fast note. Even though I couldn't see the entry, I knew the one they called Kelto had just bubbled to the top of Jake's concern list.

"Well," Harlan drawled, "we better do somethin', and we better be doin' it fast." He turned to Jake. "Think maybe we oughta see how many guys we can round up and start combin' that stretch of beach from the motel on down past the pier on out to the Carson place?"

"Does that include the cave area?" I asked.

"Most of 'em," Jake grunted. "There's only a couple down on George Daniels's place."

"Why are you askin' about the caves?" Caleb inquired.

I shrugged. "Call it a gut feeling."

"What about it, Jake? Think we oughta make a sweep through that area?" Harlan asked.

The big man drained the last of his coffee and nodded. "Don't think we have much choice," he admitted. "We can't just stand around while this thing wipes out the whole damn village. I'll call Lieutenant Langley over at the Waverly post in the mornin' and see if he can send us some help. Then I'll call an open village meeting for two o'clock tomorrow afternoon and tell the folks what we need to do."

I looked over at Brenda. She was watching Madden, and there was a different kind of look on her face. Maybe haunted is the word I'm searching for.

Outside again, the earlier chill wind had died off, the rains had ceased, and the cloud deck was lying right on the surface of the bay. A heavy, smothering cloak of fog had settled over Chambers Bay. We were standing on the curb in front of Madden's office, and I knew the silver Z was parked at an angle not more than 20 feet away—yet I couldn't see it.

Caleb and Harlan said good night, and within seconds both were swallowed up by the fog. Brenda was standing next to me with the blanket still wrapped around her, shivering.

"Think you can find your way back to the motel in this soup?" Jake grunted.

"Shouldn't be all that difficult." Even as I said it, I knew there wasn't a great deal of conviction in my voice.

"I'll be happy to run you out there," Jake offered.

I took a long look at Brenda, who was the next best thing to a basket case, and decided to take the big man up on his offer. We crawled into his four-by-four, and Madden inched us out and onto the highway. Twice I checked and twice I confirmed that we were clipping along at less than seven miles per hour. As far as I could tell, the village, the streets, the road, even the diner looked deserted.

The choking blanket of misty greyness had closed in and captured us, bending Jake's yellow fog beams back up at us in a nightmarish swirl. Brenda laid her head on my shoulder, and I could hear her sob softly in the darkness.

Somehow, Jake knew when we were there. He pulled off into the motel parking lot, and I could hear the grating sound of wet gravel crunching under the tires. Even though I knew we couldn't be more than 30 or 40 feet from the entrance to the motel office, I couldn't see a thing; it was like being dropped off on another planet. The neon signs, both the one out at the road and the small one over the office door, were completely obliterated. The combination of mist, drizzle and fog confused every-thing—direction, distance, even my equi-librium.

I coaxed the sleeping B.C. down out of the cab of the truck, put my arm around her and headed in what I hoped was the direction of the motel. I kept looking back to see if Jake was still there. He was fading, and finally he too was gone.

The cold, heavy dampness of the fog can do strange things to men's minds. Images often materialize—of things that aren't there. Ghosts appear and just as suddenly are gone, leaving us to deal with the question of their return. Fog always catapults me back to the reality of those long and lonely nights. Then there was the reality of the bitter, mind-numbing cold. Now it was a clinging dampness, summoning up a chill that permeated to the very marrow of the bone. Fog, I have often thought, makes us question the existence of our tomorrows.

When my foot made contact with something solid, I prayed it was the step up to the sidewalk in front of the units. Good old number eight was my sanctuary. It was all too easy to remember that somewhere out there in the fog, someone or something was lurking that killed for no apparent reason. When I turned around, Jake was now completely lost from sight.

I took out my lighter, felt along the wall until I found a door and then traced across the surface until my fingers found the raised plastic numeral; it was a six. A still shivering Brenda was little more than an ill-defined image shuffling along in the grayness in front of me.

By the time we got to good old number eight and I managed to get the door open, Brenda had completely given up. She slumped up against the wall and protested that she couldn't go any further.

It took some fancy footwork, but I managed to maneuver between the two rooms and set her down on her bed. She did the rest on her own. Rolling to one side, then curling her legs up and under her, she twisted herself up into a tight little ball, and I covered her up.

Back in my own room, I turned on the light on my dresser and began to peel out of my damp clothing. I was again berating myself for leaving my prized survival kit in the Z. Twice in one day was proof that I was getting careless. I whipped out a blank file card and scratched out the word KIT in big bold letters with a felt tip. Cosmo was right; senility is a bitch.

Everything I needed was stowed in that damn kit behind the driver's seat in the Z. The momentary reflection on the kit set me to thinking about the antique Mauser that Papa Coop had given me the night we celebrated selling my first novel. It was intended to be a trophy. Instead, it had become the cornerstone of my now famous survival kit. The Mauser had swung the argument in my favor more than once.

A hot shower had the effect of partially invigorating me, and I meandered out of the bathroom with a towel wrapped around me. I glanced at my watch. It was almost midnight, too late to catch the news and too early to turn in. I decided that a quick review of the file cards would be just the thing to slide me off into another dimension.

It had been a busy day, and I had accumulated quite a stack. If I ever intended to construct any kind of a story out of all this, I had to spend the time giving the cards some semblance of order. I laid them on the dresser top, reached for the half empty bottle of Black and White, glanced in the mirror and saw him.

Kelto had situated himself in the darkest corner of the room with his back to the wall and his hands stuffed into the pockets of an old army issue fatigue jacket. He was leaning indolently against the wall.

"What the hell are you doing in here?" I barked.

"Bert said you were looking for me."

On balance, I tend to be a somewhat placid individual with an incredibly high threshold for the inconsiderate vagaries of the human species; there are a couple of things, however, that tend to send me right off the charts. One is loud noises; the other is the invasion of my cherished privacy. In other words, I was tired, a trifle cranky, and pissed over the fact that young Kelto had let himself in unannounced. "That was twelve hours ago," I said testily. "Now, I know it's an absolute bitch out there, so why don't you go get lost in it? There can't be anything either of us has to say that can't wait until tomorrow."

Kelto held up his hand in a halting motion. "You've been asking questions about me, Mr. Wages, so I asked a few questions about you."

"Just who the hell are you?" I snarled.

I don't like indolent people, but I like the word indolent because it perfectly describes the demeanor of people like Kelto. He was sleek, constructed like a greyhound, with the natural grace of a dancer, yet here he was with his perpetual pout lowering himself slowly, almost clumsily, into a chair. He had no intention of leaving. "I know what you think," he whispered huskily. "I know you're wondering what I found out about you." He paused, all too aware of the stress level. "I learned quite a bit. Would you like to know what I learned, Mr. Wages?"

I was still trying to get my temper under control. I walked over to the dresser and strapped on my watch, then sat down on my bed. "You've got five minutes. Say whatever it is that you've got to say and get the hell out of here."

"You're E.G. Wages," he began in his malevolent voice, "a writer who writes stories about things like this. You make people uncomfortable with your focus on the bizarre and supernatural."

"Four minutes and counting."

"You came to Chambers Bay because you suspected that there would be a repeat of a series of atrocities that began forty-four years ago. You are many things, Mr. Wages, but you most certainly are not a casual tourist."

I didn't have to ask for the source of his knowledge. My files were all too casually stacked on the top of my dresser and all too carefully labeled. I glanced at my watch for effect.

"You see, Mr. Wages, we, you and I, share a common interest in these unsavory episodes from our history."

"All right, I'll bite. What kind of common interest?"

"I too have been following these events. The difference, you see, is that I have been doing it far longer than you."

"How much longer?" The little bastard was beginning to intrigue me.

"Twenty-two years." There was no hesitation in his voice, only the element of something haunted and mysterious.

"That would have been about the time of Battle Harbor."

"I was at Battle Harbor," he said evenly.

It's strange how some words or statements or admissions can zero right in on your personal gyro. Kelto just had. I was off balance with a funny taste in my mouth. I did a couple of quick calculations; if he was actually at Battle Harbor, he was older than I had him pegged. "You were," I repeated in amazement, "at Battle Harbor? You mean you actually saw what happened?"

Kelto nodded somberly. "I not only saw it, Mr. Wages. I *lived* through it."

The funny part about it was that I halfway believed him. I pushed myself forward. "Tell me, what did you see?"

"If you mean you want me to describe what I saw, I'm afraid I cannot."

"Why not?" I insisted.

"I was seven years old at the time, Mr. Wages. I had pleaded with my mother to let me go on that retreat. At first she was reluctant, but my sister, Jenna, was attending and good old Reverend Bell was there in the capacity of both a chaperone and a spiritual advisor—so she relented. It was only a two-hour journey from the church to the retreat site, and there were games and singing. I remember only that I felt very grown-up. It was to be a whole new adventure for me."

Kelto's story began to unfold, and as he told it, his voice developed into something quite different from the grainy, almost tortured rasp of our first meeting. Now it seemed as though it was detached, almost apart from him, speaking through images coming back through the shadows of his mind.

"I remember that I was sitting next to Reverend Bell, who was driving the bus. He had wisely kept the smaller children to the front because there were three boys in the back who were being quite rowdy. When he pulled off of the main road and began to head down a rather narrow lane back toward the retreat site, we all heard a loud noise. It sounded like something exploded. Quite suddenly, the left front end of the bus pitched down. The Reverend got out of the bus and studied the situation. When he got back on the bus, he broke us up into two groups. The first group consisted of mostly the younger children, and he put Jenna in charge. I can still recall how the Reverend instructed us to stay close together and follow the path. He kept the older boys with him. We were several feet from the bus, walking down the path, when he called out to us that he would be along just as soon as the problem was solved."

Kelto had also accomplished something else. His story forced me off my self-imposed one pack a day limit. I got up, poured myself another drink, opened a fresh pack of cigarettes and returned to my perch on the edge of the bed.

"I have no way of knowing how far we had walked or how long it had taken us, but I suddenly realized that Jenna was alarmed. She had us huddle together and hold hands. We could all hear strange sounds. The trees there are mostly scrub, not much height to them; the soil is pockmarked and cluttered with large boulders. I was holding onto a little girl named Anita, and she was crying.

Suddenly Jenna screamed, and I saw something in the thicket. I was terrified," he said softly.

"Go on," I pushed, now disregarding his time limit.

"To this day, I don't know what it was that came out of that underbrush. I was petrified, a frightened little boy with his eyes shut and praying. Apparently I got knocked down, and that must have been the thing that saved me. They found me three days later, wandering around in a state of shock." He recited the events without emotion, as though it had happened to someone else.

"Why isn't any of this in the official record?"

"It's quite simple, Mr. Wages. Everyone thought I was dead. There was no way for the authorities who conducted the investigation at Battle Harbor to identify one child from another. In most cases they were dealing with little more than mutilated bits and pieces of my classmates. When I was discovered, they decided to keep my survival quiet. They didn't know what they were dealing with and they were afraid of what the maniac would do if he knew that someone had survived. They thought he might even come after me."

There have been no more than a handful of times in my life when I was speechless, but this was one of them.

For Kelto, the floodgates of his mind were open. "My mother was a widow. The experience broke her heart. I know that she loved me, but Jenna was her chosen, the very reason she lived. She died shortly after that, and I was shuttled off to an orphanage."

I'll admit to having been around for a while and over the years having observed a good many men describing and living through all kinds of personal hell. It is unusual for a man to relive a traumatic experience of the nature and magnitude that Kelto had just described without some sort of inadvertent demonstration of the fires that kindle that emotion. Yet there he sat, describing an atrocity of shocking proportions, and his face, his manner, his speech pattern were all devoid of passion. I kept thinking that what he was telling me was unreal, nothing more than a horror story. There would have been more. It was, after all, the cathartic ramblings of a tortured soul.

I started to ask him a question, and he again held up his hand in that halting gesture.

"When I was fifteen, I ran away from the orphanage. The nightmares were unbearable. I couldn't make it through the night without reliving those few terrifying minutes and suffering through the agonizing days that followed. I kept seeing it over and over in my mind—that horrible foul-smelling something, plundering, destroying."

"When did you realize that what happened at Battle Harbor wasn't a singular event, that it was actually one in a continuing . . . ?"

"I was twenty, working in the cannery in Saint John's. A friend, named Concha, told me about a sister that lived in a small commune in Quebec. She said the commune was decimated by a madman. Somehow, Concha's description of what had happened to those gentle people catapulted me back into my own memories, and I saw similarities. I wondered even then if this madness would continue. I began to read, and it wasn't long till I came to the same conclusions that brought you here. You see, Mr. Wages, I too knew that they would return, and like you, I know the time is now."

"Are you aware that they killed a man this afternoon, a local fellow by the name of Percy Kramer?"

Kelto accepted the news stoically. "I find it interesting that you refer to them as 'they'," he offered evenly. He sighed and closed his haunted eyes. "You see, Mr. Wages, I did not come here to solicit your help. Quite the contrary, I came to ask you to stay out of it. I understand now. I know what I must do." Satisfied he had said all he wanted to say, he pushed himself erect, offered me a wan smile and turned toward the door. He paused just long enough to button the collar of his jacket, quietly opened the door and turned back to face me again. "Tell them to stay out of it, Mr. Wages. I know what must be done. If others become involved, the situation will only worsen."

He stepped silently out into the empty gray stillness of the night, and the door closed behind him.

It took longer than usual for me to slip into my world of troubled sleep. And even when I did, the images that danced in the shadowy world of my subconscious were little more than amorphous and half-born nightmares. I saw Kelto's stoic and somehow unreal face and the unforgettable sight of Percy Kramer's violated fat white body hanging from the dead tree. Woven throughout were frightening and forbidding glimpses of the vast cold and barren polar plains. I was in total synchronization with a tortured psyche, yet I had no idea what it meant. Finally, there was the young woman, slim and yet somehow pregnant with hate and fear. She was laughing, and she had a knife. She was holding the knife out . . . no, at me.

I woke up twice, sweating, each time groping my way to the dresser in the darkness to grab a cigarette. Each time I returned in a kind of halfway world between awareness and fear.

Outside my door, veiled by a cold gray curtain of choking fog, was an indescribable homicidal maniac, a pathological, knife-wielding creature, a marauding, unthinking thing that terrorized. It had returned. I shuddered, closed my eyes and hoped against hope that the frightening images would not return to haunt still more dreams.

It was later, in the early hours of the morning, that I felt it. There was the slightest movement next to my bed. I felt the covers pull back as B.C. slid in beside me. She pushed her slender body up close to mine, and I heard her sob softly. Protege of Cosmo Leach or not, I curled her sweat-dampened head in the crook of my arm and pulled the sheet over her. She mumbled incoherently and curled her hand into mine. "Sleep tight, little lady," I whispered. "Maybe we'll make it through this night yet."

I used to refer to it as the curse of the Wages; my father and his father before him, in fact all of us, were always up at the first light of the new day.

It was dawn, I was certain of that. Eventually I would look at my watch to verify it, but for now it was enough to just know that I had made it through another night. I slipped my arm from under B.C.'s head and inched my way toward the edge of the bed. By the time I made it to the window to make my ritualistic assessment of the new day, I knew it was pointless. The heavy gray pallor still choked the landscape. I could see to the edge of the concrete walkway, but that was as far as it went.

I gathered up pants, shoes, socks, and my favorite golf shirt (the dark blue one with Harbor Springs embroidered on the left sleeve), slipped into the bathroom, got dressed and managed to slip out of the room without waking her. I had a hunch Brenda Cashman wouldn't have awakened if a bomb had gone off.

The horizontal visibility was still what the boys who run the weather bureau call "condition totally obscured." Suffice it to say that I could see large objects, if they weren't more than ten feet or so in front of me. Keeping to the sidewalk in front of the units, I groped my way down to the office. Bert was there, feet propped on a waste can, chair tilted back, watching the early morning news. When I knocked, he waved me in.

"You're up early," I observed.

"Had to. Polly had a rough night. I got up to draw her a hot bath and couldn't go back to sleep." Bert pointed to a lime-crusted Mr. Coffee and invited me to help myself. I did, laced it with a powdered cream substitute and dropped into the chair beside him. "Did you ever find Kelto to talk to him?"

"Last night," I muttered, hoping the curt response would satisfy him. It did. Bert wanted to talk about other things. When he started in on the fog, I knew that Jake had been at least partially successful. It was obvious the word on Percy Kramer hadn't yet made it as far as the Chambers Bay Motel.

"Ever see fog like this before?" Bert groused.

I shook my head. To be honest, I wasn't really interested in casual conversation; Bert's only real attraction for me was his coffee. I fully intended to hit him up for a second cup, get my still snoozing brain in gear and begin formulating plans for the day. There were two things uppermost in my mind. One was a second go around with the mysterious Mr. Kelto, and the second was a chance to look into this person they called the Widow Austin. During the course of the long night I had tried repeatedly to reason out how and why these attacks seemed to be occurring in both a chronological and geographical pattern. I had taken for granted that our creature or thing was one in the same—that is to say, the same individual. But somewhere along in the dark hours, between fitful hours of half-sleep, I realized that I might be guilty of jumping to one very erroneous conclusion.

It might not be an individual at all. What if it was a cult, or some Satanic society working to some sort of other-world calendar that dictated that mutilations and murders be carried out according to some sacred order? Under most circumstances, I would have reached over and turned on the light and uttered this new thought into my voice recorder, but with B.C. just finally drifting off into an untroubled sleep, I was afraid it would wake her. Luckily, the fringe-area thought stayed with me till the dawn.

All of which leads to the lady they call Widow Austin. How, I asked myself, would this cult or group or whatever know what was going on? Given that, how did they select their victims? Or was it a random thing, mere vagaries of fate? In the cases of both the incidents at Battle Harbor and the Coalition commune, they were able to perpetrate their crimes because they were able to isolate their victims—in both cases, youngsters without adequate supervision. But the question still remained, did they have some sort of advance notice about where these children were going, or were these nothing more than terrible co-incidences when the victims stumbled into their grasp?

Taking my long shot hypothesis one step further, if the cult needed a contact with the community, there would have to be an advance party—and that advance party would be someone the community didn't suspect. What better cover than being a 70-year-old widow? Long shot? Leap in logic? Probably, but I've learned that the logic of the ordered and civilized world seldom applies to situations like this.

I poured myself a second cup of coffee, thanked Bert for his hospitality and stepped back outside into the fog. I detoured just long enough to try the door to Kelto's unit, but it was locked, so I went on back to number 8. When I got there, B.C. was perched on the edge of the bed with a sheepish look on her face.

"Relax," I advised her. "I've had a few bad nightmares myself."

She tried to smile, but when the effort fell short, I handed her what was left of the second cup. It took her less than ten seconds to drain it. "Worst night of my life," she muttered. "I don't know what I would have done if you hadn't been here."

I wanted to avoid a pity party and the string of time-wasting apologies that are usually part of that libretto. Instead of commenting on her tough night, I sat down on the edge of the bed next to her and whipped out my stack of file cards. "It's a new day and we've got things to do. Here's the agenda." I really hadn't thought it out all that well, so I was rapidly scribbling notes as we went through the stack. "We're going to do some checking on our friend

Kelto and the lady they call Widow Austin. After that, we're going to meet Jake Madden and go to that village meeting he intends to call. After that, I want to talk to somebody at the Waverly RCMP post."

Brenda looked at the stack of cards, then up at me. A small smile played at the corners of her mouth. "Thanks, E.G.," she whispered. "I was a basket case and needed a friend."

PART 5

So far, B.C. had managed to survive the cultural shock of Chambers Bay, the discovery of the three victims, an attempted rape, and two days in very close proximity to yours truly. She was road tested and proving fairly serviceable. On the third morning we did what writers do best, hopefully, we wrote. That is to say, I organized my stack of file cards, and Brenda entertained herself by diligently constructing a logic tree, an old Cosmo device that tests the theory that everything related to the events traces back to one tap root. There was one curious thing about it. I had to show young Brenda how to do it because, she indicated, Cosmo never covered it. It was doubly curious when you consider that the logic tree is one of the old boy's pet testing devices. On the other hand, maybe the old geezer had a new gimmick.

At any rate, the results of the logic tree exercise did confirm one nagging suspicion, and that was simply that so far there was no logic to the pattern. We had victims who were brutally assaulted and still others who had been carved up with near surgical precision. We had young victims and old victims, boys and girls, men and women, and our creature hadn't confined his activities to humans, either—witness the destruction of two sheep and a horse. And, if that wasn't enough, we had situations involving total destruction and still others where the only thing disturbed was one or two vital organs.

B.C. stayed with her snowballing list of variables longer than I would have, but finally she demonstrated her frustration by throwing her pencil down and muttering an emphatic "damn."

By nine-thirty the fog had peeled back slightly, and I was able to see all the way across the motel parking lot to the dense growth of pine on the other side of the highway. It was just enough to make me decide to give it a try. It had cleared enough that B.C.'s constitution was renewed, and our accomplishments were going to be minimal if we continued to sit in our motel room, reviewing old data and waiting for the sunshine to break through.

Our first stop was at the Chambers Bay community office building, an ancient edifice constructed of crumbling brick surrounded by a landscape that consisted of mostly hardpan occasionally interrupted by patches of grass. The young lady behind the desk informed us that her name was Angie and readily expressed an interest in helping us in any way she could. We told her that we were doing research on a family tree and were interested in talking to a woman that we believed might have some information that could help us. The woman, of course, was the Austin widow.

"Dumb old me," Brenda gushed in an embarrassingly poor imitation of a Southern drawl. "We drove all the way up here, and I left her name and address on the dresser—dumb old me."

Angie dug into her files while I scowled at Brenda. She shrugged her shoulders and quietly pointed to the fact that we were getting the information we wanted.

The Austin widow turned out to be Glenna Hoyt Austin, 67 years old and most recently a resident of Fort Albany on the southwest shore of James Bay. Her husband, an outfitter on the Albany River, had been dead for a number of years, and she had come to Chambers Bay in search of a long lost niece identified only as a Miss

Harris. The aforementioned Miss Harris, Angie informed us, was no longer a resident in the area and had left no forwarding address. The widow Austin, however, had stayed on, and Angie gave us instructions on how to get to her place.

Despite the fog, we found it. The surprise was that the old lady's house was just down the road and up the hill from the very spot where Percy Kramer had made his ill-fated pass at B.C.

The ramshackle old house was in an advanced stage of decay. It was shuttered (all broken) and badly in need of paint. The front porch sagged, and if ever a house could be described as lonely, this one qualified. There wasn't another structure visible in any direction. I looked over at B.C. She was apprehensive about the whole thing, and it had begun to show—wrinkles of concern, my mother used to call them.

"Ready?" I grinned. "Research is the fun part of writing, meeting new people in new places and learning new things."

I trudged up the hill with B.C. close behind. It took several solid raps before the door was grudgingly opened a scant four inches. A squinty, dull brown eye peered around and out at me and a twisted, uneven whisper masquerading as a voice asked, "What'cha want?"

I stepped back out of the long shadows so that the old woman could see my face.

"Mrs. Austin, my name is Elliott Wages and this is Miss Cashman. We were wondering if you could spare us a couple of minutes to answer a few questions."

"About what?" she snapped. The response was almost a whiplash.

B.C. stepped forward, all sweetness. "We're doing some research on this area of the province—social research, needs of the elderly, quality of the available medical services, things like that."

Brenda had hit the old woman's hot button. The Austin widow opened the door another four inches. The shielded face bobbed up and down as she appraised us from head to foot. "You ain't from the church, are ya?"

"No," B.C. said calmly, "we're from the Canadian Research Bureau." She reached into her shoulder bag, pulled out her American driver's license and handed it to the woman. The widow snapped it out of her hand, held it up close to one eye, studied it momentarily and handed it back. "All right," she hissed, "but be quick about it."

Brenda nodded. "We'll be as brief as possible," she replied sweetly.

With B.C.'s assurance, the door creaked open and the old woman waddled into the darkened room ahead of us. Two flickering candles served as the only illumination. The cluttered room was a montage of gray on gray unrevealing shadows. When she got to the center of the room, she turned around and stared at us defiantly.

Most folks who have been around me any length of time accuse me of stereotypical thinking, and while I'll admit to a certain amount of this decidedly universal human failing, I will not apologize for the habit. Over the years it has served me well. It is seldom necessary to start from ground zero in assessing new situations. Right or wrong has nothing to do with it. The fatal flaw in this practice, of course, is that one or ten or whatever percent that pops up deviating from the norm. All of this leads up to the fact that I knew I was confronting a 67-year-old widow—hence, she should have been white-haired, with kindly blue eyes, slightly stooped, sheltered by a shawl and happily offering us chocolate chip cookies. Nothing could have been further from the package we confronted.

To be sure, she was small and somewhat stooped, standing less than five feet. She was the unfortunate possessor of greedy, mud-colored pinched eyes, an ugly squat face and a mouth that was little more than a humorless slit across an ashen and wrinkled face. Her whole demeanor betrayed her perpetual conflict with the world that surrounded her.

"Now, ask yer questions quick-like and get outta here," she hissed.

The room itself was a chaotic collection

of primitives and junk, all focused toward a white-clothed, waist-high round table in the middle of the dimly lit room. The table itself was decorated with a tall, white, tapered candle, a sprig of pine and a grotesque figurine of a black, pear-shaped creature with a bloated belly.

Beauty, they say, is in the eye of the beholder. To me, the little statue was, in a word, disgusting. Brenda, however, reacted quite differently. She bent over and gazed at the eight-inch-high statuette with what amounted to a degree of reverence. The old woman's eyes watched Brenda intently, and a sinister little smile began to play upon her ugly slash of a mouth.

"What is it?" Brenda asked softly. For some reason, I had the feeling B.C. already knew.

"Beautiful, ain't it?" the old woman rasped. Even at that, her voice seemed to have somehow softened. She moved in closer to the figure as though it was her mission to protect it from B.C.'s penetrating appraisal. "You are gazing," the old woman raptured, "at the sarcophagus of Sate, Ancient of Ancients."

B.C. repeated the pronouncement and looked up at me. Her eyes were glazed, and then suddenly she seemed to regain her composure. "Lovely," she repeated, her voice drifting off again.

"Is this a good time to answer our

questions?" I interrupted.

"Get it over with," the old woman bristled.

For the next several minutes, B.C. spewed out what sounded like a well-prepared list of very official, typically bureaucratic questions all relating to health services. If I hadn't known better, I would have sworn that the whole act was a carefully rehearsed and frequently practiced routine. She concluded by thanking the old woman for her time and bidding her a good day. She wasn't even subtle about hustling me out of the house.

We were safely back in the Z and headed back for the village before she quit scratching out her own notes and allowed me the luxury of a few questions.

"How did you know the old girl couldn't read? That little routine with the driver's license was beautiful."

"Long shot," she admitted, "but it paid off."

"And that list of questions—fantastic! You sounded official as hell."

B.C. looked straight ahead, her face furrowed into a frown. "Not bad for a flat-chested broad who snores, huh?"

She never cracked a smile.

I've heard it said that one of the secrets of winning teams is that there is always someone on the team who is willing to step forward, take charge and fire the team with enthusiasm. At the moment, B.C. was in charge. We aimed the Z into the fog and back for the motel. I was anxious to get on the phone to Lucy.

B.C. had already scribbled out a list of questions, most of them relating to what she informed me was a sixteenth century lesser deity called Sate. This time my mumbled instructions were even more vague than usual. I couldn't give Lucy much to go on from B.C.'s all too terse summary. I knew very little about Sate; in fact, I'd never heard of him.

Lucy must have picked up on my vibrations because she kept her small talk to a minimum. She hung up with a promise to get back to me as soon as she could come up with something.

While I was on the phone, Brenda practiced her pacing. She patrolled back and forth between the two rooms, from time to time pausing just long enough to assess the still dismal day droning on outside the shelter of our motel room. It was equally apparent that she had developed a taste for my Black and White; the Scotch supply was dwindling rapidly. Finally she slumped into the same chair that Kelto had occupied a few hours earlier, folded her hands under her chin and stared at me.

"Tell me what you know about this Sate stuff."

Brenda's face creased itself into something akin to a reflective frown, and she slumped deeper into the chair. "I'm digging back," she admitted. "He was a lesser Mongol deity that was supposedly chased into the great swamps of Pullan. The way I remember it, he and his band of true believers were run off because the authorities believed they were flesh eaters."

A piece of the puzzle tumbled into place. "When?"

"I just don't remember," she said with an air of apology. "It wasn't the focus of what we were studying at the time, more of a footnote curiosity in an Ancient Cultures class."

My mind was already off to the races, B.C.'s offhand comment and admittedly vague recollections were just enough to spur the old theory developer into some unplowed territory. Already my mind was conjuring up images of Sate's zealots laboriously working their way, island by island, up the Aleutian chain toward the frozen wastelands of the north. "What else can you remember about the old boy?" I urged.

B.C. ran the tip of her index finger around the top of her glass and closed her eyes. "Nothing of any importance," she said lazily.

"What did that old girl call it? Ancient of Ancients?"

B.C. nodded.

"Wish we had some more information on the old boy," I added impatiently.

"Well," Brenda purred, "why don't we just wait for your little pet—what's her name, Lucy? I'm sure she'll be calling you back soon."

Madden's open village council came off as planned. By the time two o'clock rolled around, we had driven back into Chambers Bay and located the old community school building where 70 or so people had gathered in the drafty old gymnasium.

Jake, along with Harlan, Caleb and a stern, square-jawed, blue-faced man in the smartly pressed uniform of the RCMP, sat at a small table on a riser at one end of the room. B.C. and I located two seats up front and prepared ourselves for more research.

We hadn't been on the scene more than 48 hours and already we had a pretty good handle on some of the locals. B.C. spotted the combination hostess/waitress/owner of the diner with the name Vernice stitched on her brown and yellow polyester uniform, and I located Bert Johnson standing nervously along the far wall. Polly wasn't with him. Equally conspicuous by his absence was young Mr. Kelto. I was about to put the Widow Austin in the same category, but the old woman slipped in at the last minute and took a chair in the far corner of the room.

She was still wearing the same baggy brown coat sweater and her eyes were still pinched into an uncompromising squint.

It was exactly two o'clock when Madden rapped the table with a gavel, and the already somber crowd grew even quieter.

"I think everybody knows why we're here," he said.

It wasn't one of those situations where the crowd responds vocally. Instead, the only indication of involvement was the way they seemed to collectively stir in their seats and incline forward. It wasn't the kind of meeting where a person wanted to miss too much of what was said.

"For those of you that don't already know, we found Percy Kramer's body in the Carson woods late yesterday afternoon."

Apparently the word of Percy's fate hadn't leaked out after all. The news was greeted with an audibly nervous murmur, as though the assemblage took a collective breath.

"He was mutilated, just like those two kids we found yesterday morning on that little strip that runs out off of Tacker Point. Now, I ain't sayin' they're one in the same, mind you, but we got four cases of this kind of thing now. Less 'an a week ago this all started when Barry Harrison's boy found those two ewes of his all butchered up and half-eaten. The next day Ruby Carson found that old work mare of hers the same way.

Now, animals is one thing, but now it's people—and I think we better be doin' somethin' about it."

Jake's oratory stirred some of the villagers into a few sporadic "yeahs."

"Earlier today I called over to the RCMP post at Waverly and asked them to send someone over. The officer sittin' up here at the table with us is Sergeant Kendall. He's here to act as liaison and offer us assistance. He's agreed to help us organize a sweep of the area to see if we can ferret out whoever or whatever is doin' this." With that, Madden stepped back and motioned for the sergeant to unveil his plan.

Constable Kendall was decidedly taller than he had appeared while sitting down. He was an easy six foot two or three and ramrod straight in his yellow striped pants and knee-high brown leather boots. Without comment he began to unfurl what proved to be a detailed map of the Chambers Bay area. With Harlan holding one end and Caleb the other, Kendall duly detailed the location of each of the four incidents. His voice was a tinge British and appropriately clipped. "This point is the Freeman Field auxiliary landing strip that Mr. Harrison leases from the provincial government for open range sheep grazing. I've put an X where Constable Madden reported the slaughter of the two sheep."

I glanced over at B.C., who was frantically scratching out her own version of the map complete with notes.

Kendall's hand traced along till it came to another X, this one with a small numeral two located next to it. "This is, as you all know, Tacker Point. This is where the bodies of the two young people were discovered yesterday morning." Again he began tracing along an invisible route until he came to another X. "This is where Mr. Kramer's body was discovered yesterday afternoon." Almost as an afterthought, he gestured to the fourth X. "And this is the location of the Carson loss." He stepped aside and made a sweeping gesture with his hand as though it would help the locals understand the magnitude of the problem of adequately covering the area.

"Hey, Madden," a voice bellowed from near the rear of the room, "how come we gotta cover it? Why don't the Mounties bring a squad in here and take care of it?"

"Yeah, Madden, why us? We don't know nothin' about trackin' some kinda madman."

Jake lumbered back to the front of the riser and stared toward the back of the room. "Because the RCMP post at Waverly is operatin' short-handed. Constable Kendall here called his superior officer at detachment headquarters and explained the situation. They promised to send in two more officers sometime tomorrow—Thursday at the latest."

The announcement brought another murmur from the crowd, this time a little louder than before.

Kendall held up his hand. "Listen to me, please. I don't think the situation as it stands now can be termed critical. I think we can control it."

It was apparent the crowd didn't agree with Kendall. To their way of thinking, the situation was already out of hand and it was time to get the Mounties out in force. The natives were getting restless. The man behind us began whispering to his wife, and around the room there was growing evidence of discontent.

"All right," Jake thundered, "keep it down. We've got a plan. Harlan here will take ten or so men and start at the western boundary over by the caves and sweep east until he comes to the Carson road. Caleb Hall will head up the second group. They'll be starting up on the highway and sweep south till they intercept Harlan's squad. Then the two groups will cover the shoreline. Constable Kendall here will do the same thing from the east side of the village, and I'll head up the group that starts at Freeman Field. According to my calculations we got us about two and a half square miles of some pretty rough terrain to cover."

Brenda nudged me with her elbow. "What

about us?" she whispered. "Think they need our help?"

Jake was still talking. "Now, it'll work out just about right if every man in this room joins in the sweep."

"That lets me off the hook," Brenda said, grinning.

"I need two or three of the women to organize places for the families to sleep tonight, and I need two other women to handle our communications network," Jake continued.

"Communications is my thing," she whispered again. "I dusted a radio once."

"Each group will have a forty channel unit. Your squad leader will appoint someone to operate it at your sweep site. Those of you that got 'em should bring whatever kind of firearm you can rustle up. We don't know what we'll run into out there in those damn woods, so we better be prepared for the worst. One last thing—we start at four o'clock sharp. Be there!"

The cavernous room was filled with the sounds of scraping chairs and partially muted mutters of discontent. I stood up and began searching through the crowd for the Austin widow, anxious to see how she reacted to the news of the search. I grabbed B.C. by the arm. "Tell Madden I'll be with his group and that I'll catch up with him as soon as I check something out."

"Like what?"

"Like old lady Austin," I shot back. "She heard Madden's plan and hightailed it out of here."

"You think she's going to warn someone, don't you?"

"I don't know what I think, but I'm going to find out."

B.C.'s face creased into a petulent scowl of frustration. I knew what she was thinking. "Okay," she sighed, "I'll tell him, but the next time I go where you go, got it?"

I threaded my way through the milling villagers toward the back of the room. There were two doors. I gambled on the one to the left since it was closest to where the old girl had been sitting. By the time I pushed my way past a handful of grumbling villagers and out into the gray afternoon fog, she was nowhere in sight.

It was hunch time again. The damp grayness had swallowed her up. The fog was densest to the west, and since she had already disappeared, I was really playing a long shot. At this point, I hadn't even convinced myself the old girl had a role in all of this. I was basing a lot of it on the discovery of an ugly little statue and an old legend only half-remembered.

Still, the Austin widow, like Kelto, remained a riddle. Like the old woman's sarcophagus, Kelto's parting admonition played over and over like a grooved record. "Tell them to stay out of it. If others become involved, the situation will only worsen."

Don't ask me why I didn't run around to the front of the building and get in the Z with the survival kit still tucked securely behind the driver's seat. For some reason, instincts were taking over. I knew, but I didn't know. I was getting a strong signal from wherever it is those signals come from that Glenna Austin was somewhere up there in the fog just ahead of me. Chalk it up to gut feeling.

Unless the Austin woman was clairvoyant, which was a distinct possibility, there was no way for her to know I was trying to follow her. Half of my problem was that I couldn't be certain she was up the fog-shrouded streets ahead of me. The other half of the problem was I was so pre-occupied trying to weave the old woman into the story that I damn near collided with someone.

It was Kelto.

He was standing there in that damned olive drab fatigue jacket like a sentinel, almost part of the fog. He glowered out at me from under that pronounced ridge like some sort of malevolent gargoyle. He had waited until I was within five feet of him before he spoke. There was no greeting, merely his raspy and ominous pronouncement. "I warned you," he said in his measured fashion.

"What the hell are you doing out here?"

I blustered. The stone-faced kid had a way of getting to me. It was the second time in the last 18 hours he had unexpectedly materialized out of the fog.

"I have been searching in the woods," he said evenly.

"Searching? Alone? In this weather? In those woods? Are you out of your mind?"

Kelto stared back at me with a look of intolerance. "It is altogether possible, Mr. Wages, that I understand what is happening much more clearly than you do."

In less time than it takes to describe it, I was down to the last few inches of the old fuse, and it was burning fast. "Damn it, Kelto, if you know something that can shed some light on this situation, you'd better come out with it before someone else gets killed. While you were out there poking around in the woods, Madden held a village council session and decided to make a sweep through that area."

"I told you to let me handle it."

"Handle it hell," I shouted. "We've got some kind of maniacal, half-crazed, depraved monster out there that butchers animals and carves parts out of people— and you make it sound like we're trying to get rid of some kind of garden pest. Just because you've got some sort of personal vendetta against this thing, you can't ignore your responsibility to . . ."

"I told you to let me handle it," he

repeated solemnly.

Grammarians will tell you there is a difference between frustration and exasperation, but to my way of thinking it's nothing more than a matter of degree. What I'm saying is that I vaulted through the former straight to the latter. Kelto not only wasn't any help, but this pointless exchange had cooled the trail of the Austin woman—if, in fact, she had ever been there. I sighed and started walking back toward the old schoolhouse. Kelto was still back there, standing in the fog.

Officially, it was going on sunset, but the time of day seemed of little importance. I had returned to the site of the assembly, jumped in the Z and took off for Freeman's Field. It took me a good 15 minutes to do so, but I caught up with Madden at just about the point his sweep team cleared through the area beyond the ill-fated spot where the young couple had died just the morning before. Before leaving, I had been smart enough to raid the old survival kit for the Mauser and a flashlight. Both items were tucked securely in my belt and concealed by a poplin windbreaker.

We worked our way steadily west. The going was tough. I had been assigned a position out on the left flank of the team, closest to the shoreline—a boulder-cluttered area laced with scrub pine, a tangle of bramble and waist-high weeds. Most of the time I couldn't be certain what the next step would lead to.

I don't really know what we expected to find, but we didn't find any blackened patches of earth similar to the one where Percy was killed. Nor did we find any evidence of broken saplings, unusual holes or gouges in the surface. Even more importantly, I encountered nothing that looked like a two thumb, three finger imprint.

There was a definite lack of what you would term the sounds of nature—no chatter of birds begrudging our invasion and no trace of any wildlife. There was only the steady, almost mocking sound of the placid water lapping against the rocky shoreline.

The whole effort, as it turned out, was a tiring, fruitless and time-consuming four-hour drill in futility. The sweep from east to west by Madden's group accomplished a big fat zero.

We intercepted Constable Kendall's group, four men and two teenage boys carrying kerosene lanterns at the junction of two sandy trails. The dancing flames of their lanterns created a bizarre flickering setting in the foggy landscape. From there on, the two squads combined their efforts and collectively canvassed the area on into where Percy's deserted pickup truck still languished. Caleb's squad and Harlan's men were still out there somewhere.

We were at the rendezvous point. Jake checked his watch, grumbled and plunked his heavy frame down on the tailgate of Kramer's truck. It was the best seat in the house, and I joined him. I took out a cigarette, offered Jake one and noted with a modest degree of satisfaction that it was only my fifth one for the day. That achievement, however, paled in comparison to the fact that Madden's entire crew, including yours truly, had survived the trek in from the Freeman boundary without some sort of encounter. There was little doubt in my mind that Madden viewed it as just another day's work, but to my way of thinking, it was akin to conquering Everest.

We had been waiting no more than five minutes when Caleb's crew began to filter out of the woods into the clearing. "We could hear Harlan's crew working out to our right," he said. "They're runnin' three, maybe four hundred yards behind us."

Jake nodded, slowly scanning the men from the last three groups. In all, I counted 23 of them. At least five of them looked as though they could be 15 or maybe even younger. There was no horseplay between the youngsters; there seemed, instead, to actually be a grimmer dimension to them than the older group.

It was a good 20 minutes later when Harlan's crew began arriving. They straggled out of the woods, one by one, most carrying shotguns, two bearing torches. This time I glanced at my watch and confirmed my suspicions; it was 7:45. The fog had now completely choked out what little daylight there was left.

The men broke up into several small groups. Here and there fragments of conversation could be detected. For the most part, comments were subdued and low-key. There was an awareness that Harlan himself still hadn't emerged from the shadowy woods, and comments began to pass from one group to another. No one could recall the last time they had seen him.

Madden and Kendall huddled near the rear of Kramer's truck, nervously stealing glances back at the woods to the west.

I checked my watch again; it was nearing 8:20. Darkness rapidly enveloped us. I looked back at Madden, who was headed toward me. The many folds of his contoured face had all collapsed into one massive, scowling frown. "Harlan shoulda' been here by now," he grunted.

The men had already started gravitating toward us. They were growing restless. Kendall began circulating among them. Flashlights and lanterns emerged. The colorless nothingness of the persistent fog caught the reflection of the still-sputtering flames and bounced them back at us in an eerie pattern of unreal color.

It was still enough that Jake didn't have to shout.

"Look, men, I don't have to tell ya that Harlan ain't come out yet. He's long overdue. Sergeant Kendall and me agree we better be startin' a sweep west to look for him."

This time the grumbles were absent. The men were tired, but they were his friends, his neighbors, maybe even relatives. A new commitment had evolved.

Kendall stepped forward again. "Okay, we've got seven torches. I want you to work in clusters—three on each side of the man carrying the torch. Take a good look at the men on each side of you. Know who they are and keep them in sight. If you lose visual contact with the group on either side of you, start hollering until you re-establish contact, then tighten up your group and go on. The clusters at each end of the line should be particularly alert to your exposed flank. Double-check everything. We don't know what we're dealing with."

One of the younger men stepped forward. His voice trembled. "You think that critter got 'em, Sergeant?"

Jake shook his head. "Don't know, Clem. We just don't know."

Kendall took the first few steps, and three ranks began to cluster up on either side of him. I had an ugly flashback of National Guard units, apprehensive, new to their roles, uncertain of their purpose—Kent State. The thought raced through my mind. What if one of these guys sees a ghost or a shadow and gets trigger happy?

Kendall and Madden were obviously concerned about the same thing. "Let's get started," he barked, "and remember, if it ain't somewhere in the vicinity of one of the torches and you can't get a response out of it, be prepared to defend yourself. Stay alert!" Jake Madden could be very convincing.

I made myself a part of the trio to the left of the torch on Madden's left flank. One of the men in my cluster carried a pump action 12-gauge, the other carried the torch. I had my fingers nestled around the reassuring old Mauser. The one with the shotgun kept looking nervously back at Madden.

The flickering lights of the kerosene torches created crazy, surrealistic patterns. The pines formed a virtual canopy over us, somehow creating the illusion that they held the fog prisoner. Twigs snapped. Shimmering gray-green images appeared, unreal and threatening. The collective mind was becoming an even greater threat than our unseen adversary. Something darted, scurrying frantically for the protective cover of the underbrush. Now and then there was a shout or a nervous laugh. "Is that you Frank?" another shouted. "Damn it Roy, when I say somethin', answer me."

Another nervous laugh.

There was no way of knowing how much ground we covered. It didn't seem possible, but this sweep was actually slower than the earlier one. Now there was the added dimension of the darkness. I stumbled and righted myself, finger inching through the trigger guard. The hair on the back of my neck had begun to bristle. The other hand had coiled tightly around the handle of the flashlight.

I had just looked over in Madden's direction when it happened. The youth to my left stopped. His arm darted out in front of him, his finger pointing into the swirling montage of the fog in the trees in front of us. "I saw somethin'," he stuttered.

For a split second I saw it too. Then it disappeared. Instinctively I reached out and touched the torch carrier on the arm. He halted, his anxious eyes nervously searching the area immediately in front of him. Now Jake had stopped. When he finally spoke, it was barely a whisper. "See what? Where?"

"It was the kid over here on my left," I hissed back.

The young man with the torch circled around behind me and moved in beside his friend. "Where'd you see it, Tommy?" He hoisted the flame higher, inclining it forward.

"There! See that?" Tommy stuttered.

There was something there, all right. I didn't so much see it as feel it. It was too brief, like a sudden cold chill, there and yet not there.

"That you, Harlan?" Jake barked.

There was no answer, only the sound of a small branch snapping.

I suppose it was the culmination of everything, of rubbing the already frayed fibers of the fearful mind, of the subtle sound in the trees overhead, of the otherwise eerie silence, of the perceptions of fear—but suddenly it was reality. The night was shattered by an almost cannonlike roar. Bolts of orange flashed out like a snake's tongue, piercing the gray blanket and slamming into their target. There were shouts, frenzied footsteps, confusion. The young man beside Madden had fired four times; now he was transfixed.

"There it is again," the boy shrieked.

"I didn't see nothin'," another protested.

Madden took a step forward. "Damn it, Harlan, if you're in there, you better say somethin'."

The silence was only punctuated by labored breathing.

"Tommy," Jake snarled, "get your butt over here."

Both of the boys sidled up to Madden.

"Show me where," he challenged.

Tommy pointed.

There was something there, all right—an

image that wouldn't crystalize, a bad dream, no beginning, no end. I shuddered.

"Researcher," Madden snapped, "over here!"

I took several steps forward, fingers cramping around the handle of the Mauser.

"Flash your light up in that tree," he whispered. "Keep your movements slow."

The index finger of my right hand was coiled securely around the trigger. My left hand clutched the cumbersome flashlight. From there on I like to think it was one fluid movement; my thumb jammed the switch forward and the beam of light pierced through the fog and darkness like a laser. I was dead on. It was still there, and my stomach began ricocheting around like a crazed pinball machine.

"Oh, my God," Madden muttered.

There were no reference points. It simply was. It had a bloated, misshapen head that was dominated by slitlike, yellow, dulled eyes that glared down at us in open defiance. All of its other features seemed to be lost in the twisted mass of variegated tissue that constituted the head. Only the crooked, cud-chewing mouth possessed its own definition; it was an uneven black slit that slashed across its face, seeping thick, oily juices as it masticated its food.

It grunted an unintelligible prehistoric threat, weaving slowly back and forth on a precarious perch high above us. The detail of its indescribable shapeless body was lost in a squatting mass, partially concealed by fog and branches. It blinked lethargically, making no attempt to escape the probing light.

"Holy shit," Madden muttered again, "what the hell is it?"

Words failed me. My stomach was churning and stale air was clogging my throat.

Slowly, almost as if oblivious to our presence, the thing worked its massive two-thumb, three-fingered claw up to its mouth and belched out a chunk of something, disdainfully discarding it like a piece of spoiled meat.

The boy with the torch leaped aside, then bent over and held the illuminating flame down to inspect the rejection. It was mangled and blackened, giving off a rancid odor.

Suddenly he reeled, his knees buckling. He stumbled forward in the dirt, vomiting. When he managed to look up, his eyes were glazed. The scream finally escaped. "Oh God, Jake," he screeched, "it's a man's hand!"

We all stared up at the beast in stunned, almost stupified silence.

Almost majestically, the creature raised its massive arm and pointed. The beam of my flashlight traced out the length of the branch until we saw the creature's gruesome prize. Harlan Gorman's long, now featureless body was draped like a giant gunnysack over the limb. At least I thought it was Harlan. A body without a head is not the easiest thing to identify.

Cosmo always said that you can tell a great deal about a man's passions by the manner in which he fires his weapon. Jake was only the first. In his case it wasn't self-defense. Self-defense had nothing to do with it. It was classic outrage. He jerked the ponderous .38 out of its holster and fired twice, two cannon shots that ruptured the silence. He fired again . . . and again. Each of the chunks of lead seered into the creature with a sickening thud. Its huge disfigured hand moved clumsily to the point of impact as the monster stared back at us in bewilderment.

Suddenly the eerie setting was a battlefield; the volley that followed was violent and instantaneous. The gray, saturated, choking air was momentarily violated by brilliant flashes of yellow and orange. The terrifying sound of gunshots thundered out all around.

The thing screamed and pitched forward, plummeting to the earth no more than 15 feet in front of me. For one fleeting moment my eyes locked on those dull, yellow slits of life and then they closed. There was a brief convulsion, an almost plaintive whimper—and silence.

For several minutes, no one moved.

PART 6

It was approaching two A.M. by the time we reassembled in the front of Palmer's Market next to the checkout stands. Old man Palmer had balked at Jake's request at first but had finally relented. The acerbic old man had gone home in disgust, sternly admonishing Madden that he and he alone was responsible in case anything was missing.

Jake walked wearily over to one of the store's large display coolers, took out a Moosehead, opened it and gulped down several swallows. With a bit of a flourish, he smacked his lips, wiped them off with his shirt sleeve and hefted his bulk up on one of the checkout counters. Somewhere during the course of events he had lost his hat, and now his shaggy blond crop of hair only added to the overall impression of disarray.

Kendall had his foot propped up on a crate of apples, supporting his clipboard on his knee. He busied himself filling out a ponderous sheath of reports. From where I stood, it looked as though the sergeant had a long way to go before he was done.

To my surprise, B.C. had lingered longer than anyone else in the huge walk-in refrigerator, fascinated by the carcass of the beast. She had already used up one pad and had left the beast just long enough to venture out in the store to find another. In addition to my trusty little Canon AF35, she had relied on Madden's tape measure. She emerged from the cooler the second time just long enough to announce that the film and measurement records were complete.

As for the creature itself, the measurements were, to say the least, surprising—if not a bit of a revelation. It measured 62 inches from the top of its ugly bulbous head to the soles of its clawlike feet. The head alone was 34 inches in circumference, 24 inches at the neck and 47 inches at its girth. Despite all this, there was a general overall impression of shapelessness.

The arms or top appendages were likewise 62 inches in expanse, muscled up close to the shoulder with almost whiplike forearms. The two-thumb, three-finger construction was the same on both its hands and feet.

The most intriguing aspect, however, was what appeared to be the creature's respiratory system. There was no apparent nose, but there was a series of flapped vents at the side of the head which seemed to be some sort of filtering device for the air it breathed. There were eyes (at least that's what they appeared to be) and a slitlike mouth a full 15 inches across. Old man Palmer had pried the beast's mouth open with a wooden block to reveal three rows of razor-sharp incisors, each row progressively more savage looking than the row that preceded them.

The skin was blackish brown in color and incredibly coarse; it had a sandpaper-abrasive quality. B.C. likened it to the skin of a shark. I happily went along with her assessment only because I have never been and never intend to get close enough to a shark to know enough to debate the issue.

Where there was hair, it was more like coarse bristles than what we have come to accept as normal for a wide variety of the species known as *Homo sapiens*.

It struck me that the creature looked like something caught in some kind of an evolutionary time warp, like something that was still making the transition from its vast watery world to that of the land. I shared that thought with B.C. only to have her inform me that to her way of thinking it looked like something cursed—suspended, if you will—and doomed for all eternity. With that rather morbid description tucked in the back of my mind, I decided her version would do nicely if and when I ever got around to trying to tell the story of the creature.

The decision to bring the remains of the beast back to the village was based on more pragmatic lines of thought. The moment the thing hit the ground there was evidence of some sort of rapid change in cell structure, as though it were still alive. From the outset there was an evident stream of a black, oily substance seeping from the gaping holes created by the bullet wounds.

Kendall had instructed Madden to find a way of keeping the body of the creature intact, and to Jake that meant, if not freezing it, at least keeping it as cold as possible. The cold temperature of the cooler, at least for the time being, seemed to stop the rapid deterioration. B.C. had gone so far as to venture the opinion that there was some indication the wounds appeared less severe than when the creature was first brought in.

Harlan's remains were stored in the same cooler. The fog was now too dense to attempt the journey to Kemper. Kendall had taken a careful head count and confirmed that Harlan had been the only casualty. There was some perversity in the fact that Harlan had been the only one to find what we had all been looking for. His savagely mutilated body was destined to stay with me for a long, long time.

At Madden's insistence, a steely jawed, white-haired man who appeared to be in his sixties had been brought in from Kemper. Hawkins had struggled 60 miles through the fog to get him. His name was Russell Ferris, and he was a doctor—the only doctor, Jake informed me, in the quad village area of Kemper, Waverly, Chambers Bay and Loma. Now he was walking out of the cooler with a pipe firmly clenched between his teeth, a frown on his craggy face. He headed straight for us.

"That's the ugliest damned thing I've ever seen," the old man assessed dryly.

Madden gave him a half-grin. "What's it remind you of, Doc?"

The grizzled old medic rolled his eyes, thought for a moment and extracted the pipe. "Guess it comes closest to resembling some sort of a gorilla or a baboon."

"My associate back there in the cooler says the hide reminds her of a shark."

Russell Ferris shoved the pipe back in his mouth and grunted. "What would a pretty young thing like that know about sharks?"

Caleb Hall drifted over to the conclave just in time to catch Doc's remarks. "Just goes to prove that little filly of yours don't know much about the things that come out of the water," he said sneering. "At least I ain't ever seen one before that had arms and legs and claws like that thing."

Ferris was in total agreement. He reached over, slipped the Moosehead out of Jake's hand, took a swig and handed it back. "Naw," he grunted, "I'd have to go along with Caleb. It looks more like some sort of gorilla than anything else."

Madden glanced at his watch and lowered his frame down from the checkout counter. His face was lined, and he looked exhausted. "What 'ya say we all get a good night's sleep and let Sergeant Kendall figure out what he's gonna do with that damn thing."

"That's pretty much up to his superiors, ain't it?" Caleb asked.

"Yeah, suppose it is," Jake agreed. "The detachment commander over at Waverly wants to get some RCMP specialists in here to assess the situation. Kendall has been instructed to get a veterinarian in here to have a look at the thing. That shouldn't take too long. With any kind of luck at all, by tomorrow afternoon we can have most of this mess cleaned up and start puttin' things back in order around here."

"That'll take a while," Caleb mused solemnly. "Ol' Harlan never had much to say, but he was an important part of this community. Same can be said for Percy

Kramer, too, since he did most of the talkin' around these parts. Folks are gonna miss both of them."

Madden nodded his concurrence with Caleb's evaluation and turned to me. "What about you, Researcher?"

I shrugged my shoulders. "It's hard to say. We'll probably stick around another day or two and make certain we've got all our T's crossed and I's dotted. There's a lot about all of this I still don't understand. We all know what happened. I can see your point, though. Now that you've got your critter stretched out back there in the cooler, your job is done. If we do our job right, ours has only begun."

Kendall finished one stack of reports, picked up another and walked toward us. The classic square-cut jaw was covered with a growth of dull brown stubble and the penetrating icy blue eyes were haggard. "I reported in," he said wearily, "and told the dispatcher that it looked like everything was under control. He'll pass along my report to the Detco in the morning. You can figure our lab boys will be crawling all over this place for the next couple of days."

Jake and Caleb heaved a collective sigh. I glanced at my watch again and noted, somewhat ruefully, that it was now going on three o'clock in the morning. Under the standard E.G. Wages sleep plan I was scheduled to be up and at 'em in another hour or so, banging away on the old word processor.

"I'll stick around here," Kendall continued, "until somebody gets here from the post to relieve me. Besides, I need to be here in the morning to make sure old man Palmer doesn't try to open the store. He won't dare sell anything out of this store until we've made certain that creature back there isn't carrying some kind of disease."

Again Madden nodded. "Standard procedure," he admitted.

With matters pretty well wrapped up for the night, I headed back for the big walk-in cooler to get B.C. She was still busy taking notes. She had borrowed a jacket from one of the men in Madden's sweep crew and had a stocking cap pulled down around her ears. Her exposed hands and face had a rosy glow.

"By now you've probably recorded every vital statistic possible. How about calling it a night?"

She turned, studied me for a moment and curled her finger at me. "Come here a minute," she said solemnly. "Look!"

"Look at what?"

"At these gunshot wounds, at the holes here and here."

"What about them?"

"They look like they've started to seal over, almost like they're healing."

"Quite natural," I expounded, trying to

summon up my most authoritative manner, which was no easy task at three o'clock in the morning. "Your friend there is obviously the proud possessor of a basal metabolism somewhere in the minus one to minus two range. Probably converts oxygen at a rate less than one-tenth the rate of a human. You could tell that by the color and consistency of the stuff being pumped by the heart."

"When I first came in here, those wounds were still weeping," Brenda protested. "Now they're almost sealed over."

"Do you have any idea what the temperature is in here?"

"Twenty, maybe twenty-five degrees?"

"Precisely! That, my dear associate, is below freezing. When things freeze they get a crust over them, a thin layer of ice crystals, but more than enough to make the wounds look less angry."

B.C. continued her appraisal, looking at me, then back again at the creature. A slow smile began to invade her face, and she laid her pencil down. "You're probably right," she admitted.

By the time I crawled into the shower, every bone in my body had filed an official protest. There wasn't a single item in the inventory that wasn't bruised, cold or aching. In recognition of a job well done and as a reward for the long, agonizing hours

I had asked the old bod to put in, I stayed in the steamy hot shower an extra five minutes. At the same time, I was convinced that soap, and lots of it, was the only thing that would get the stench of the creature off of me.

Following that, I spent a few minutes mugging in the mirror, inspecting a whole new crop of gray hairs and trimming back a beard that had grown a tad shaggy from several days of out and out neglect. It worked. In a matter of minutes the old gray-green orbs were at half mast. The last thing I remember was sinking down on the edge of the bed.

The next thing I remember was an ungodly, unwelcome and totally uncultured sound. I rolled over and scissored my head between the two pillows, burrowed my shoulder back under the covers and faked a condition known as death.

It didn't work. I heard it again.

Somewhere, off in another land, some asshole was calling me by name. I ignored it. It was too garbled and too far away to be important. Besides, I knew it couldn't be important. After all, they could see I was dead.

"Damn it, Elliott, answer your door."

I reached over and slapped the far side of my bed. It was a woman's voice, and I don't know any women. Go away!

There was the clicking sound of a lock,

then midly protesting hinges and muffled voices.

"He's out like a light," a voice said.

I rolled over and squinted one eye open. They were staring down at me.

"Is he always this hard to wake up?"

"Hey," Brenda protested, "don't ask me. We just work together."

I was still trying to grope my way to the surface. At the moment they were little more than blurry images. My brain was still trying to figure out which button to push. B.C.'s presence was a matter of record. It was the other one I was having trouble cataloging.

"Wake up, Elliott. Jake wants to talk to you."

That did it. That was the button I was looking for. Now I had a reason for coming out of my cocoon and facing what was left of the day. "What time is it?"

"Almost eight-thirty," Brenda hissed.

I propped myself up on one elbow and gave them the evil eye. Brenda was still blurry but the jeans with the knee out gave her away. She was wearing a white turtleneck with some sort of sailing craft emblazoned across her chest and a Detroit Tigers baseball cap.

"We just had a run-in with this guy Kelto," Jake announced. "Thought you'd be interested."

My eyes darted around the room, hoping

against hope that there was some coffee available. Ever alert B.C. recognized the signal and handed me a lukewarm styrofoam cup. I took a sip and grimaced.

"Let's not hear any grousing," Brenda warned me. "I walked all the way down to the diner in this fog just to get this for you."

The statement was designed to make me feel like a heel, but I didn't. In my finest Cosmo Leach impression I declared it cold and unfit for human consumption.

"I ran into Jake here," B.C. continued, "and he was telling me about what happened with Kelto. We both thought you'd be interested."

"What about Kelto?"

Jake lowered his bulk down on the edge of the bed and picked up the cup of cold coffee. "You're right about that kid," Jake declared. "He sure is strange. When I got down to the market this mornin' he was screamin' at Kendall, tellin' him we had to burn the carcass of that damn thing we shot in the woods last night."

"Burn it? What for?"

Jake shrugged. "How the hell should I know why? I just ran him off, told him we were under strict orders to turn the remains over to the RCMP."

"Then what?"

"Then nothing. He just stood there glarin' at me, tellin' me that if I didn't believe him I better be talkin' to you."

"I hate to sound like a broken record, old buddy, but why should you be talking to me? I don't know any more about all of this than you do."

Madden drained the cup and stared gloomily at the floor. "Under most circumstances I'd figure that this kid was just one more weirdo that drifted into town, keep an eye on him while he was here and be thankful when he drifted out. But there's somethin' different about this one. I want you to talk to him and find out what's goin' on in that screwball mind of his. When I told him we were turnin' this whole affair over to the RCMP, he started screamin' that we were makin' a big mistake. I asked him what he meant by that, but he wouldn't tell me."

"Why didn't you detain him?"

"On what charge? Bein' weird? Hell, everybody in the whole damn village is as nervous as a whore in church." It didn't take Madden more than a microsecond to realize what he had said. He blushed and muttered an apology in Brenda's direction.

B.C. was standing there, taking it all in. It occurred to me that neither of them had any regard for a man's privacy, so I shoved the covers back and crawled out of bed. If they weren't going to be embarrassed, neither was I.

I pulled out the uniform for the day, a pair of fresh wash pants and a faded kelly green golf shirt with the words "Runner

Up" stitched above the pocket. In a matter of minutes I had donned them and located my Reeboks. With that accomplished, I headed for the door.

"Hey, where ya goin'?" Madden inquired.

"To find Kelto."

"Just like that?"

"What other way is there? I sure as hell won't find him if I hang around this room."

Jake jacked his frame up off the bed and followed me to the door. "Do ya mind doin' this? I know this ain't your problem, but I know you been talkin' to this kid."

"I'd mind it a whole lot less if I had some hot coffee," I admitted.

Madden was a silent observer while I made my routine first weather assessment of the day. Brenda was right; it was still foggy. I could see across the motel parking lot, but that was about it.

Jake tugged down on the brim of his hat and started for his four-by-four. "I'm headed back to the market to see what them Mounties are gonna do with that thing in Palmer's cooler. If you find that Kelto kid, let me know what you learn." As he crawled into the cab, he gave B.C. one of his big affable smiles and drove away.

When I looked at Brenda, she had a perplexed "what's our next move?" look.

It was easy enough to check Kelto's room. I did, and he wasn't there. There was a brain game in all of this, a variation on the old logic riddle, but I wasn't sure I was up to playing it. A quick check at the motel office revealed that Bert had relieved Kelto at seven o'clock. Instead of going back to his room and getting some sack time like most sane citizens who work the graveyard shift, Kelto had taken off. It was a half-hearted effort, but I started working my way through the riddle—boy gets off work, boy doesn't go to his room, boy hikes into village, boy tells the local gendarmes they should burn the body of the beast, boy implies that bad things will happen if they don't, boy disappears. Where has boy gone?

Nothing.

The riddle fell flat on its face. There was nothing logical about any of my conclusions. Boy goes for another hike in the woods? Dumb in this fog. Boys goes to . . . ?

As Cosmo used to say, when logic fails, follow that little voice that comes up at you from the gut. The voice from the gut was telling me that I ought to talk to the Austin woman, but that was nothing new. It had been telling me that for some time now, and maybe that was reason enough to do it.

Brenda was waiting for me when I got back to the unit. The transition was complete. We had converted from bumbling, half-awake tourists to bumbling, half-awake researchers. With no small amount of urging, I convinced her that we had to go back into the village and promised to stop just long enough at the diner to get us some coffee. The bribe worked.

When she crawled back in the Z carrying two oversized styrofoam cups, she had an announcement. "Remember the gal that waited on us the first night we were here?"

I pried the lid off the cup and greedily went after the contents. "Uh-huh."

"Her name is Vernice."

"Nice name," I grunted, trying to get the Z's cranky old gearbox into first.

"Jake Madden is sleeping with her."

"That's nice. Everybody ought to sleep with somebody," I declared.

"Oh," Brenda replied, arching her eyebrows, "and who does the infamous Elliott Grant Wages sleep with?"

"None of your business," I snarled.

About that time, the Z relented, leaped into first and we were back on the road headed into town. I didn't say anything, but the question bothered me. It had been a long time since Gibby. Images were starting to materialize, and I didn't need that now.

Despite the fog, the journey from the diner to Palmer's Market took no more than five minutes. Again I had B.C. do the legwork. While she went into the store to check on Kelto, I grabbed a cigarette and polished off the coffee. When she crawled back in the car, I already knew what the answer was.

"No sign of him, huh?"

"No, but you ought to see the hunk that relieved Kendall this morning." She let go with a decidedly feminine expression of pleasure that again brought back memories of Gibby. I ignored it and asked the inevitable.

"What's his name?"

"Tom. Tom Gregory. Officer Tom Gregory." There was a note of reverence in her voice.

"Tommy? That's a helluva name for a Mountie!"

"I didn't say Tommy," she said, pouting. "I said Tom, very masculine, like in primitive jungle drums."

It's a struggle in the low-slung seats of a turbocharged 280 ZX, but somehow I managed. I fished a quarter out of my pocket and once more relied on the oldest decision maker known to man.

"Heads we set sail for the Austin woman's pad; tails we go back to the motel and I call Lucy to see what she's dug up on what you so quaintly term 'a lesser deity'."

The alternatives only intensified B.C.'s pout. "Can't I just stay here and talk to Officer Gregory? I might come up with something new."

Heads.

We headed for the widow's house with B.C. slumped in the passenger seat. The whole situation was rapidly developing into one of the weirdest entries in all my years of keeping journals. A 44-year-old puzzle had been destroyed the previous night without a solution. The way it stood now, the whys and hows of the riddle were about to disappear into the dusty annals of time without ever seeing the light of day.

The drive gave me time to reflect. We live in a bottom-line world—and the bottom line on Chambers Bay was simply that the killer had killed again and now the killer had been killed. What was it all about? If I was ever going to make any sense out of all this, I had to know a great deal more about it.

"Why don't we just go home?" Brenda pushed. "What you don't know, you can hypothesize. Isn't that what it's all about?"

"My curiosity has been tweaked," I admitted. "Besides, you don't have enough to write your dissertation—or have you forgotten about that?"

The all too blunt reality of my assessment only served to drive her further down into her seat. Her sensuous lower lip was now protruding a good quarter of an inch. "So why won't you talk about your love life?" she mumbled.

In front of the delapidated old gray house again, I began having second thoughts. What if Glenna Hoyt Austin was nothing more than what she appeared to be—a pathetic, dislocated bag lady. Maybe I was making too much of her cackling mumbo jumbo about the sarcophagus of Sate.

Maybe I wanted nothing more than a second look at that grotesque little figurine. Maybe I wanted nothing more than to dispel the nagging little suspicion that had haunted me since I got a good look at the creature stretched out in Palmer's cooler.

After I parked the Z, we trooped up the hill, threaded our way across the sagging porch and knocked—not once, but three times. I did it loud enough that if the old girl had actually had neighbors, they would have been fearfully peeking out from behind their curtains to see what kind of creature was making all the racket.

"Obviously, no one's at home," B.C. offered, a bit testily.

"Obviously," I agreed—and twisted the knob.

"What are you doing?"

"I think the technical term is 'trespassing'—or is it 'breaking and entering'?"

"You can't do that."

"Now look," I snapped back, "don't start developing lofty ethics on me. We need information, and if the old girl isn't around to answer our questions, maybe we can poke around and find it on our own."

"For what reason?" Brenda insisted. "What could an old woman like Glenna Austin have to do with that . . . that thing down in the meat cooler?"

To me, the answer was obvious.

I grunted, butted the door gently with my

shoulder, and it flew open. The trick has nothing to do with leverage, power, or even technique. It was simply a flimsy, half-rotten door.

Apparently Glenna was still too busy to tend to her chores. The house was a mess. We sifted through the clutter until we uncovered the table with its starkly simple shrine. "There it is," I muttered, pointing to the brooding sarcophagus.

B.C. watched while I picked it up and rotated it in my hands. It was surprisingly heavy and intricately detailed.

"Elliott," she hissed, "are you going to tell me what this is all about?"

"Look! Look closely. What do you see?"

Brenda sighed. "Oh, all right, I'll play your little game. I see the same thing I saw the other day—an ugly little chunk of carved stone that's supposed to represent some sort of second-rate, half-forgotten deity. Okay?" B.C.'s voice was getting testier by the minute.

"More than that. Look again!"

The young woman must have detected something in my voice. She retrieved the sarcophagus and looked at it again, this time a little more critically. "All right, I'll admit I'm obviously missing something. Just what is it I'm supposed to be seeing?"

"But you were fascinated with it yesterday," I reminded her.

"That was yesterday. Now I just want to

get out of here before that old lady comes marching in here and finds us trespassing. For all we know, that little old lady could be carrying a very big gun."

I put the statuette down, carefully positioning it just as I had found it in proximity to the tapered candle and the sprig of pine. That same gut voice was talking to me again. Glenna Austin very well might not be able to find her kitchen in all this clutter, but I had the distinct feeling she would know immediately if someone had been tinkering with her little altar.

"Can we get out of here now?" Brenda pleaded.

"Let's hit the road."

We didn't head directly back to the motel. In fact, we didn't make it back there until midafternoon. From the Austin widow's decrepit old house perched on the hill, we headed for Caleb Hall's marina to find out what, if anything, he knew about the old woman. While Caleb professed that it was his wife who kept him tuned in on the local gossip of Chambers Bay, I figured he knew more than our friend Madden. Jake knew who people were, but Caleb seemed to know what they were doing.

We found Caleb huddled by an old kerosene heater in an unpainted clapboard shanty at the far end of the public pier. He was bent over some charts, knee deep in conversation with a heavily whiskered old-timer in bib overalls and sloshers.

There was no pretense at social exchange. Caleb looked up, acknowledged us, finished his business with the man and walked wearily over to us.

"Figured that now that the excitement is over, you and the little lady would be pullin' out."

B.C. was standing somewhat behind me; nevertheless I could feel her stiffen at the reference to "little lady."

"We've got a few loose ends to tie up before we can say we're done."

"I think it's a shame we had to kill that creature before we found out what this was all about," B.C. offered.

Caleb nodded. "I was tellin' Mary Beth this mornin' at breakfast that it may take a while before I can eat anything that I know has come out of old man Palmer's meat cooler. Why, I've seen him makin' hamburger on that very block where we got that thing stretched out."

"Caleb, there's just a couple of things I still want to get straight."

The skipper wasn't any different than the rest of the locals; he took his own sweet time, loading, tamping and relighting his pipe. "Don't know as I can add anything to what you already know, but I'll be more than happy to try."

B.C., shoulders slumped and hands

clasped behind her back, wandered over to a dirty little window and stood looking out at the foggy bay. Caleb watched her intently. There was a look of consternation on his lined face, as though there was something he wanted to ask her.

"Do you remember when that woman you call the Austin widow arrived in these parts?"

Caleb rolled his eyes, then closed them momentarily. "Can't say as I do. Spring maybe . . . maybe early summer. Strange old lady. Sorta seems like part of the local scenery now, though."

"Who knows her? Does she have any friends? Does she attend one of the local churches?"

"Ya know, it's funny you should ask me those questions. Them's the same questions Jake told me that strange young fella works for Bert asked him about the old woman."

"You mean Kelto, the Johnsons' night man?"

"That's the one," Caleb confirmed.

There wasn't much doubt now that Kelto and I were racing toward the same conclusion. The difference was, at this stage, he knew a little more about it than I did. It was becoming clearer all the time that Kelto was the one who had the answers I was looking for. I had to pin him down and find out what he really knew. Otherwise I had a story with a beginning and an end but no middle, nothing that tied the two together.

Beyond that, Caleb was reticent. I had to remind myself that even though B.C. and I had been a part of probably the biggest story to ever unfold in Chambers Bay, we were still outsiders and newcomers.

We thanked Caleb, crawled back in the car and, with the fog intensifying again, crawled back to the motel. B.C. got out again at the diner to get us sandwiches, and I drove on, hoping to catch Kelto in his room. Once again it proved fruitless—no Kelto. A check with the Johnsons confirmed that they still hadn't seen him since he got off work. I declined Polly's offer of a cup of coffee and decided to take a gamble. Since the motel was deserted and there were no other guests, since Bert was pre-occupied with adjusting his television and Kelto hadn't responded to my first knock, I figured the risk was small.

I used the old ice ploy again. While Bert went to get me a bucket, disappearing behind the curtain and down the dingy hall-way, I slipped around behind the desk and rifled through the drawers until I found the master passkey. With that little gem securely tucked in my jacket pocket, I slipped back around to the front of the desk and waited. When Bert returned, he handed me the ice bucket and went back to his chore. I tried to exchange one or two more pleasantries, but he was too engrossed to do much more than respond with a couple of cursory grunts.

I went to the room, desposited the ice on the dresser and quickly slipped back up to the opposite end of the complex. This time I didn't even bother to knock. I just unlocked Kelto's door and went in.

Another surprise. The room was immaculate.

But there, right in the middle of his dresser, just like the one sitting on the small shrine in the old woman's house, was a sarcophagus of Sate. The old woman's description came back to me—"Ancient of Ancients." I picked it up and confirmed my darkest suspicions; it was an exact replica of the one in the house on the hill.

The pieces suddenly tumbled into place. The statues owned by the old woman and Kelto and the beast lying on the chopping block in the back of Palmer's market were all one in the same.

I returned the passkey with the feeble excuse that it must have been left in the room by the cleaning lady, and I went back to my room with the express purpose of calling Lucy.

B.C. arrived with the sandwiches, and we spread the three-by-fives out on my bed while we ate. Somehow the whole thing seemed anticlimactic and yet, deep down, I was getting a gut-wrenching signal that the worst was yet to come. I tried telling B.C. how I felt, but it was obvious she didn't understand. She hasn't as yet learned to listen to that silent, secret and all too often painfully accurate signal emanating from somewhere deep within her. She'd learn— in time.

I still had a mouthful of ham salad when I dialed. Lucy answered on the third ring. "Where the hell have you been?" she snarled.

Leave it to Lucy. "Can I tell you that's an unacceptable way to answer the telephone. How do you know it wasn't someone important like the President of the United States, maybe?"

"You're the only one who ever calls in on your unlisted number," she grumbled. "In fact, you're so damn secretive about it you're probably the only one besides me that even knows you've got it."

As usual, I chose to ignore her. "Look, this whole thing is winding down, but I've still got my hands full."

"Full of what?" she shot back. She still hadn't let go of the fact that I was traveling with someone she considered to be a threat to my morals.

I ignored her again. "What were you able to dig up?"

"You're referring to Sate, I take it?"

"No," I snapped back, "let's talk about how damn difficult it's going to be for you to get another graduate assistant's job if I don't give you a good recommendation."

"Testy, aren't we? I hear that comes from not getting enough sleep."

"Damn it, Lucy, what about Sate?"

"I went right to the top. I went over to see your friend, Doctor Freeze at the Culture Center."

"Good man," I confirmed, "piss poor poker player, but other than that, a good man."

"He couldn't keep his hands off me," Lucy bragged. To hear Lucy tell it, every man who ever laid eyes on her wanted to take her to bed. "But I finally convinced him that I was there on business, and he settled down."

While Lucy was meandering through the fantasy world of her preamble, I fished the voice recorder out of the survival kit and attached the input cord to the telephone with a simple clamp. If it was a typical Lucy fact-finding mission, the data would start pouring in and there would be no way I could keep up with her.

"Ready?"

I grunted.

"According to your friend, Doctor Freeze, there was a Tarpann warlord by the name of Korbac, circa year one thousand. It seems our boy Korbac started eating his Wheaties at a very early age and decided to build himself an empire. The only problem was that he had some neighbors called Tobors, who didn't share his dream and controlled the lands north and east of him.

"Also, according to Freeze, Korbac was not only super aggressive, he was also super smart. He knew he couldn't defeat the Tobors without some help, and we're talking serious help, because the enemy outnumbered Korbac's troops four to one.

"Freeze's version is that this hunk called Korbac went up on a nearby mountain to meditate and pray the night before he launched his campaign. There, so the story goes, he ran into this strange-looking little monk who went by the name—wanta take a wild guess?—that's right, Sate.

"Freeze paints him like your prototypical apocryphal monk—sack cloth robes, long stringy beard, thong-wrapped feet, the whole nine yards. Supposedly, Sate told Korbac to study his own weakness and he will know his enemy.

"Korbac plunges into a fit of confession and confides that his biggest fear is that he will be outwitted in battle because he has heard that the Tobors are brilliant war strategists. Sate then calmly informs him that the only way Korbac can overcome this disadvantage is through the process of fortification, and that through this process he will be brilliant in battle. Pretty heady stuff, huh?"

"So what's this fortification bit?"

"This part will knock your socks off,"

Lucy continued. "Sate tells our boy Korbac that he will be assured of victory if he, now get this, slays the truly wisest man he knows and consumes his brains after a twelve-hour fast. How's that for gross?"

"You're kidding."

"Uh-uh, not one single word is changed, boss baby. I think your friend Freeze really digs this stuff. He's even got etchings of Sate, Korbac and some of the troops, and you ought to see them—real stomach flippers."

"So what happened?"

"Honest to God, it gets worse. It turns out Korbac thinks his father is the wisest of all, so he sends out one of his warriors to trek back to the ranch and do the old boy in. The soldier returns just before dawn on the day of the battle with the old man's head—and you can guess the rest."

"And of course our boy Korbac was victorious."

"Resounding victory, routed the Tobors. By nightfall the battlefield was littered with literally thousands of Tobors dead and wounded. During the course of the victory celebration, Korbac confides to his generals how he achieved his great victory. The idea spreads like wildfire, and the Korbac generals figure if it's good enough for their leader, it's good enough for them. The bottom line is Korbac and his staff have this big feast with the wounded and dead Tobors as the main course."

"Can you be a little less flippant about all of this?" I groaned. "My stomach just did a one-eighty on me."

"Don't tell me you buy all of this hogwash?" Lucy chided.

"You'd have a little different perspective on all of this if you were here," I scolded.

"Well, there's more," Lucy continued. "Korbac is proud as a peacock. He tromps back up the hill to share the news with his friend Sate. This time, Sate's mood is a little different. Sate lays it on him that he, Korbac, will have to continue to fortify himself or he will die, and if he dies, he will have to submit to the ordeal of atonement."

"And the atonement is?" I felt like I was playing Lucy's straight man.

"Don't know, because the last we heard about Korbac, he was still tromping through the countryside doing his gastronomic thing, trying to avoid atonement."

"That's it? No big ending?"

"Not really. Your buddy Freeze says there are two theories about what eventually happened to Korbac. One is that he flew into a rage, killed Sate and fled with a handful of his troops into the mountains. The other theory has it that the locals, fearing for their lives, banded together and mounted a military campaign that chased the old boy into the swamps and caves of Polan."

"That's it?"

"I'm afraid so. It's a good thing Freeze was plugged into all of this, because I haven't been able to come up with anything through our normal channels."

"Did you try Cosmo?"

"Didn't think this was his kind of thing."

"It isn't, but I'd still give him a crack at it. Besides, it'll brighten his day. He likes to talk to pretty girls."

Lucy giggled. She loved it. "Okay, I'll give him a call. I'll be back in touch with you if he has anything to add."

As usual, there were no good-byes, just a click followed by an irritating buzz. I hung up.

B.C., who had heard nothing more than my limited input during the course of the call, unplugged the monitor, rewound the tape and played it back. At appropriate times she made the appropriate faces of revulsion and disgust.

When the tape was finished, she laid back across the bed and stared up at the ceiling. "Know something?" she mused. "I've about decided to give up my dreams of a doctorate in this field and go on to something a little more tasteful, like bullfighting or prostitution."

"It ain't exactly the stuff Disney films are made of," I agreed.

Brenda's voice fluttered, and I could tell that the combination of the late night, the stress and being rousted out by Madden had taken its toll. When her eyes finally drifted shut, I picked up my windbreaker and the survival kit and slipped out the door. Two and two don't always make four, but the sum of my knowledge about that thing peacefully reposing on the butcher slab at Palmer's market added up to a whole lot more than I knew when I had gotten up this morning.

The Z coughed to life and I aimed it toward Chambers Bay.

If you've never had the experience of arriving at the scene of a bad accident 30 seconds after it had happened, you're never quite sure how you'll handle it. Do you rattle? Are you the kind who panics? Some people come unwrapped. Some respond appropriately—cool, calm, measured, efficient. Unfortunately, I don't fit in either category. My best reactions are gut reactions. Sometimes that's good; sometimes it isn't.

Reflecting on it, the fog probably saved me because I had slowed down more than normal for the corner and had dropped into second gear when it happened.

I was sure of two things. It sounded like the initial volley at Gettysburg, and it was too damn close.

Instinctively, I ducked.

The Z veered sharply to the right, crashing into the eight-inch-high elevated sidewalk and slamming my face up against the steering wheel.

There was a typical, if brief, E.G. Wages response to the mishap—a string of un-bridled profanity punctuated by frequent checks to see if the old proboscis was splattered all over my face. I'll admit to being a little paranoid about the afore-mentioned beak simply because it has been battered out of shape so many times over the past half century.

The other reflexes were still working, though. I unsnapped my harness, thrust my shoulder into the door and tumbled out onto the damp asphalt surface of the street. Three more shots shattered the stillness, and I started clawing my way toward the curb. In the murky twilight up ahead of me, I could see Madden's four-by-four sitting at a right angle to the street and steaming; one tire was flat. Jake was hovering off to one side, the long-barreled .38 clutched in his ham-sized fist. At this distance I couldn't tell much else about the situation.

I was still trying to catch my breath and trying to get a reading on the situation. "What the hell's going on?" I shouted.

Jake gave me a shushing motion, finger to the lips, and stared at the front of Palmer's store.

At that point I started to inch myself up on the curb next to the steaming Z. The engine was still running, but the sudden encounter with the cement curb had ruptured a gas line. A pool of pungent pinkish fuel was starting to trickle toward me.

"Stay where you are," Jake thundered.

I peeked up over the curb and felt the gasoline seep into the sleeve of my jacket. Except for the sound of the sputtering Z, the street was silent. Nothing was moving. Gradually the chaos began to fragment into isolated bits of discernible detail. The front window of the market was shattered. Huge shards of splintered glass cluttered the sidewalk. Across the street, behind Madden, a man darted from one building to the next. He had a rifle. Then I saw another, but he disappeared in the fog.

"See anything?" Jake bellowed.

"What the hell am I supposed to be looking for?"

"That damn thing we shot in the woods— it's alive!"

The words sent a cold chill rocketing up my spine and into my neck like a runaway freight train. What was he talking about? That thing we shot in the woods was dead. I'd seen it—cold and stiff and very, very full of big gaping holes. I'd even touched it.

A response was probably forthcoming, I'm still not quite sure, because it never got past the formulation stage. It all happened too suddenly. There was a sound like an explosion followed by a sudden rain of bricks and debris. I could hear them plummeting down on the Z and everywhere around me. One of them caught me a glancing blow on the side of my head.

Jake started firing again, this time in my direction but up above me. I heard one of the slugs rip into the sheet metal of the Z, and I started praying that it didn't ignite the escaping gasoline.

There were other sounds, more frightening than that of bullets spraying all around me. There was a gaping hole in the brick wall, and suddenly the thing emerged, half-stumbling, half-crawling, but very much alive. It's ungainly bulk was looking for some sort of sanctuary.

Elliot Grant Wages was in the wrong place at the wrong time.

The thing leaped clumsily down on the Z, glowered at me and took a swipe at my head with its massive paw. Instincts took over. I made one frantic attempt to slide under the Z. It was too late. The creature's viselike grip clamped around my leg and dragged me away from the only thing that possibly promised safety.

I remember a terrible cramp in my foot, pain in my right leg, my head thumping merrily along the rough pavement, the sound of more gunshots, the guttural sounds belching from the foul-smelling thing, and last, but not least, sheer, unmitigated terror.

Just as suddenly, and, as far as I can determine, for no apparent reason, the thing let go of me. It must have figured I wasn't worth the effort.

The chaos continued. I could hear shattering glass, frenzied shouts, footsteps and more gunshots.

Suddenly another shadow blocked out what little light my swollen eyes weren't filtering. It was gray and confusing and accompanied by lots of heavy breathing.

"I'll be damned surprised if he ain't dead," Jake grunted.

"Naw," someone else assessed, "I can see him breathin'."

My brain was doing its best, but the short-circuiting continued. Shouts. Footsteps. A world gone mad, out of control. Strange discordant music played in the background of my befuddled mind. I was looking down at me. I was a mess. Better tidy up. The same note kept playing over and over. I could see somebody getting out a blanket and covering my head. Wait a minute. You're wrong. But the protest was stuffed into a murky gray envelope along with everything else. Now silence. Now nothing. A world of gray on gray.

"His eyes moved," someone observed.
"He may make it," another said.

"I think he's startin' to come around," still another opined.

"How long has he been out?"

"Forty-five minutes at least."

Voices—just a lot of voices.

Through my squint, heads were taking shape, heads outlined by blurry lights that gave off a spooky, pale, fuzzy-colored yellow glow.

"Elliott," a softer voice intoned, "can you hear us?"

I could hear, all right, but I wasn't about to make any commitments. There were a whole bunch of other components that still had to be tested. At this point I figured surviving from one minute to the next was all I could hope for.

"He'll be all right," another voice evaluated. "He took a pretty good pounding, but I can't find much more than some contusions and a nasty whack on the head, maybe a minor concussion. He'll be pretty sore for a while, but he'll live."

By my standards, someone was being rather glib with my prognosis, and I wanted them to stop. If I was going to defend myself I had to crawl kicking and screaming back into the world. I forced one eye partially open and then the other. The circle of faces was grim.

"Where the hell am I?"

Madden was towering over me, glowering. He talked too slow and too loud, like he considered it a distinct possibility that the thing had fractured my ears. "You're . . . still . . . in . . . Chambers Bay . . . at . . . Palmer's . . . market."

It was now or never. In another ten minutes I would be too stiff to even attempt it. I pushed myself up on one elbow, heard someone tell me to take it easy and started recording facts. I had been in the halfway world long enough. They were all there— Madden, Caleb, B.C., Kendall and Ferris— plus a bunch of others that I suspected were there purely out of morbid curiosity.

"Is it true? Is that thing really alive or did I just dream it?"

"That can all wait until you're on your feet," B.C. cooed.

I swung my legs over the edge of the checkout counter and pushed myself into a sitting position. "Will sitting up do?" The sick little grin I forced didn't fool anyone.

Madden was the one who understood. When a man needs data, he needs data. "You're gonna find this tough to swallow, Researcher, but you were mauled by that thing we shot last night."

When you've had somebody pounding on your cage with a big stick, sometimes the things people tell you don't hang together. This was one of those times. "Will you repeat that?" I muttered.

Kendall moved in beside Madden. His

uniform was in disarray, and there was a fold of swollen, discolored tissue under each eye. His voice was still a little shaky. "I came back on duty at four o'clock and relieved Constable Higgins. We talked for a few minutes, and he brought me up to date on tomorrow's schedule. He made some comment about the fog getting worse and decided to bunk down and get some sleep back in the store room. About an hour later old man Palmer came by and did some more grousing about us keeping the store closed another day while the forensic team from headquarters gets this thing squared away. He poked around for a little while, then said he wanted to go back and check the temperature in the cooler. I didn't see any harm in it so I went back with him. After all, it's his store.

"We hadn't been back there more than a few minutes when he walked over to the carcass and started poking around on it. I was just about to tell him to quit when all of a sudden one of those big black arms flies up and wraps around Palmer's neck. Before I can even shout a warning, the thing flings the old man across the room like he's some kind of rag doll. All I hear is the sickening sound of that old man splattering up against the wall of the cooler.

"By that time I've pumped four shots into the thing. I can see the slugs ripping into it, but it was almost like shooting into a bowl of Jello. It wasn't affecting it at all. The things just turned and looked at me with those hideous yellow eyes and raised its arms like it had conquered something.

"I could tell Palmer was dead, and when I saw the four shots hadn't slowed the critter down one bit, I hightailed it for the door, slammed it and threw the dead bolt. Even then I could hear it raging around in there, growling, screaming, breaking things, like it was having a tantrum.

"There was a kid peeking in the window, and I started screaming at him to find Madden and Hall. The kid's eyes were as big as saucers, but he got the job done."

I sat through Kendall's breathy dissertation, shaking my head in disbelief. "Wait a minute," I finally interrupted, "do you expect me to believe that the beast that bounced me around in the middle of the street out there is the same one that was stretched out back there in the cooler?"

Madden nodded grimly. "Told you it would be tough to swallow."

B.C. was still holding my hand, nodding right along with Madden and Kendall. "It's not there, E.G. I looked for myself."

"Things don't die and come back to life," I said flatly. "The world doesn't work that way."

Brenda let go of my hand, and with some trepidation I lowered myself down off of the counter. The minute my feet hit the floor I knew the little white-haired man with the paternal look on his face was right; my gyro had been scrambled. I staggered, knees buckling, regained my equilibrium and wobbled toward the cooler.

The door was massive, made of steel and a good six inches thick. It had been ripped right out of its casing, its steel hinges splintered. The dead bolt, a piece of steel rod three quarters of an inch in diameter, had been sheared in half. From its location and condition, the why and how was all too obvious. It had been hammered out from inside the cooler.

I fumbled my way around the door and went in. Palmer's crumpled body was coiled up in the corner with a blanket not too discreetly concealing it.

The creature was gone, all right.

By the time I worked my way, wincing with each step, back up to the front of the store (B.C. had her arm around my waist and my arm over her shoulder), the battery of questions was starting to formulate.

"You must have gotten here in a matter of minutes," I said, looking at Madden.

Jake nodded. "Me and Caleb got here at about the same time. Just as I pulled up, that damn thing come plowin' through the big plate glass window. I started firin' even before I got out of my rig. Kendall was already across the street, emptyin' his rifle at the thing."

"Right about then," Kendall interrupted, "the mercury vapor lights started coming on up and down the street. For some reason the thing tried to shield its eyes and crawled back through the broken window into the store. I reloaded, and every time I saw something move, I started firing."

"And that's when I stumbled in?"

"Exactly," Kendall confirmed.

Madden was shaking his head. "Between us I know we nailed the bastard at least ten times. I don't miss at that range."

"It never even slowed down," Kendall said dejectedly.

"All right," I pushed, "after he got through pounding on me, what happened?"

Jake pointed at the sergeant. "Me and Kendall followed it down toward the pier where Caleb has the Lady Mary tied up."

"Then what?"

"It headed west up the beach into the scrub brush."

"Did you follow?"

Jake looked at me as though I was slightly addled. "In this fog? Are you kiddin'? You saw what happened to Harlan out there in that damn woods, didn't you?"

By ten-thirty, the streets of Chambers Bay were deserted. Word had gotten around, and I could just imagine what was going on behind the shuttered windows and locked doors. The fog had closed in again and even the streetlights were little more than blurry indications of man's age-old feeble attempt to fend off fear of the dark.

Madden had managed to round up 18 or so of the heartier souls in the village to help him conduct a hastily concocted, combination patrol and vigil.

Kendall had succeeded in getting two additional officers down from Waverly post, and the men arrived with a small arsenal of weapons that were promptly passed out to the patrol.

The three Mounties and Madden held a strategy meeting at the back of the store, and when they came out, Kendall assembled the men around him.

"Gentlemen," he began stiffly, "this is Constable Gregory and Constable Hawkins from the Waverly post. These men are here to serve as squad leaders and maintain contact with our detachment headquarters in Thunder Bay.

"We'll organize our patrol network pretty much on the same concept we used to conduct our sweep last evening. Constable Gregory will set up a command center down at the old school house, and Officer Hawkins and I will head up the two patrol shifts. Each patrol will cover four square blocks and report in to Officer Gregory every thirty minutes. The group that goes out now will be replaced at three o'clock, and we'll rotate again just after dawn."

Suddenly an agitated voice rumbled out of the back of the room. "There's a story goin' around that you and Madden shot the thing several times earlier tonight and it didn't even slow it down."

Kendall held up his hand in an attempt to quiet the murmur of voices. "That's true," he admitted.

"Then what the hell good are these rifles you gave us?"

Madden elbowed his way to the front of the circle. "Look, ain't nobody sayin' this is gonna be a cakewalk. We know two things. We know our round of fire knocked him out of the tree last night, and we know we scared him off with gunshots tonight."

Another voice grunted. "Yeah, and we know that we ain't got no one gun that'll stop the damn thing."

Madden was undaunted. "Doc Ferris took a good look at that thing when it was back there in the cooler, and he figures we're dealin' with somethin' altogether different here."

"Like what?" the voice shot back.

"Well . . . Doc figures this thing has some real low-functioning respiratory system with such a low basal metabolism that it would be virtually impossible to tell what condition it was in. He figures we only stunned it."

"Then how the hell are we gonna stop it?"

"The object," Madden persisted, "is not

to kill it, but to keep it away from the community and under control until we can get some help in here. Now, we got most of the folks from the outlying areas rounded up and bedded down here in town. Look at it this way. All we gotta do is keep Chambers Bay secure until sun-up."

Kendall took over again. "We've got a couple of things in our favor. This thing, whatever it is, is slow; its mobility is limited. On the other hand, we know it's strong and that it can climb, so it could be anywhere. But—and I think this is important—it's probably scared and confused, and like any caged animal, it'll attack if it's provoked."

Kendall was still talking when Madden started toward me. "Do you feel good enough to help us?" he asked.

"Like a virtual powerhouse," I lied.

B.C. shook her head. I heard her mumble something about a form of macho insanity.

"Besides, I need to talk to you. Your lady friend here tells me you've learned something else about this critter."

Connecting Lucy's research with the events that were unfolding in Chambers Bay seemed slightly ludicrous even in light of what had just transpired. For some reason I was convinced that the human brain could leapfrog the logic of all those shots only stunning the creature, but I was reluctant to unfold a story that had the thing surviving for centuries and wreaking all this havoc.

"I don't even know if it's relevant," I answered.

Madden glared back at me. The look on his face indicated that he thought I was holding something back from him.

Even with that I was reluctant to parade out my theory. I wasn't even sure I believed it.

"Tell you what I'll do, Jake. If we make it through the night, I'll run out to the motel in the morning and get the tape for you. Then you can judge for yourself. Deal?"

Madden nodded and motioned for me to follow. "Come on," he grunted, "we're servin' as back-up for all the patrols. It's gonna be a long night."

PART 7

It was a long night. The patrols, much to my surprise, performed with admirable precision, and by the time that the first shift change was effected in the early hours of the morning, a good deal of the early apprehension had dissipated. In one of the groups there was actually an exchange of some light-hearted banter.

Kendall had put the less experienced Constable Gregory in charge of the command post. He was a tall, blond, angular young man with piercing blue eyes and a quick, flirtatious smile. I am told some women actually find that type appealing. And each time that Madden and I checked in, Brenda had discovered a new way of fawning over the young officer. She had regaled him with coffee, some cookies from Palmer's rapidly depleting shelves, some clever repartee, and was now dazzling him with her multifaceted personality. All of which wasn't lost on Madden; with each report, the big man became a little more surly.

Twice following the two o'clock shift change we altered our patrol routine, once to check with Hawkins and Caleb Hall, who were working the four square block eastern quadrant of the village, and the other to briefly check out the darkened marina.

Kendall's makeshift communications network was more than adequate. We were working with standard 40 channel citizens band units of the handheld variety, and the patch-through buddy system had effectively kept everyone in touch. The too frequent, too nervous, too excited transmissions of the early evening had settled into a series of terse, almost laconic "all's quiet" and "nothing to report" static-laden crackles. Still, Madden manfully monitored each and every one of them. He systematically recorded each one on a battered clipboard that lay on the front seat beside him.

The frequency of conversation between Jake and myself had deteriorated over the course of the long night until it became little more than a series of cryptic grunts. The coffee was gone, and I was down to my last cigarette.

The creature had simply vanished.

By the time the first faint traces of dawn began to penetrate the long hours of fog and darkness, Jake had parked the four-by-four at what the patrols had been referring to as quadrant W.E. He turned off the ignition, slumped down behind the steering wheel and shoved his hat forward down over his eyes. The look of exhaustion had crept over his lined face. "Well, Researcher, it looks like we're goin' to make it," he sighed.

I was still gratefully fondling the arrival of the new day, and it was easy to agree with him. Somehow the threatening combination of darkness and fog and knowing that the foul-smelling thing was still freely roaming around out there in the shadows had made the night seem all the longer. I had already seen the monster muscle his way through one brick wall, and it was a sight I had no desire to witness a second time. So it was symbolic, if nothing else, that the darkness was giving way to the dawn; one of the three obstacles to survival had been, at least temporarily, overcome.

Through it all, it occurred to me that I still knew very little about the mountain of a man who sat slumped in the seat beside me. I had developed a great deal of respect for Jake Madden over the past few hours. If he was going to be accurately characterized in whatever this affair turned out to be, I had to know a great deal more about him.

"Are you a native to these parts, Jake?" It was the kind of question that doesn't change anything. One man's assessment of another is based, to a large extent, on what he sees, and what I had seen in the way of actions from the man indicated integrity, concern and commitment—solid elements, indeed.

Jake pursed his lips and took his time unwrapping a small cheroot. Like everything else the man did, it evolved into a kind of miniature ritual. He tucked the cellophane in his shirt pocket, used his pocket knife to cut off the tip, wet it, lit it and took a deep drag.

"Naw," he drawled, "come from up north of Calgary. Used to be a Mountie myself. Came home one night and found this note on the door—she was gone. She'd had enough of it. Can't say as I blame her. It's no life for a woman, especially a pretty one who likes female doo-dads." His gruff voice trailed off, and he took a drag on his cheroot.

When a man begins poking around in the attic of his memory, you give him time. For most of us it's a little like probing the old body the morning after a street fight. It's done with a great deal of caution, gingerly testing the bruised areas, seeing how much they hurt. Then, and only then, does a man determine how much further he is willing to probe, how much he's willing to reveal. Some old hurts never heal.

"I was thirty-seven at the time. Saddle sore. Broke. And just beginning to come to grips with the fact that I was a natural-born loner. So one morning I just marched into the Detco and resigned. He had me fill out a bunch of forms, and when I was done with all that nonsense, I crawled into my old pickup truck and headed east. Oh, I stopped a couple of times along the way, got to know a few people, spent a little time in Winnipeg—and then one day I landed here in Chambers Bay."

"Why did you stay in Chambers Bay?"

Madden gave me a sideways glance and an easy smile. I had the feeling it wasn't the first time he had been asked that question.

"It was a Sunday mornin'," he reflected. "I'd been drivin' all night and had stopped down at Vernice's diner, the same place where I met you folks. When I went back out to my truck I had a flat tire. There I was, my right rear flatter than a fritter, the gas tank empty, and I had three dollars to my name. Even if I solved one problem, I still had the other—so I just stayed."

"And?" I knew there was a bottom line, and I instinctively knew I was supposed to ask.

" 'Bout a year later, four bikers showed up, real bad dudes. They strutted around, raised a little hell, intimidated a couple of the local folk and started bustin' up Vernice's diner. I was washin' dishes in the back at the time. When I heard the ruckus they was raisin' I went out the back door, out to the shed, got myself a crowbar and pried the spokes out of the wheels of their bikes. They didn't like that much and got a little surly about the whole affair, so I used the bar on them."

He took time out to enjoy another drag.

"Harlan saw the whole thing, and the next thing I know the village council was offerin' me eight hundred and fifty bucks a month to sorta keep the lid on things around here. Up until now it ain't been all that much trouble."

"Do you like it?"

Jake shrugged. "What the hell," he groused, "it's a job, and a man's gotta do somethin' with his time. Never have found a substitute for eatin'."

The interlude was interrupted by the crackling of the radio. Jake was suddenly alert again. A voice began transmitting without identifying itself. "Just checked with Ben Hart who says his gear's out. Says he ain't seen nothin'."

Jake depressed the transmit button on the side of his unit. "Where are you, Phil?"

"On Chestnut, down by the stone quarry."

"Seen anything?"

"Nothin' but the goddamn fog," the man snapped.

Madden grunted, released the button and laid the mike on the dashboard. For a moment or two he stared off in the grayness. "Know what Vernice told me?"

I shook my head.

"She says you not only research this weird stuff. She says that when you figure out what's happenin' and come up with some logical explanation for it you write about it. That true? Do you write about ghosts and stuff like that?"

"Everybody knows a ghost story or two," I said, smiling. "If we didn't have ghost stories, we wouldn't need campfires. If we didn't have campfires, we wouldn't need marshmallows. If we didn't have marshmallows, the whole economy would collapse."

Jake didn't smile. "How come you didn't tell me that? How come you told me you was a researcher?"

"Minor detail. Besides, it didn't seem important."

"You came here knowin' that somethin' unusual was gonna happen in Chambers Bay, didn't ya?"

"Call it a hunch. But when I read the news reports about the animals, it more or less confirmed some suspicions."

"Guess in a way we can be thankful for

the fog," Jake mused, "otherwise this old town would be crawlin' with reporters and officials breathin' down our backs, tellin' us what to do."

"For the most part, I figure the world's pretty much unaware of what's going on here."

"How about it? You got it figured out yet?" He was like a big kid looking for an easy answer to a complicated puzzle.

"Well, at this point, we haven't got very much, just a bunch of seemingly related bits and pieces that don't add up to very much. A person would have to have one incredible imagination to gather all of this into something meaningful."

"Try me," Jake drawled.

"Well, I've already told you that the things going on in Chambers Bay are similar to incidents that happened in other places over the last several years."

Jake was nodding. "Go on."

"There are any number of possibilities at this point. One, of course, is that none of these incidents are related, that they're really nothing more than a bizarre set of coincidences. At the other end of the spectrum is the possibility that we've been plunged into some prehistoric nightmare that has to do with things we'll never be able to explain."

"Which way ya leanin'?"

"First you've got to promise you won't

throw me out of the truck."

Jake grunted.

"I think we've got something going on here that transcends everything that's logical, defies the imagination and makes people real, real uncomfortable."

The lawman took one last drag on his cigar, rolled down the window and flipped it out into the fog. "I got one more question."

"Shoot."

"What's goin' on between you and Brenda Cashman?"

I started to laugh, then decided against it. I had a sneaking suspicion it was not a laughing matter for Jake Madden. "Take my word for it. It's strictly business."

The big man's expression didn't change all that much. And maybe it was nothing more than my imagination, but it did seem that there was a little less tenseness to the set of his jaw. If there was a comment in the offing, it never materialized. The emergency channel was suddenly a storm of static. Kendall's voice boomed in loud and clear.

The men of the RCMP had called another meeting. This one had a decidedly different flavor than the previous one. For one thing, most of the women and children were now secure in an area that could be easily patrolled. Secondly, we had made it through the night without—as far as anyone knew—

any further casualties. Thirdly, a dimension of fatigue was beginning to surface. Most of the men were working with less than four hours of sleep. As Kendall was stepping back up on the riser, those same men sat dejectedly in a semicircle of folding chairs.

Sergeant Kendall had rejuvenated the area map used in the first briefing session. It was taped to the wall again.

By this point, much of the spring had gone out of Kendall's step. He paced back and forth in front of his maps, sporting a two day stubble and looking for all the world more like a fugitive than an officer of the RCMP.

"Okay," he began hesitantly, "we made it through the night without any further incidents. We made it because we were organized, we were careful, and we followed our plan. It's important that everybody keep that in mind, because that's going to be the thing that gets us through this whole nightmare."

As it turned out, Kendall was just getting warmed up. From there he went on to inform us another sweep was being organized. "We'll follow the same routine we used in our first sweep, the only exception being that Constable Hawkins will head up the team coming in from the western boundary."

One or two of the men still had enough energy to mumble minor protests.

"We'll launch the sweep at exactly ten o'clock, and we'll rendezvous at the clearing where we found Percy Kramer at twelve noon. Bring any kind of weapon you feel comfortable with, but remember, be darn certain you know how to use it and what you're firing at. Be especially aware of where the other members of your sweep team are at all times. We've got our hands full with that creature. We don't need to be shootin' at each other."

Kendall's plan had the ring of organization about it, but one discouraging fact kept bubbling to the forefront of my thoughts. I knew it had to be on the minds of the men as well. The question had already been asked. Namely, what were we going to do even if we did find the creature? So far, bullets were accomplishing little more than keeping it awake.

Kendall must have known what the men were thinking. "This time we'll use the portable radio gear, and we've added two more weapons to our arsenal. One is a portable ensnarement device, a trap blanket made of woven fiberglass and magnesium. The ensnarement net is encased in a large payload cartridge propelled by a T-47A. Both Officers Gregory and Hawkins are proficient with the device." Kendall was beginning to sound stiff and hopelessly military.

"How do we know that newfangled net of

yours is gonna work any better than anything else we've tried?'' one of the men
groused.

"It'll stop a tank,'' Kendall responded
confidently.

"So what?'' another snarled. "What you
aimin' to do with it after you've caught it?''

"Constable Gregory has also managed to
round up four 731 tranquilizer guns. I've
ordered that they be loaded with Selphon
3431—enough to knock down anything that
walks, crawled or exists on the face of the
earth. Each of the groups will have one of
the tranquilizer guns. It's as simple as we
know how to make it. If you see the thing,
open fire and keep firing until the man in
your unit with the Selphon cartridge gets
there. The minute you've got the beast on
the ground, have your radio man get in
touch with Officer Gregory; he'll get there
with the T-47A and get the trap blanket over
the thing. As soon as the trap blanket is in
place, anchor it, cage it, kill it—whatever's
necessary to prevent any further loss of life.
Any questions?''

This time the men were silent. No one had
a better plan.

"All right,'' Kendall barked, his voice
getting more hoarse by the minute, "step up
here and I'll assign each of you to one of the
four sweep teams. Then each of you will
have till ten o'clock to check on your
families and get yourselves ready. In the

meantime, I've assigned Constable Hawkins and four other men to continue the patrol of the perimeter of the village."

It was a struggle, but I finally managed to heft my weary body out of the chair and went looking for B.C. It was her job to find out where I would be most likely to locate the Austin widow and young Kelto. Some things hadn't changed. I still wanted to talk to both of them.

Brenda was just walking through the door when the Kendall briefing began to break up. Despite the long night, there was still a twinkle in her eyes that made her look a whole lot better than the majority of Chambers Bay's walking wounded. She was sporting a smudge on one cheek and her hair was mussed, but other than that she looked surprisingly fresh. For the most part, it was the moon child element that was still with us.

"Any luck? Locate either of them?"

B.C. shook her head. "Nothing! Not a trace. It's like they just disappeared. I've checked every place in the village that housed people last night."

"Damn," I muttered, "you'd think someone would have seen at least one of them. Kendall was certain we had everybody rounded up."

"Kendall is wrong," she announced. "Remember that skinny little gal that works in the village office? The one that gave us directions to the Widow Austin's place?"

"Angie. Her name was Angie."

"How interesting. You remember her name, huh?"

"Easy name to remember," I lied. Actually I didn't have the foggiest idea why I remembered the girl's name. "Why?"

"Thought you didn't like flat-chested women?" B.C. purred.

"Damn it, B.C., I'm too tired to play games. What about the girl?"

"From what I'm told, she's the one who went out to get Bert and Polly. She supposedly took a van so that they could get Polly's wheelchair."

"And?"

"Well, apparently nobody has seen her since."

"What about the Johnsons?"

"No one has seen them either."

Madden's reaction was the same as mine. The three of us jumped into his four-by-four and hightailed it for the old motel. The whole process of informing him on what we had learned and racing the mile and a half to the motel took less than five minutes, even with the fog.

It took no more than a couple of steps to hit the motel's front door, throw it open and half-hurdle my old body into the tiny lobby. Bert had the shotgun at waist level, finger on the trigger, ready to fire. The look on his face read more terrified than committed to shooting whatever it was that was coming through the door, however, and we stood there looking at each other.

"Damn," he sputtered, "you don't know how close I came to emptyin' both barrels."

There was still too big a lump in my throat for me to say much of anything.

Bert had no more than gotten the words out of his mouth when Madden hit the door with B.C. right behind him. The look on Jake's face was a mixture of surprise and relief.

"What the hell happened?" he thundered.

Polly wheeled around from behind the lobby desk, her normally placid face mirroring the stress of the long night. "Angie here came out to tell us that the RCMP wanted everyone in the area to move into town," she explained. "But we couldn't get the car started."

"Don't know what's the matter with it," Bert groused.

I had that funny feeling you get when you think someone isn't giving you the straight story.

"Never did that before," Bert grumbled. The feeling intensified. He wasn't at all convincing.

"Why didn't you call into the village?" Jake asked. "We'd have sent someone out to get you."

"The phones are dead," Polly said calmly.

"We always have phone problems when one of these fog blankets settle in like this for several days."

"What's the situation in Chambers Bay?" Bert questioned.

Jake shoved his hat back and leaned against the counter. " 'Bout the only thing for certain is that we made it through the night. We got some eyewitnesses that say they saw the thing head down to the pier and veer off into the woods. Too foggy and too dangerous to follow it through."

"Anything I can do to help?" Bert inquired.

"The RCMP is organizing another sweep of the area that starts at ten o'clock," Jake informed him.

"If you can help me get Polly and Angie into the village where they'll be safe, I'll be there."

There was a fleeting moment when I read something into Polly's expression other than wifely concern, but I let it pass without comment.

We made another unsuccessful effort at getting Bert's car started, but after several minutes of grinding, Angie's van finally coughed to life. Jake muttered something about damp plugs, which I had a little trouble buying, but the bottom line was that we got them back into the village and Jake and I headed for Freeman Field to catch up with the sweep effort.

We still had 30 minutes to spare when Jake pulled off the main road and stopped at the diner. He drove around to the back door, produced a ponderous set of keys, sorted through them and opened the door to the diner's kitchen.

"Vernice gave it to me," he said a little sheepishly. "Said I might never know when I'd need it."

It was obvious the big man knew his way around the kitchen. He fired up the front burner on the big gas range, dug through the pantry until he found a jar of instant coffee, put some water on to boil and leaned casually up against the cooler with his arms folded. "I can rustle you up some bacon and eggs if you're hungry," he offered.

At the moment I was having trouble conjuring up visions of anything except a platonic relationship between Jake and the hawk-faced Vernice, but I'd be the first to admit that the libido does funny things to people.

"I know what you're thinking," Jake began defensively. "It just sorta happened. Started right after I took over this job, 'bout the same time she bought this place. We was both puttin' in fourteen and sixteen hour days. I'd stop by here for coffee in the mornin' and a cold one the last thing at night. One night it didn't make much sense to go on home. Been an off and on thing ever since."

"Where is she now?"

Jake gave me one of his casual bull-shouldered shrugs.

"In town, I reckon . . . we don't keep close tabs on each other." Somehow I had the feeling Jake thought he knew, but he wasn't about to lower his defenses and admit it. He pushed himself away from the cooler, went through the swinging doors into the dining room, crossed it and went over to the window overlooking the bay. I followed. The room smelled stale and greasy.

There wasn't much to see. The water was placid, the sky a dreary gray. Both were void of detail. Together they blended into a monotone of colorless sameness. We stood there for several minutes, staring out at the featureless seascape, feeling the effects of the long, sleepless night.

"Think we'll find that damn thing out there?" Jake mused.

"Been wondering the same thing myself," I admitted absently.

Jake studied me briefly, then turned his attention back to the bay.

Men, I have observed over the years, approach even the most difficult of situations from a great many different perspectives. For me, the head-on approach has always been the most rewarding, and most of the time, solutions just generate more questions. For others, solutions are the end-all, and then they turn to something else. For me, Chambers Bay was simply one more adventure, one more exploration into the fascinating world of the bizarre and unusual, one more unexplainable situation to be defused with logic. For Jake, it had evolved into something decidedly different. My detachment was my sanity. His involvement was his reality. For me, Vernice, Jake, Caleb, Harlan, Bert and Polly were all living, breathing human beings, but there was a time, still some way off, when they would be little more than carefully scribed recollections over Scotch in front of a crackling fire. For Jake, they were a very real part of tomorrow—and the day after and the day after.

The big man checked his watch, sauntered back into the kitchen, fixed each of us a cup of coffee and drifted out on the back porch. He stood there for several seconds before I heard the protest. "Oh, God . . . no," he cried.

He stared across the narrow expanse of oil-stained gravel at the front door of Vernice's faded silver and gray house trailer. The front door was open. On the top step was Vernice's robe-clad body.

Jake bolted for her with me on his heels.

He bent over the woman's lifeless body and tenderly cradled her head in his bear-like paws. The look on his face betrayed the unbridled gamut of his emotions—disbelief, loss, sorrow, outrage.

I reached down and touched the woman's hand. It was cold and stiff; she had been dead for several hours. The faded cotton robe was damp from its nightlong exposure to the blanketing fog.

Jake was sobbing. Absently, he tugged at the robe, trying to smooth it, and stroked her hair, trying to coax it back out of her unseeing eyes. All the while, tears trickled silently into the furrows of his craggy face.

I had a feeling down deep inside me that Jake Madden, a man who didn't claim much for himself in this world, had just lost something more precious than he dared to admit. Finally, he slumped back against the side of the trailer, buried his face in his hands and sobbed like a schoolboy.

Even in emotionally charged times, my mind has the disturbing tendency to logically chronicle facts. It bothers some people, but over the years I've learned to accept it. Such was the case now. Vernice Hutchins was dead, but as far as I could tell there wasn't a mark on her. And for some reason I was already convinced she hadn't died of natural causes.

It took Jake several minutes to regain his composure. When he did, he leaned over, picked up Vernice's lifeless body and carried her out to the four-by-four. He covered her with a blanket and crawled in the cab without saying a word. His face was drained of color, and there was a discernible tremble in his lower lip. A tremor dominated his voice when he finally spoke.

"Never knew that woman to be sick in all the years I've known her," he managed.

"Call it anything you want to, Jake," I said uneasily, "but I've got a feeling this is tied in with the rest of this weird stuff."

"You think somebody killed her?"

"I don't know what I think, but we'd better have a look around."

Jake still paused, transfixed by the lifeless form stretched out under the worn plaid blanket. "Who would want to harm her? She didn't have an enemy in the world. Everybody liked her."

While Jake tried to cope with the ebb and flow of his emotions, I began looking around. Something was bothering me, but I couldn't put my finger on it. Maybe it was the fact that she was wearing a robe and was outside. Maybe it was the fact that she hadn't gone into town as she was instructed to do. Or maybe it was simply the fact that Vernice looked like one of those wiry little women that would seem to live forever.

I gave the rutted gravel drive the once-over and went back up to Vernice's trailer. There was no sign of blood on the porch, and once inside, it was evident that there were no signs of a struggle. The tiny quarters were immaculate. A pair of men's white boxer shorts and two white crew-necked tee shirts had been laundered, carefully folded and stacked on the end of the bed. They were obviously Jake's. The bed was still made, and a full cup of coffee was sitting on the kitchen table.

It was easy to conjure up a scenario. Vernice Hutchins was ready for bed, decided to have one last cup of coffee, heard a sound in the drive, thought maybe Jake had finally arrived, went out to greet him, and . . .

I was on my way out the door when I glanced up at the top of the cabinet in the tiny kitchen area. I stopped dead in my tracks, a cold chill racing down my spine.

There it sat—a small vase with a sprig of pine, a single tapered candle and a statuette of the sarcophagus of Sate.

One thing was now painfully clear. Vernice Hutchins hadn't died of natural causes. The only questions now were—who, how and why?

By midafternoon all teams had completed the sweep and come up empty-handed. Hawkins's crew had worked their way east to the Carson farm road, concentrating their efforts along the coastline. They had intercepted Kendall's group at what had become known in the last few hours as the rendezvous point—the spot where Percy Kramer had died.

Madden, in a state of shock over Vernice's

death, had taken her body into the old schoolhouse and solicited B.C.'s help. I joined up with what would have been Madden's team and hooked up with Caleb on the sweep effort. All the reports sounded the same—saw nothing, heard nothing, no creature, no nothing.

The men milled around the area in a kind of robotlike daze; most of them hadn't slept in 36 hours. They were operating on coffee, cigarettes and frayed raw emotions. What little banter there had been earlier had now disappeared completely.

Kendall was aware of the situation. He clustered the 20-odd men around him and signaled for silence. "It's a little after three," he began in a voice worn thin by the mounting hours of strain, "and most of us are out on our feet. I intend to initiate the same security plan tonight that we had last night. Everyone who isn't assigned to one of the patrol efforts will be restricted to the village."

Kendall's speech mirrored his own growing uncertainty. The situation was deteriorating. He knew it and the men knew it. The repeated failures to find and capture the wounded creature only compounded the problem. The men were losing confidence in both the man and his plan.

The trek back to the marina gave me some time to think. I didn't know how or why, but I was convinced that both Kelto and the old

Austin woman knew a great deal more that could help us. The trick was going to be to find out what. There were all kinds of questions bouncing around in my mind—questions like, where did Kelto go when he disappeared for hours at a time? What did he know that he wasn't telling me? What was his relationship to the Austin woman? Maybe even more importantly, where were they last night? And why didn't they feel obliged to come into the village like they were ordered to do?

The questions continued to rattle around. No one single element seemed to be related to another. I was still harboring the uneasy feeling that Bert and Polly hadn't wanted to come into the village where they would have had the protection of the patrols. Why? And Angie—why had she stayed there with them? True, it had taken a little coaxing to start the van, but there was a gaping hole in all of it and I wasn't finding it. By the time the sweep teams had returned to the marina I was still muddling through the same seemingly simple questions. Finally, I decided to chalk off the lack of answers to nothing more than being too tired to think clearly.

By the time we worked our way back to the old schoolhouse and checked in, I had decided to venture back out to the Chambers Bay Motel and grab a couple of hours of much needed sleep. I retrieved the survival kit and conned one of the locals into dropping me off at the now deserted motel.

I had no more than dropped the kit on my bed and poured myself a drink when there was a knock on the door.

"Come in," I snarled, still savoring the warm surge the B and W was bestowing on my chilled innards.

The door opened, and Kelto stood there with that damnable sullen look on his face.

Suddenly all my pent-up emotions snapped.

Battered body and all, I took one ballet-like leap that carried me across the room. Just like that I had him by the front of the jacket, brought the knee up, and chopped down. He was on the floor, beside the bed, half-propped against the wall, a dazed expression replacing the perpetual sneer. All of this would probably have elicited some kind of response if I had given him time.

I didn't.

Pissed-off gesture number two was the old knee to the belly shot. It slammed into his flat stomach, and he was pinned to the floor. The air belched out of him, and he went through the age-old agony of a man who has had the wind knocked out of him and who truly believes he'll never breathe again.

"Okay, sonny boy, have I got your

attention?''

Kelto stared back at me, dazed and gasping for breath.

I got off of him, swaggered to the dresser and poured myself another drink. I was secretly wondering how Mike Hammer or Travis McGee would have improved on my little routine.

It was destined to take him another four or five minutes to marshal his scrambled senses. In the meantime, I slumped down on the edge of the bed, casually reached into my survival kit and fished out the Mauser. For effect, I exercised the nine-cartridge clip and rebolted it. Kelto's eyes were as big as golf balls.

"What . . . what's this . . . all about," he finally wheezed.

"Let's just say I'm pissed."

"About what?"

"Look, Tinker Bell, you slip into my room without knocking, you make veiled threats, you give me some kindergarten story about being the only survivor of the Battle Harbor carnage. Then you manage to get in the way while I'm following the old woman in the fog and I lose her. And if that isn't enough, you expect me to buy some half-baked story about you out tromping happily through the woods while the rest of the community is being carved up like a Thanksgiving turkey." I paused just long enough to reach down, jerk him to his feet and shove him across the room into the chair. Through it all, I made sure he never lost sight of the Mauser. "Talk to me, Kelto—and this time, talk to me straight."

It won't come as any surprise when I tell you the sullen look was gone. He blinked a couple of times and cautiously reached up to wipe off his mouth where a tiny trickle of crimson was oozing from his bruised lower lip. "I don't know what you're talking about," he stammered.

"See that little black thing over there?" I was pointing toward the telephone. "How would you like it if I walked over to it, picked it up, dialed the boys in the striped pants and told them you were withholding information about this whole ugly mess? Let me tell you something; if they happen to discover that you knew one thing that could have prevented just one of these atrocities, you won't take another hike to the woods for another thirty years. The way I see it, you're already an accessory to mass homicide." It sounded pretty bad, but the truth was, I had no idea what kind of charges the Mounties could drum up. I was bluffing. All I could hope was that he didn't know I was bluffing.

Kelto leaned forward, his eyes watering and puffy, still dabbing at his lower lip. "You can't do that. You can't interfere now."

"Watch me." I started to reach for the

telephone.

Apparently he didn't know the phones were out because he appeared to be buying it.

Kelto held up his hand. "Wait a minute," he pleaded.

"Straight story, that's all I want, the straight story."

"We are approaching the Sabbat of Sate," he whispered, "the year of the fallow fields and the year of the feast, the year for an appeal of the fates."

"Look," I sputtered, "the jury is still out on you. Watch my lips; talk to me. Talk to me straight. Knock off the cult crap. What's going on here?"

Kelto tried to clear his throat and folded his long feminine fingers into a prayer pyramid; his eyes were closed. He began again, this time with his voice coming through as little more than a muted whisper. "We are about to witness the equinoctial awakening of Sate. It is the eleven year cycle of birth and death . . ."

"All right," I fumed, "hold it right there. You're talking about Sate, the Mongol, the one they call the Ancient of Ancients?"

Kelto nodded, eyes still closed.

"Come on," I sighed, "surely you don't have the audacity to sit there and tell me some second-rate Middle Ages witch doctor has survived all these years?"

"I speak the truth," Kelto replied grimly.

He opened his eyes, and they were slightly glazed. It was as if he had slipped into some kind of trance. "There is much you do not know."

"Enlighten me," I snapped, giving him another glimpse of the Mauser.

"Sate is not a product of the Middle Ages. The Ancient of Ancients reaches back into the dawn of all civilization, even before the time of the great celestial storms. He is a consort of the very Prince of Darkness himself."

I got up, poured myself another drink and tried to decide whether Kelto needed another bop on the beak or a straight jacket. All of this talk about the dawn of civilization and the Prince of Darkness was more than I could handle. He was rapidly being reclassified in the Wages reference file from weirdo to wacko.

"So you're telling me this guy Sate is several thousand years old?" It was becoming more and more difficult to keep a straight face.

"That's exactly what I'm saying," Kelto insisted, "but you still don't understand. Sate is not a mere mortal. He is a cursed force, an extension of the most evil one, and he has great powers."

I slumped back down on the bed, managed to locate a cigarette and took a swig of the tepid Scotch. I had just about decided Kelto's mumbo jumbo would make more sense if I was half in the bag. "Let's go back to the beginning," I sighed. "Tell me again. Why are you here?"

"The faithful have been summoned," he answered without hesitation.

"But I thought you said you weren't one of them."

"Quite the contrary. I am the vehicle of retribution."

"In other words, you figure this is your chance to get even with this Sate character."

"I see very little humor in all of this, Mr. Wages."

"Don't get pompous on me, buster. Like I said, the jury is still out on you."

Kelto blinked. "This may be the only chance we have to rid ourselves of this evil force."

It was play-along-with-Kelto time. "Okay, you tell me what makes you think you can get rid of this thing called Sate, when we couldn't bring him down with half the damn guns in the province pumping away at him."

Kelto's confidence suddenly began to return. His nearly flawless face inched its way into a sinister half-smile. "I know what to do," he assured me. "I alone know how it must be done."

"Let's go back to something you said earlier." I had calmed down to the point where it was at least possible to establish a rational sequence to my questions. "You said the faithful had been summoned. Are you telling me there are others here who believe in all of this nonsense?"

"There are many," he said evenly.

"Like who?"

"Can't you see? The true believers are all around us. It was my own research, my search for the truth, that led them to believe I was one of them."

I sighed, set my drink on the floor beside the bed and leaned back on my hands. "I hate to admit it, Kelto, but I think I'm starting to make some sense out of all this. What you're saying is you wanted to get even. You saw a correlation between what happened at Battle Harbor and the Coalition commune. You started digging into it and came to the same conclusion I did—that these incidents have been happening every eleven years and that Chambers Bay looked like the site for the next episode in this nightmare."

"I was uncertain until I was summoned."

"What do you mean, you were 'summoned'?"

"I was in the old library at Camberbie doing research. A strange-looking little man walked up to the reading table where I was seated. He laid a note on the table and walked away. The note was nearly illegible, but finally I was able to decipher it. It said, 'You are called, the chosen must serve, Chambers Bay at the time of the equinox.'

By the time I read the note and went to look for him, he was gone."

"Okay, but that doesn't prove anyone else is here. How do you know anyone else was informed?"

"I'm certain of it. This is a momentous occasion for the followers of Sate. A true believer in the religion of the Ancient of Ancients believes that he will be allowed an audience with the great Sate only once in his lifetime. It is the only time he will have the opportunity to appeal for Sate's blessing."

"Okay, if there are others, who are they?"

"So far, I am certain of only one."

"The Austin widow?"

"She is a true believer," he confirmed. "I am not surprised that you know it. She talks too much."

"But you don't know of any others?"

Kelto shrugged. "The Emissary has not yet revealed his identity."

"Emissary?"

"The Emissary is the appointed one, the one responsible to see that the way has been prepared."

I took another swig of my drink, jotted down a few more notes on my growing stack of three-by-fives and pushed on.

"So at this point you don't know who the Emissary is, and you don't know who the other true believers are, except for the Austin woman."

Kelto nodded.

It was pacing time. I got up and started. I had more questions. "Okay—why the woods routine? Do you think that's how they'll make contact with you?"

Kelto nodded again. "The autumnal equinox draws near. I have tried to make myself accessible, but so far I have not been contacted."

"Maybe they're wise to you. Maybe they realize you're not one of them."

"I don't believe so," Kelto said guardedly. "I have been able to venture into the woods without incident. I have to believe that if they were onto me, I would have been attacked like the others."

"So what's your next move?"

Kelto dabbed at the crust of dried blood near the corner of his mouth. "To continue as I have been doing. The equinox draws near. It is my only opportunity."

Surprisingly enough, I was beginning to believe him.

Kendall's seven o'clock session was a repeat of the previous two. The patrol routes were designated and the teams appointed. For some reason, Madden was missing and the youngest of the trio of Mounties, Constable Gregory, was designated to take Madden's place. I begged off by telling Kendall I had uncovered some additional information that I wanted to check out. He didn't like it, but he bought it.

The Z was worse off than I thought. In addition to a ruptured fuel line, it had a broken tie rod and the right front wheel was bent. Nevertheless, I managed to maneuver it across the street and down the block to a decrepit, grease-caked garage that looked far better suited to housing an anvil and forge than a lube rack. The proprietor was probably at Kendall's meeting so I pushed it up next to the old structure, locked it and left it.

The Austin widow was still on my mind, and the prospect of hoofing it out to her place in the fog lacked a certain amount of appeal. I went back to the schoolhouse, scouted around and finally spotted Percy Kramer's pickup truck. It was still parked in front of the darkened drugstore with the keys in the ignition. Wherever Percy was now, I didn't think it mattered much to him who used it.

It took all of 20 minutes to thread my way back out to the Carson road and start to work my way back up to the old woman's house. The fog seemed to be settling in again, and the encroaching darkness only compounded the situation. Lights didn't help. The road seemed to end abruptly no more than 30 or 40 feet in front of the truck.

The whole effort evolved into a guessing game. I hadn't been clever enough to record the mileage in previous visits and now, no

more than 30 yards off the main road, I had
already lost my orientation. In desperation,
I jerked the pickup to a halt, crawled out,
grabbed my survival kit and continued on
foot.

Another 100 yards down the road, I
realized Elliott Grant Wages had made a big
mistake. The gravel path narrowed, and the
fog began to close in; strange sounds began
taunting me from both sides of the tree-
shrouded path. A twig snapped. A branch
swayed ominously overhead. There was a
subtle movement in the underbrush. Then,
suddenly came the worst thing of all—an
eerie, unreal, perhaps deadly silence. I
stopped, forced to listen to the sound of my
own triphammer heart. It was augmented
by strained and shallow breathing.

I made an anemic, half-hearted attempt
at a whistle. It fluttered out over bone dry
lips and sounded a lot like a sputtering
steam engine. At the time, it seemed like a
futile gesture, but there was some comfort
in getting my fingers coiled around the
Mauser. When I had it in my right hand with
my index finger coiled around the trigger,
I felt even better.

Thinking back about it, I don't know why
I found any security in that cherished chunk
of carefully crafted metal. So far, bullets
hadn't proved to be all that much of a
deterrent. The twisting, rocky path up the
hill to the isolated old house of the Widow

Austin was just on the other side of the creek. So, when I felt the ground slope away to the creek bank, I knew about how far I had to go.

The incline was gradual at the base and steeper near the top. My world had been gradually reduced to a gray on gray landscape completely devoid of features. The flashlight was practically useless.

There was no indication of light.

And no indication of life.

I stepped up on the porch, crossed it and knocked.

There was no answer.

Somewhere off in the distance I was aware of a dull roar, the kind water makes, like a waterfall or a rushing river. The shore was several hundred yards away, and yet it sounded near. I tried to conjure up a mental picture of the location of the house in relation to the shoreline. It was, if I remembered correctly, at least a quarter of a mile away. All that notwithstanding, the bay was dead calm. The surface was like a sheet of cloudy glass, tranquil, no wind, only the thick, stifling fog hovering over it.

Despite the darkness, I stepped down off the porch and circled around to the back of the house. The weed-choked yard was cluttered with the debris of time—fallen limbs, undergrowth and a tangle of twisted vines, broken boards and dead trees.

Then I saw it.

The old house was situated no more than 15 yards from a cliff that plummeted away into a yawning pit of blackness. Below, in that absence of light, I could hear the thundering sound of churning water. I shoved the beam of the flashlight out over the edge, but it was swallowed up by the nothingness. The swirling fog created a dance of twisted ghostly shadows.

Somehow the water had to be working its way through some kind of channel or underground entrance into a walled canyon, and if there was a canyon, if there was water, then there were caves. Bingo, Elliott old boy, another piece of your puzzle has just tumbled into place.

Apparently no one knew about this canyon. The sweeps had been made from the shoreline in, across the natural bridge that sheltered the hidden inlet. The teams had confused the sounds of the rushing waters with the natural sounds of the bay, and the fog had done the rest.

It was information that had to be shared.

I went back around to the front of the house and knocked for a second time. When there was no answer I did a repeat of the old shoulder to the door trick. It swung open without a protest.

My eyes were still trying to adjust to the minimal light of the flickering candle when I heard the ominous click-click of the old woman's double action 12 gauge.

"You know what happens up in James Bay when we catch somebody tryin' to break in one of our homes?" the raspy voice crackled.

I shook my head.

"We don't take time to ask questions, Mr. Wages. We start shootin' and leave the talkin' till later."

PART 8

She had situated herself in a creaking old rocking chair on the far side of the cluttered room. The shotgun was propped on the arm of the chair with the index finger of her gnarled right hand curled determinedly around the trigger. Beyond that, detail was lost in the shadows. The single candle on the table that held the sarcophagus wasn't equal to the challenge.

What now seems like 100 years ago, the infamous Gibby Marshall taught me a ploy that under the circumstances sounds perfectly iudicrous. The premise is a simple one; no matter how bad the situation, disregard the other fellow's advantage and act just like you have control. Considering the situation and the size of the barrels of the gun glaring up at me, it was worth a try. If the Widow Austin squeezed that trigger, it was all over—and at the moment it looked like the old girl could go either way.

"Why the hell didn't you answer the door?" I blurted out.

Glenna Austin didn't answer. On the other hand, she didn't shoot, either. She rocked back and forth, her wretched old face mercifully hidden by the room's shadows. The latter, of course, meant there was no eye contact, and if you take Elliott Grant Wages's eye contact away from him, you've partially disarmed him.

"Maybe I should be the one askin' questions," the old woman growled.

At this point I figured I had already won round one. If she hadn't pulled the trigger by now, the odds were at least 50-50 that she wasn't going to. Pulling the trigger on another human being when they're breaking into your home is an impulse thing, and once the impulse passes, you've won the first round.

"What 'cha want here?" she groused.

The mere fact that she was talking instead of shooting was another hopeful sign. I felt my jaw relax, and the lump in my throat started to go away.

"It's the sarcophagus, ain't it? That's what you came for, ain't it?"

It was time to come up with a response

that sounded at least halfway intelligent. If I didn't, there was a good chance that finger of hers could get a little nervous.

"I didn't come for it," I explained. "Actually, I came here to talk to you about it."

"What about it?"

There were two ways to approach it—head on or try to gain the old girl's confidence with a little preliminary chatter. Rightly or wrongly, I figured Glenna Austin wasn't big on the social amenities. James Bay didn't exactly conjure up impressions of a place where the emphasis was on the social graces.

I decided on the no-nonsense approach. If I kept her talking, she would be thinking about what she was saying and not about pulling the trigger.

"The true believers are assembling, aren't they?"

"Who told you about that?"

I pointed to the ugly little statue with the bloated belly. "I've done some homework."

"Sate, Ancient of Ancients," she repeated. "We ain't supposed to have them sittin' out where folks can see it, but I think it's too beautiful to keep hidden."

"Are you a true believer?"

The old woman nodded dreamily. "Me and the husband was both blessed."

"Your husband was a true believer, too?"

She nodded again. This time she tightened

her shawl around her throat as though she was experiencing a slight chill. In the darkness I could read little else into the gesture.

It was time to let her off the hook momentarily. The one thing I didn't want to do was to put her back on the defensive. A defensive attitude could result in a squeeze, and I couldn't think of anything I wanted less than a twitch in that gnarled old finger of hers which was still tightly coiled around the trigger. I decided to do a little more talking and give her a breather.

"We were intrigued with the replica of the sarcophagus of Sate, intrigued enough to start asking some questions."

"Then you already learned that it's the time of the equinoctial awakening?"

I gave her my best E.G. Wages quizzical expression and hoped she'd catch it.

The old woman somehow managed to contort her twisted features still further. She began what was essentially an affirmation of what Kelto had already told me. "The eleven year cycle of Sate has begun again. The Prince of the other-world domain will rise again." It was all too obvious she was merely parroting the words she had so carefully memorized.

It was time for quizzical look number two.

"You know nothing of this?" she rasped.
There was a momentary lull in the conver-

sation while she tried to decide just how much it was safe to tell me. She may have been ugly, but she more than made up for it in caginess. So far her patterns weren't the standard "I'll follow the cause at any price" attitudes. She was reticent. Most true believers won't shut up once you get them started.

"I'm told you have to be chosen."

She came back at me with a barely perceptible nod.

"How do you know you've been chosen?"

She still kept her finger on the trigger, but the other hand reached up and loosened the shawl. Beneath that was a high buttoned blouse. She opened it to reveal what appeared to be nothing more than a small discoloration of the skin, a tiny bruise in the V of her throat. "We are all marked," she said solemnly.

"When?"

"At the dawn of time, an ordinal process, an allocation with the assignment of souls."

"What do you mean by the assignment of souls?"

"The planning of events," she answered evenly.

"So what does this equinoctial awakening mean to you?"

"It means that among all the blessed, I am chosen. I am Sate's choice. Of the many who are so blessed, only a handful of true believers will be called upon to serve, to attend to the Ancient of Ancients."

"What about your husband?"

"If he had been among the chosen, he would have lived to see this day."

"What's your role in all of this?"

"My mission will become known to me as the great hour approaches."

"Are you saying the hour is near?"

She closed her pinched little eyes as though she was savoring the thought of the momentous event. "It is an occasion of great joy for the true believers. It is the time of the cycle; it is so ordained."

"Something in your voice tells me you think this so-called awakening is somehow different than the rest."

The old woman nodded dreamily. "Eleven times eleven." For one brief moment the rasp disappeared from her voice and assumed an almost celestial quality. "On the calendar of Sate this is indeed a special occasion."

"How do you know these things?" I pushed.

"These are revelations from the Great Book of Comprehensions," she answered flatly.

"You have such a book?"

She nodded suspiciously.

"May I see it?"

"Are you a true believer?"

I was tempted to tell the old girl that I couldn't be sure until I went back to the motel and gave the V in my neck a closer inspection. On the other hand, it didn't seem to be the time or place for one of E.G.'s flippant remarks. The old girl just might squeeze.

"No," I answered, knowing full well I couldn't have produced the evidence to support my contention even if I had lied to her.

Somehow the convoluted old face conveyed a look of sympathy, as though she felt sorry for me.

"Then I cannot reveal the contents of the great book to you."

"When will we witness this so-called great hour?"

"It has already begun," she announced solemnly.

Suddenly there was a chill in the room, like a cold draft. The tapered candle next to the sacrophagus flickered, and the sprig of pine swayed perceptibly. The old woman closed her eyes and appeared to lapse into what cultists like to call a state of deeper communication, a dialogue with another dimension. Her face seemed to relax, and for a fleeting moment there was a trace of a smile. Then her eyes opened.

"I have counseled with the Power," she announced. "He informs me that you are a skeptic and that you cannot be trusted with further revelations."

"I take it then that our little conversation is over."

The Austin widow nodded. She had the gun, and I was tempted not to even try to plead my case.

Still, as Cosmo would say, "No risk, no reward," and I barged on. "Well, then, who is the Emissary?"

The faint, almost discernible little smile was long gone. A twisted mask composed of distrust, confusion and cultism was all too much in evidence. She glared back at me without responding.

"If you can't tell me that, at least give me the rundown on Kelto."

The old woman was obviously weighing her answer. "I am told he is one of us, but I do not trust him. The Emissary will put him to the test."

"The test? What kind of test?"

"No more questions," she snapped. Just like that I was back to square one. "Go!"

I shrugged, turned and started for the door, hoping the Emissary wasn't sending a message that could be interpreted as "shoot." The door was open and I was halfway out before she spoke again.

"Do not come back again, Mr. Wages. The Emissary has spoken. Skeptics are to be regarded much the same as we regard the nonbelievers. They are not to be trusted. And if you cannot be trusted not to interfere, then you will be treated the same as those who seek to intervene."

I had the distinct feeling that I had taken

it as far as I could. I didn't bother to respond. There was only one thing for me to do and I did it. The door swung shut behind me.

The fog was worse, only now I had to contend with the pitch-black darkness and the penetrating chill of the ghostly Chambers Bay night.

On the journey back to Percy's pickup, every movement of every branch, every snap of every twig, every unidentified sound made the hair on the back of my neck stand up. The black, featureless darkness of the northern night was never worse.

It was a stumbling, groping trek and took no more than ten minutes, but seemed like an eternity. The flashlight was virtually useless, and my fingers ached from the death grip I maintained on the old Mauser. When I finally stumbled into the side panel of Percy's truck, I uttered a sincere prayer of gratitude.

Having to drive five miles an hour with the window open so I could hear the crunch of the sometimes gravel under the tires was equally disconcerting. If anything, it was worse than the journey from the old woman's house to the truck, and it seemed both slower and longer.

My mind was racing. I fished the the voice recorder out of the survival kit, inserted a new tape cartridge and started tumbling a litany of random thoughts, observations and questions into the little device.

Click. Who is this so-called Emissary? One of the locals? An out-of-towner? Is there such a thing, or am I dealing with some kind of cult hysteria? About the Emissary, what does he, she or it do? Click.

Click. Why doesn't old Glenna trust young Kelto? Better yet, do I trust Kelto? Is Kelto's version of things as they really are or how his Battle-Harbor-twisted mind perceives them? Click.

I lingered for a moment on the so-called Book of Comprehensions, wondering if the library back at Saint Francis had or could get hold of one for me. Maybe it was too late to help me sort through this mess, but the old girl had tweaked my curiosity. Click. Call Lucy and see if she can hustle up this so-called Bible of Sate. Click.

The gravel had quit crunching. Damn!

I sucked up my gut, held my breath and cautiously opened the door. With a firm grip on the Mauser, I crawled out and my feet hit the solid surface of the asphalt blacktop. Percy's truck was sitting crosswise in the middle of the road and clear of the gravel lane.

I jumped back in, hoping against hope that some other clown wasn't foolish enough to be out driving in this soup and about to plow blindly into my exposed flank. I could already see it in big print in the Saint Francis daily student newspaper: "E.G. Wages Dies on Fog Shrouded Canadian Highway." Then I had a second, even more disconcerting thought. What if my flaming final moments didn't even make the student newspaper at all?

I jumped back in, jammed the clunker in reverse, slid momentarily back on the gravel, inched back out on the highway and turned east toward Chambers Bay.

It didn't take long to lapse back into thinking about what the widow had said. "The hour is at hand. The time has come. Eleven times eleven. A one hundred and twenty-one year cycle." Click. "Lucy, my dearest research resource, find out what's so special about this particular emergence. Is this one destined to be even worse than the others? Does that explain why this particular event seems to be so strung out and the others all appeared to be one day shots?" Up until now, up until Chambers Bay, these tragedies seemed to be confined to one event, one massacre, one episode of monumental proportions. Now, thinking about it, there were a great many aspects of this whole affair that were markedly different from previous ones. Click.

There was a light ahead, not well defined, but blurry, vague and uncertain. A streetlight? Was I at the edge of town? Had I made it?

The impact stopped the pickup cold.

For the second time in two days, my face ricocheted off the steering wheel, and again the old vision went cloudy. A salty hot fluid began trickling down my throat and out my nose, but most of that was immediately forgotten. I had another problem, more immediate and a great deal more monumental.

My unexpected impediment had rolled up over the hood and crashed into the windshield with a sickening thud. Fracture lines now raced across my field of vision like a crazed jigsaw puzzle, and for the briefest of moments, I was face to face with a hideous, bloated prehistoric face, twisted in rage. The thing rolled backward, regained its equilibrium and sat hunched like a brooding gargoyle on the crumpled hood; its long, black, apelike arms were outstretched, while it belched out a kind of putrid, black, oily substance.

My brain was short-circuiting.

It was pure survivalist instinct. The Mauser had a mind of its own. It was out, and I was firing point-blank. The decimated windshield was no barrier. Despite the shattered, diffused glass, despite the blurry vision, despite 101 other reasons why the torrent of shots could have gone astray, I was right on target.

The beast took the first slug in the right side of its face, erupting tissue and a thick black liquid like a volcano. One of its massive, two-thumb, three-finger paws groped at the missing part of its head like it was belatedly swatting at a mosquito. The second shot caught him in the ugly hairless expanse of the chest, and the third assaulted the lower part of his face. Each bullet destroyed something, yet no single shot seemed to do the job. It lurched forward again, outraged, slamming its angry bulk up against the shattered windshield. One of the ponderous fists crushed the glass, penetrating it, blindly groping in the darkness of the cab, inches from my face.

The fourth shot blasted another hole through the glass. It caught the monster in the left temple and created a hole the size of a golf ball. Again the head seemed to erupt, and another geyser of the black fluids began to gush down the side of the twisted face. This time the beast cried out, a terrifying sound that somehow reached back into the nothingness before time itself.

I twisted the ignition key and the engine sputtered back to life. Then I slammed the gear shift lever straight down, and the truck leaped forward. The beast catapulted forward, up and onto the roof. The sheet of steel separating us buckled under the impact, and I heard it roll into the bed of the pickup and out, the unreal sound of its bulk tumbling out onto the pavement behind me.

Almost instantly the temperature gauge

rocketed past the red line into the danger zone; pieces of twisted body panels began bending back and slapping violently as the pickup hurtled through the darkness like a wounded bull. There was an explosion under the hood and then another. Fragments of disintegrating engine spewed out of the chamber that had once housed it and flames began leaping out from under the dash panel, scorching my legs, pumping a torrent of blistering heat into the cab. The wiring caught on fire and acrid, choking smoke engulfed me.

When you can't see, you can't breathe, and you're hurtling blindly into a dense fog bank at something close to 50 miles an hour in a truck that's belching out flames and smoke from what was once called the hood and cab—you need a plan. My standard repertoire does not happen to include one that covers this type of situation, so I reverted to my baser instincts and decided to get the hell out of there. What little bits of logic that were managing to filter through told me that that foul-smelling, antisocial mountain of hostility that had twice tried to rearrange my face was sprawled somewhere, dazed and full of big ugly holes, three blocks or more down the highway. If that was the case (and even if it wasn't) my options were still limited; get the hell out or barbecue my long-cherished main frame.

I slammed on the brakes and felt Percy's pathetic pile of mangled metal rattle to a halt, tires squealing.

I threw my shoulder against the door, tumbled out onto the street, regained my footing and made ready to run.

It was like diving head first into a brick wall.

The thing grunted, shoved and pitched me backward like a pushover toy. I went one way, the survival kit went the other. My shoulder hit first and then my face. I could feel the grainy surface of the damp asphalt peeling off layers of what my mother had so endearingly termed my "cute little face."

With the exception of that one prehistoric grunt and my labored breathing, the only evident sound was the hissing, popping and still burning pickup. Flames were every-where, leaping, dancing and surging. The world was cast in an unreal orange-yellow glow, layered by billows of black acrid smoke trying to copulate with the shroud of clinging fog.

The thing was out there, hovering in the darkness, and I couldn't see it.

How the hell could it possibly still be alive?

But then, how could it have survived the escape from Palmer's market? All that not-withstanding, how the hell did it get from back there to up here, full of holes, chasing a truck going 50 miles an hour?

When the truck finally blew, it blew big. There was a low throaty rumble; it was building to a grand finale, and I knew it. Suddenly it erupted into a blinding ball of blue-orange that consumed the night. The world was transformed into bizarre half-images and distortions. There was an eerie, ear shattering shriek, the smell of gasoline, the sound of a thousand thunders, a stench, a terrifying, paralyzing roar, a rain of shrapnel, and the truck was consumed in a flaming orgy.

At first I didn't see it, didn't realize what was happening. Maybe it was the agonizing, near human scream that alerted me. It sounded like something out of a Saturday morning cartoon show, almost electronic in origin yet totally terrifying.

But there were no lasers or high tech, only fire—angry, consuming, deadly, defeating.

The stunned monster stood there, its yawning, gaping, prehistoric face all too visible. It was on fire, watching in a kind of stupefied awe as the fire engulfed and consumed it.

The air went out of me. My eyes went shut, and I struggled to begin breathing again.

The voice was intelligible, but a trifle strident and damned unsympathetic. "Every time I turn around we're scraping this guy up off the pavement somewhere and trying to patch him back together. He must be accident prone."

There was no response.

Here I was, again hovering at death's door and someone was badmouthing me. It wasn't fair. The thought occurred to me that all I had to do was pick up my ball and go home. The problem was, I'd lost my ball. I was trying to think of something downright surly and biting, but nothing came to mind.

Something large and sinister again dominated my world, hovering over me; it was Madden.

The gesture was tentative and revealing. My hand crept up to my face as if it was afraid of what it was going to find. "You guys wouldn't be so damn flip," I snarled, "if you'd have been here."

Ferris was a little more solicitous. "Actually," he appraised, "I can see why he's hurting. There's not a lot of hide left on the left side of his face."

I pushed myself up on one elbow and surveyed my unsympathetic surroundings. Percy's truck wasn't a truck anymore, and the critter was gone as well. "Where the hell am I this time?"

"I don't know how you managed to do it, Researcher, but you've wrecked a truck right in the middle of the street not two blocks from the old schoolhouse. Now what the hell happened?"

"You can ask him questions later," Ferris

scolded. "First thing we'd better do is get him out of the middle of the street and over to the command post to see if anything is broken."

"Think you can walk?" Jake asked.

I tried pulling one leg up, hinging it at the knee. To my utter astonishment, it worked. It hurt, but it worked. Jake slipped one of his massive arms under mine and tugged. All of a sudden I was vertical again. Unhappily, I discovered that in the upright position, everything hurt. The business end of the Mauser was jammed down into my groin area, and I fished it out, muttering a small prayer of thanks that it hadn't gone off accidentally.

Madden, Gregory and Ferris, along with a pockmarked face perched atop a human beanpole, gathered around me. Big Jake had a flashlight and was still checking to see if there was yet any sign of pupils floating in the morass of bloodshot gray-green I call eyes. I punched one leg out in front of the other and it worked. When I tried it the second time, Jake let go and I amazingly remained upright.

"What the hell happened out there?" Jake insisted.

Limping along between the two gendarmes with Doc and the beanpole following, I began to recount the whole gruesome episode. By the time I worked up to the climax, they were ushering me through the side door of the old school. I was deposited in a folding chair next to a long, cluttered table piled with the debris from the search party. A little gray-haired lady with the milk of human kindness coursing through her veins offered me a cup of coffee.

"And you say that damn thing rolled right up over the hood, caved in the roof and fell off on the surface of the road?"

"If that bucket of bolts wasn't sitting out there little more than a mass of molten metal, you could see for yourself," I shot back.

Kendall joined in the interrogation. "How far do you figure you traveled after that?"

A shrug seemed adequate. I had no way of knowing, and I wasn't really concerned. "Hell, I don't know. I was somewhere inside the village limits because there were street-lights all around me when I hit the sucker. After that, I must have traveled another three, maybe four blocks. Who knows?"

Madden and Kendall exchanged knowing looks.

"Why not let me in on your little secret?" I groused.

"First, let me make sure I've got your story straight," Kendall said straight-faced. "You say you first encountered the—"

"Encountered, my butt, Sergeant," I spat back at him. "I plowed right into the sucker. The impact mangled the front end of the truck. That's why it came unglued on me when I tried to get away."

Jake put his hand on my shoulder to settle me down.

Kendall went right on. "Then, after it smashed your windshield, you fired three times and all three shots hit their target. Right so far?"

"What's this all about?" I asked angrily. I wanted to know why they were picking at my story.

"Then you traveled some additional distance before you stopped the truck, crawled out and encountered the beast again. Right, Mr. Wages?"

I looked at Madden. "What's going on here, Jake?"

The big man didn't answer.

"Did you get a good look at him during the second encounter?" Kendall continued to dig.

"Now wait a damn minute," I simmered. "Why, all of a sudden, are you double-checking everything I say? Tell me if I've lost my credibility with our little group and I'll be happy to gather my things and clear out of this crazy town."

"We got a problem," Jake finally admitted.

"With my version of what happened?"

"What we're coming to," Jake muttered, "is a conclusion that scares the hell out of us. After you shot the thing, ran over it and raced away from it, it was still right outside your truck. That leads us to only one logical conclusion."

"Oh, my God," I finally muttered. "There's more than one of these damn creatures, isn't there?"

Madden sagged down in the chair beside me. "That's precisely what we think," he sighed.

PART 9

By dawn, a steady stream of casualty reports began rolling in.

The theory that we were now dealing with more than one of the prehistoric creatures had pretty much become a reality. There was more than enough good, solid and verifiable evidence to substantiate what only a few hours earlier had been little more than a dreaded possibility.

For all intents and purposes, Chambers Bay was isolated, cut off from an unknowing outside world. The phones had been out now over 24 hours, and the choking blanket of gray, damp fog yielded little more than a few begrudging feet of horizontal visibility.

Twice during the early hours of the morning, two-man teams in four-by-fours attempted to head north on the highway to Waverly. One had crashed 300 yards outside of the village limits; the second was found abandoned by one of the patrols. Both men were missing.

During the night, the makeshift communications network set up by the RCMP began to fail, and by dawn only three of the original eight units were still operating.

The 0614AM transmission of the Everett-Forrester team was cut short, and Madden and Kendall took two men and hurried out to check out the situation. Both Everett and Forrester were found hanging from a tree near Clyde Everett's pickup truck. They were dead and stripped.

Madden and Kendall returned with the news and summoned what was fast evolving into a war council—Caleb, the other two RCMP officers, Gregory and Hawkins, Doc Ferris, Bert Johnson, and yours truly, who was still referred to as Researcher.

"How many men can we muster for another sweep?" Kendall began.

Gregory, the tallest of the three, picked up his clipboard and began to toll off the names. He came up with 13, then counted again to verify his figure.

"Christ," Madden muttered, "how many have we lost?"

"We've lost fourteen people since this

nightmare began," Doc confirmed, "and four more are unaccounted for."

"What the hell good does a plan do us if we can't stop the damn thing?" Jake grumbled.

Kendall held up his hand. "I've been thinking about something Elliott said. Remember how he said the thing burned like an inferno last night, which got us to questioning how many of them there actually were?"

Everyone appeared to nod in unison.

"Doc thinks," Kendall continued, "that the reason the bullets don't do anything but destroy what appears to be lifeless tissue is because the damn things are operating on an essential base of plasma."

"Plasma?" Madden repeated.

"Plasmodium, to be more specific," Doc interjected.

"Highly volatile once the membrane is penetrated. We simply shrink it with heat," Kendall said triumphantly.

"Before everybody goes off half-cocked, I need to remind you that it's only a theory," Ferris cautioned. "But from E.G.'s description of what happened to that thing out there when the truck blew up, we just may be on to something."

It was time for me to play "yeah, but," and I did. "Yeah, but I don't know what actually happened to the thing. It turned into an inferno, all right, but we aren't one hundred percent sure that put an end to it."

"Sounds too simple," Jake protested.

"What are you proposing, Sergeant?" I wanted to hear Kendall's plan.

"Different plasma forms react differently to excessive heat," Ferris warned.

"I'm not talking heat," Kendall maintained. "I'm talking fire, and lots of it."

"What are you gonna do?" Jake grunted. "Set the whole damn woods on fire and hope and pray those damn things are in there?"

"I think we'd all be interested in your plan, Sergeant," Ferris mumbled. The old man had a habit of talking around his pipe, and there were times when no one could understand him.

"There's nothing wrong with the scheme we used in the second sweep. We had a good plan—knock the thing down with the tranquilizer darts from a 731 loaded with Selphon 3431 and then get the trap blanket over it and anchored."

I glanced around the room to get a reaction to Kendall's plan. Everyone was nodding except Jake and Bert. Jake looked skeptical. Bert was wearing an expression I couldn't read.

If anyone had bothered to ask me, I would have told them that I was just as dubious as Madden. As far as I knew, yours truly was the only one who had actually survived a face to face encounter with a creature, and I had misgivings about the so-called tranquilizers and trap blankets. At the moment I wasn't sure there was anything that would hold that thing. In my book, Kendall's plan was tenuous at best.

"Since we now believe we're dealing with something that is essentially constructed of a plasma base, entirely different than anything we've ever experienced, we're not going to take any chances. The minute we knock it down we're going to douse it with gasoline and put a torch to it."

There was another nervous exchange of glances.

Jake was more to the point. "I'd feel a lot better about this scheme of yours, Kendall, if we knew where the damn things were."

"Or how many of them we have to contend with," I added.

Kendall was implacable. "Look, we've got to do something. We can't just sit here and let those things pick us off one by one. The only thing we know for certain is that conventional means won't do the job, so let's use that knowledge to our advantage. Let's play our hunch and go straight for the big heat."

Madden was nodding. "I agree with Kendall. We can't just wait for those damn things to make their next move. We'll be sittin' ducks if we do."

Ferris took a long drag on his pipe. "Keep in mind that we have to be prepared for more than one of them."

Kendall was undaunted. "We'll organize it a little differently this time. Gregory is concerned that we don't have much more than a handful of men we can depend on. Those ten men plus the six of us gives us very little operational latitude. We'll have to leave one group to patrol the perimeter of the village, another group will do a house to house, and the third will man the command center here at the schoolhouse to make sure the women and children are all right."

"Hell," Madden protested, "we need twice that many just to get an effective sweep of the area between Caleb's marina and the Carson road."

For the most part, I had demonstrated a certain amount of wisdom by staying out of it. Every part of my body from the hairline down was either battered, bruised, broken, bleeding, or otherwise malfunctioning. The thought of charging off into a fog-banked forest after something I knew my trusty Mauser wouldn't stop had little or no appeal. The bottom line was that up to this point in the unfolding Chambers Bay drama, I hadn't seen anything that would stop our foul-smelling tormentor. Kendall's rapidly devised plan with the gasoline and torches sounded good in theory, but I'd have been a whole lot more comfortable if I'd actually seen it work in a true-to-life, practical demonstration.

"I can't agree with you," Doc interjected. "Looks to me like we'd be a whole lot safer if we made sure everybody was safe and secure in the old schoolhouse and waited for help. This fog has got to lift sooner or later."

Kendall shook his head adamantly. "We can't afford to wait," he repeated.

It was Caleb's turn. He had been strangely silent up to this point. "I agree with Doc. It makes sense to me. Get everybody into the old schoolhouse. That gives us only one place to protect. By now the authorities must realize we've got something drastically wrong here. Kendall hasn't been able to report in to his post, the phone lines are all down, and they know the fog has thrown a blanket over this place and trapped us."

"I don't know how long we could hold out if we did sit tight," Jake countered. "I've seen this damn fog close in up here on the northeast corner of the coast for a week at a time. This is only day three, and we've already picked the shelves clean over at Palmer's market."

"I understand the psychology of mass confinement," Kendall shot back. "We won't be able to control the people in another day or so. I say we don't have any choice but to go out there and destroy these creatures. If we don't, Chambers Bay is likely to come apart at the seams."

Kendall had convinced them. This time there was no apparent dissent; there wasn't even an exchange of haggard looks. My most recent bout with the creature hadn't completely reduced me to the role of a bystander, but it had significantly curtailed my enthusiasm for a return match.

I listened attentively while Kendall passed out the assignments and issued the order to have everyone who hadn't been assigned to a specific detail secured in the old schoolhouse. The order, he concluded somewhat dramatically, was going to stand for the duration of the siege.

While Kendall went over the details, I pushed myself to my feet and searched out another cup of coffee. It occurred to me that I'd probably be more concerned about the supply situation if someone had told me they were running low on coffee. In the process of walking over to the coffee, I took a general inventory of Wages's body parts. On the whole, everything worked, albeit a little stiffly, and by the time I returned to the conclave for Kendall's wrap-up, I was convinced I could make a contribution.

In the finest of military traditions, Kendall had us synchronize our watches. It was seven-thirty, and there was enough light in the street to indicate that there was, for a fact, a sun up there, struggling valiantly to get through. Somehow, though, I knew it wasn't going to make it.

"I think we can be ready to go by noon," Kendall summed up. "Any questions?"

There were no questions.

There was, instead, an aura of resignation.

"Okay," he said wearily, "everybody knows what they have to do."

As luck would have it, I ended up on the detail assigned to conduct the search outside of the village. The thought of dragging what was left of old E.G. body parts over the rocky terrain and around through the trees and sand wasn't all that appealing. On the other hand, if there was going to be a big, socko climax to this saga, I wanted to be there to see it. It would be a shame, I decided, to come this far and not see the last act.

I squandered a few minutes reflecting on some of my more sane friends who sat at their word processors and dreamed up bizarre tales of witchcraft and monsters—secure, creative, comfortable and with no real threat to life and limb. What I was feeling was envy. If I could do it, I reasoned, I would. Then there would be no reason for

.ne to go thumping around in some foggy woods taking my life in my hands.

With four and a half hours standing between me and the invasion of the woods, I had two things to accomplish. Concern number one was good old Brenda, who I hadn't seen for hours. After several discreet inquiries, I was fairly well able to determine that the lady's whereabouts were somewhat of a mystery. The hairs on the back of my neck had that funny little twitch to them, another signal (almost as good as the one from the gut) that there was reason for concern. I told Madden about it and Doc Ferris as well. They both agreed to keep an eye open for her.

My driving record was already marred by two wrecked vehicles, so I was somewhat reluctant to ask Madden if I could borrow his four-by-four. The bottom line was, I didn't ask; I just took it. Given the situation, who was going to know? Madden had his hands full, getting supplies rounded up for the search.

It took me a full ten minutes to slip down the alley behind Palmer's market and two foggy blocks to the highway leading out to the motel. It was a long shot, but my instincts told me that if everyone else was in town, Kelto would be where everyone else wasn't.

Along the way I cursed the fog, the

phones, my battered body, and the suddenly elusive B.C. Where the hell was she? Vernice's place looked dark and deserted, and I realized that Madden hadn't said anything more about the unfortunate woman. I knew the big guy was hurting, but I hadn't seen anything to indicate it was affecting his performance. Jake Madden was fast becoming, in my frame of reference, one of those rare creatures men like to call "a man's man."

The motel was only a couple of hundred yards down the road from the diner. By slowing down to a virtual creep, I was able to locate the motel driveway, turn in and inch my way back to the general area of the office. The lights were off, and the door was locked. This time the Johnsons had complied.

I tried Kelto's room, knocked three times and got no response.

Just to make certain I hadn't overlooked something, I managed to get one puffy paw wrapped around the handle of the Mauser and did the old patrol bit around the entire motel unit.

Bert and Polly had done a thorough job. All of the units were locked. One more exercise in futility.

By the time I worked my way back to good old number eight where the rapidly dwindling supply of Black and White was waiting, I had decided to fortify myself with one quick drink in preparation for my afternoon in the woods. It took a while, but I fished around in the contents of my duffel bag until I came up with the battered old flask Gibby gave me as a going away present the day we called it quits. ("Get out and stay out!" she screamed, and threw the flask at me. As usual, her aim was off, and I retrieved the flask as sort of a memento.) I rinsed it out, filled it with the B and W and plunked myself down on the edge of the bed.

One sip.

Suddenly, the previous night and all the days preceding it began catching up with me. Three days in Chambers Bay had turned into an eternity—an ugly eternity. The shoes came off real easy, and lying back across the bed seemed like the natural thing to do.

Maybe Elaine was right. Maybe I ought to pay homage to my mounting years and quit chasing around the countryside sifting through bizarre situations to find a story. Instead of chasing shadows, I could chase women. That's it; write romance novels. Why not? Romance from the man's point of view. Maybe it would sell. Then I suffered a good dose of instant recall and discarded the idea. E.G. Wages writing romance? Get real. Good old Elliott Grant couldn't write a romance if his life depended on it. This was the same old Elliott Grant that Gibby once termed a "sexual mutant between the sheets." Bad idea, writing romances.

Twenty winks couldn't hurt.

As I plunged headlong into a shadowy world of semiawareness, I could feel what was left of me sink deeper and deeper into an uncomfortable world of chaotic thoughts. Where was B.C.? Where was Kelto? How many of those damn things were out there tramping through the woods? And perhaps the most troubling thought of all: Where was Gibby?

The old internal clock didn't fail me. I rolled over, glanced at my synchronized watch and mentally recorded ten minutes till eleven. The near two hour tussle with the sheets helped, but it was still foggy both inside and outside my head. I spent several minutes staring at the darkened ceiling, slowly becoming aware of the uncomfortable feeling you get when you know you're supposed to be alone but you're all too aware that you aren't.

Once again I had proven that Thelma's only son was indeed a clever lad and very much predisposed to caution. Just before slipping off into never-never land, I had tucked the old Mauser under the pillow. Now it was just a simple matter of a good acting job—roll over, slip the hand under the pillow, grip that dependable old hunk of cold steel, sit up and confront my un-invited visitor.

The Mauser was gone.

Now I bolted upright out of fear.

Jake Madden was slumped in the room's only chair with a frown deeply etched into his furrowed face. "I could charge you with grand theft auto," he said a little testily.

Remember the old Gibby trick? When you're on the defense, attack. "How long have you been sitting there?" I snapped, equally surly and equally taciturn.

"Ten minutes, no more. Figured you'd be here. When I found my truck missin', I put two and two together."

"I figured I might get lucky and find that Kelto kid. If I could get him to give me some straight answers, it might save us some grief."

"What's your fascination with him?"

I swung my legs over the edge of the bed, reached down and searched around till I found the half-empty glass of B & W, took a swig and tried to get myself oriented to reality. It wasn't all that easy in a room composed of half-shadows and what appeared to be a coat of thick gray paint obscuring the world beyond the dingy windows of the rented cubicle. The thought tumbled through my mind that it might be now or never. Either I brought someone in on everything I had learned up to this point or went along with Kendall's plan intact. And at this point, I had the uneasy feeling that there was a better way than the one Kendall had proposed.

"I need one more shot at him," I repeated. Madden managed to somehow slouch down even deeper in the overtaxed little chair. It was protesting its burden. He shoved his hat back, folded his hands in front of him and shoved his legs out in front of him. "I don't have the slightest idea what the hell you're talkin' about," he muttered.

"I've already filled you in on what I think is happening here in Chambers Bay—that it's a continuation of a strange string of atrocities that have been happening every eleven years since 1943 and maybe even further back in time than that."

"That's what you told me," Jake grunted. He didn't say he was buying any of it. He simply acknowledged that it was, in fact, what I had told him. "Listen, Researcher, even you have to admit that whole yarn of yours sounds pretty far-fetched."

"If you think that's far-fetched, you may not want to hear the rest of my theory."

"Try me. I can always quit listenin'."

I sucked up my breath, finished off the Scotch and embarked. Jake was right. It was the first time I had heard it out loud, and it sounded pretty ludicrous, maybe even impossible, and definitely off the wall. But a funny thing was happening. The more I hauled it out, the more convinced I became I was on the right track. The terminology of the group that called themselves the true believers was sprinkled liberally throughout the lengthy dissertation, and by the time I ground to a finish, Big Jake had heard it all.

If the reality of the Vernice episode hadn't been weighing on his mind, I wouldn't have been surprised if that mountain-man face of his would have collapsed into a smile. Instead he scowled. I meandered over to the bureau, poured myself another drink and waited for his reaction.

It never came. His hard, thin lips were pursed into an expression I couldn't read.

"Well," I blustered, "say something."

Madden blinked a couple of times and carefully shifted his bulk in the overtaxed chair. "I guess I could see how you'd come up with most of that stuff. I ain't sayin' I buy it, mind you, but you sure do raise a whole bunch of questions."

"Like?"

"Like how did they get from there to here? And what the hell is this all about? And, if you can answer those for me, who is this Emissary they keep referring to? Beyond that, how many of these monsters are crawlin' around the countryside out there? One? Two? Ten? What the hell are we dealin' with?"

"The answer to your first question is all theory at this point. If the phones were working and I could get through to Lucy, I could get that part verified."

"You're outta luck," Madden pointed out needlessly. "Them phones are still out."

"The answer to your second question is a little more complex. We're dealing with a religious sect that goes back hundreds, maybe thousands of years. Some people would call it a cult. Others would call it Satanic. Whatever you call them and regardless of how long they've been around, we're dealing with some very, very committed people—committed to a cause we don't even begin to understand."

Jake was still listening.

"The answer to number three is—I don't know. I've got a hunch this so-called Emissary is someone we know. On top of that, I've got a hunch it's someone we would never suspect. Both Kelto and the Austin widow refer to the Emissary as some kind of priest."

Jake shifted in his chair, starting to get restless.

"As to how many of these things we're dealing with, your guess is as good as mine. Up until you and Kendall found the bodies of Everett and Forrester hanging in that tree this morning, I'd have given you ten to one odds there was only one of them. The only logical explanation I had up to that point was that we were dealing with some mutant, some prehistoric throwback, something that just never evolved beyond that stage where it crawled out of the slime of some pit."

Madden sighed deeply. It was obvious I hadn't convinced him. It was equally obvious the whole situation was too bizarre for him to comprehend. He was a practical man, trained to look at empirical data, and nothing that had transpired in Chambers Bay in the last 72 hours could be construed as practical, routine or normal. He was dealing with something far beyond the realm of drunks and poachers and traffic accidents and family squabbles. People were dying at an alarming rate. Chambers Bay was being terrorized by something that defied description. And to make matters worse, for all practical purposes, Chambers Bay was cut off from the rest of the outside world.

Finally the big man let out with one of his own half-growl, half-grunts. "Okay, Researcher, so now you've told me all of this. What do you expect me to do?"

"I want you to go back and convince Kendall to hold off on his plan until I've had one last chance to talk to this kid, Kelto."

"That's all?"

"That's all," I assured him. "All he has to do is delay his sweep an hour, maybe two, just enough time for me to find Kelto.''

Madden waited impatiently while I rounded up my survival kit, then hustled us back to the old schoolhouse, grousing about Kendall, the sweep and the fog. He went into conference with the three RCMP officers and left me to my own devices. I had a hunch he didn't want them to hear what I had to say simply because he wasn't convinced himself. On the other hand, he wasn't ready to totally disregard everything I had told him.

While all of this was happening, Ferris ambled toward me, looking for all the world like a man with nothing of consequence on his mind. He reached into the pocket of his coat, hauled out a piece of paper and handed it to me. It was folded and stapled.

I recognized B.C.'s handwritten scrawl.

> "E.G.:
> *Kelto came here to find you. He has finally been contacted by the Emissary. I'm going to the Austin widow's house with him.*
>
> *Brenda.*"

"When did you get this?" I barked at the old man.

Ferris rolled his tired brown eyes, glanced at the wall clock and took a drag on his pipe. "Couldn't have been more than an hour ago," he drawled.

It didn't take me more than a few seconds to race across the room and cram the note under Madden's nose. In the same motion I had him by the arm, dragging him toward the door. Kendall was still voicing his objections to any delays in implementing his plan when we went out the door.

Jake stopped just long enough to shout back. "Don't start the sweep until we get back."

It wasn't until Big Jake was once again hurling the four-by-four down the fog-choked road toward the old woman's house that I started reflecting on the more mundane aspects of B.C.'s hasty communication. Where, when and how had Kelto received his marching orders? And probably the most mundane concern of all, how were they getting out to the old woman's house? Kelto didn't have a car, and B.C. had been totally dependent on the Z. But by the time Madden cranked his machine off the main road and started down the narrow, twisting strip of rocks, sand and gravel known as the Carson road, I had forgotten those matters and returned to the primary concern of getting out of this mess alive.

The Constable of Chambers Bay knew his territory a lot better than I did. We slid to an abrupt halt and bailed out, leaving the machine in the middle of the so-called road. "We're close," Jake panted.

I fell into step (limped is more accurate) beside the big man, and we searched along the west side of the road until we found the path that headed up the hill. Halfway up I had to stop to get my bearings. My run-in with the quarrelsome creature was taking its toll on me. The legs were working, all right, but not that well. While I caught my breath, Madden unstrapped his .38, twirled the chamber, gave the hunk of crafted metal a critical appraisal and slipped it back in his holster.

"Ready?" he grunted.

I lied and said "yes." After all, at this point, we weren't more than 30 or 40 feet from the old woman's door.

Every scenario imaginable flashed through my mind on the way up that hill— Kelto and B.C. held prisoner by that maniacal mountain of madness . . . or, worse yet, both dead . . . or . . .

Madden didn't even pretend to knock; he kicked, and the door flew open.

If Kelto's face was white, B.C.'s was even whiter. They were in a state of shock.

Glenna Austin was again positioned on the far side of the room in her rocking chair, still wrapped in her mismatched shawls designed to shelter her from the chill. As usual, she was glowering, but this time, there was a difference. Her mouth was slack and her tongue protruded. The perpetually pasty face was bloated and discolored.

"What the hell is going on here?" Madden fumed.

"That's the way we found her," Kelto protested.

B.C. raced across the room and threw her arms around my neck. She was shivering and crying. Her words were racked out by sobs.

Consolation has never been my long suit. It's not that I don't feel compassion; it's just that I'm not very good at expressing it. Besides, in this case, there wasn't much to do but hold on, and B.C. was doing that. I patted her on the back and mumbled something inane like "everything will be all right."

Kelto was equally shaken. His haunting brown eyes darted from Madden to me and back to the lifeless form of the old woman. He was frantically searching through the maze of pockets in his tattered old fatigue jacket.

"I heard from the Emissary," he blurted out. "I've got his note here somewhere." Finally his trembling hand emerged with a crumpled piece of paper which he shoved at me.

It was a piece of waterlined graph paper, torn in half and carelessly folded. It said simply:

ANCIENTS

*THE DAY OF THE EQUINOCTIAL
AWAKENING IS AT HAND. ALL IS
PREPARED. WE WILL ACHIEVE ALL
THAT IS GLORIOUS.*

There was no signature.

I read it a second time and handed it to
Madden. He had to hold it down by the
flickering light of the candle to read it.

"What the hell does this mean?" he
grunted.

"It's from the Emissary," Kelto answered
piously.

"And just who is this so-called
Emissary?" Jake came back at him.

Kelto dejectedly shook his head. "I don't
know." He shoved his hands down in his
jacket pocket and glanced over at the lifeless form of Glenna Austin. "I simply know
that every eleven years there is an emergence, and that the Emissary is the one who
prepares for the reawakening of the Ancient
of Ancients."

Madden turned and looked at me. He was
frustrated. More than that, he was uncomfortable with the mystical elements of
Kelto's pronouncements.

"How did you get this?" I asked, pointing
to the piece of paper.

Kelto shrugged. "I found it on my pillow
when I returned to my room last night."

"Then you don't know who left it?"

Kelto shook his head.

"What the hell were you doing out there?" Jake fumed. "I gave orders that everyone was supposed to be housed in the village last night. Any one of my men could have mistaken you for one of those damn things and filled you full of holes. Or worse than that, you could have run into one of 'em and you wouldn't be any better off than that old lady over there."

"I have nothing to fear from your so-called creature, Constable Madden. They believe that I am one of them."

"How do I know you're not one of them?" Jake growled.

"I think he's telling the truth, Jake. Everything he's told me so far has checked out."

"What about the old lady?" Jake insisted. "Isn't she supposed to be one of the chosen?"

"She thought she was." I tried to slip in a sly grin, but it didn't work.

Jake was glowering at me again. "If these so-called true believers are supposed to be safe from this damn thing, how come the old lady is sitting over there very, very dead?"

"The thing you keep referring to as the creature didn't do that," Kelto said calmly.

"Then who did?" Madden was right up in the young man's face.

"The Emissary!"

Madden stared back at the young man, his

mind rebelling. It was obvious Kelto's cool demeanor and almost academic approach to the situation annoyed him. "You want me to believe this incredible yarn, yet you can't even tell me who gave you the damn note."

"I can assure you that the Emissary walks among us," Kelto said confidently. "Otherwise, he would arouse too much suspicion as he made his preparations."

"Preparations for what?" Madden fumed.

"Sate will awaken; it is so written in the Book of Commitments."

Madden turned away from the young man in disgust and walked back over to the body of Glenna Austin. He studied her for a moment, then turned to B.C. "Okay," he began, his voice softening, "tell me what you saw when you came in here."

Brenda Cashman was hugging herself against the pervading chill. In the long shadows of the flickering candle, she somehow looked thinner and even more vulnerable than usual. She walked over to the door, her finger pensively stroking her lower lip and began to retrace her steps. "We just came in. We didn't knock because the door was ajar. We both commented that it was strange that the old woman would leave the door open because it was so damp and chilly. We could see that there was a candle burning, and we figured she had to be here."

Kelto confirmed it all with a nod.

"Kelto saw her first. From just inside the doorway it looked like she was just sitting in the rocking chair, maybe sleeping. I went over to wake her and, well, you can see what I found."

Madden's deeply furrowed frown had turned into a face mirroring compassion. Now it was Brenda who was caught up in the ugly little scene, and it made a difference.

"Did you check her?" he asked.

B.C. nodded. "She's been dead awhile. As E.G. well knows, I'm no authority on this kind of thing, but her skin is cold and hard to the touch. With all those wraps around her, I can't tell if there is any swelling or discoloration to anything other than her face."

Jake was still staring at the dead woman when I interrupted. "There's something you need to see."

With B.C. and Kelto following, I led the trio out the door and around to the rear of the cabin to the cliff overlooking the hidden inlet. Jake stared down into the fog-choked crevice with a puzzled look on his face. "I discovered this last night."

The look on Madden's face told me he hadn't put the two events together.

"You were still tending to Vernice when I came out here to talk to the old woman.

When she didn't answer, I started poking around the house, looking in the windows, doing anything I could think of to learn something about what was going on here. I could hear the rushing and surging of water. I knew I was several hundred yards from the shore, but I was certain about what I heard. That's when I discovered this hidden inlet. There's water down there, and it's rushing in either through some underground cave or the land west of here is a natural bridge."

Jake stared down into the yawning blackness, listening to the dull constant rumble of the swirling waters. "Damn," he muttered, "all these years and I had no idea there was anything like this back here."

"Well, it's sheer speculation on my part, but I've got one of those gut feelings."

"What's your gut tellin' you this time?" Jake asked.

"I figure that inlet down there is the very reason old lady Austin was here in the first place."

Madden stared back at me blankly. My theory was a long way from empirical.

"It just stands to reason. Lucy tells me the geological profile and the topographical features of each place that these incidents have occurred were all networked with caves and subterranean caverns. I don't think it's a coincidence that this old woman comes to town and ends up in the very house that has access to this hidden inlet. Put two and two together. Kelto believes that the true believers were all sent here to help the Emissary make the preparations for the coming of Sate—and this house is perfect."

"Okay," Jake sighed, "but why is she dead?"

"I think the so-called Emissary, whoever he, she or it is, knew the old girl was doing a lot of talking and was afraid she would reveal something she wasn't supposed to reveal. Everyone knew I was asking her questions."

The look on Madden's face told me that he was trying to sort through what had to sound like a highly speculative, half-baked theory. "What you're tellin' me is that this house, this place and this time are no accident, that they were chosen by the one you call the Emissary?"

I nodded. "I know it stretches your imagination, but it's actually starting to come together for me."

"Let me get this straight," Jake said. "Are you telling me that these ugly critters that we've been chasing around through the woods are down there in that inlet?"

"That's what I think," I admitted. "Look, it makes sense. Think back about how each of those sweeps were organized. Each time a group has come in from the west, they've used the shoreline as the starting point. The group that worked its way in from the highway used the Carson road as its western boundary. In other words, both groups missed it simply because no one on the sweep teams even knew it was here."

"Are you tryin' to tell me Kendall organized it that way?"

It was easier to shrug my shoulders than admit I wasn't certain about anything, including Kendall. "I guess the question has to be, are we sure he didn't?"

Madden again walked to the edge of the precipice and peered over the edge. It was like looking into a monochrome kaleidoscope, a fascinating world of churning and ghostly grays that hid the angry, swirling waters. I knew what he was going to say when he turned back to face me.

"We're gonna have to go down there, you know."

"There is only one way to do it," I protested. "Go down to the shore and work our way along the coast until we find the cave that accesses back into this inlet."

"The coast line is sheer thirty-foot walls along this section. We couldn't spot the passageway from the top of the cliff."

"We sure as hell can't scale over the edge here," I insisted.

"The goin' might be a little rough," Jake

assessed, "but it could be done."

B.C. was still shivering, so we went back around to the front of the house and back into the room where Glenna Austin maintained her sightless sentinel. There was something different about the room from the first time B.C. and I first visited the woman, but I couldn't put my finger on it.

Madden had escaped into a world of detail, the kind he could handle. "How many men do you figure we need to go down there and start searchin' through those caves?"

"Only people you can trust," I admonished him.

Jake looked at me as though he didn't think it was really possible that the Emissary could actually be someone he knew. "I can trust all of them," he grunted, but there was a definite lack of conviction in his tired voice.

"You must be very careful who you reveal your plan to," Kelto warned ominously. "The Emissary could be anyone."

Madden looked past me at the young man, the look of uncertainty now more evident than before. "I've known most of these people for years. Hell, I'd lay down in front of their trucks. They're all trusted members of the community."

"Reverend Bell was a trusted member of the Battle Harbor community, too," Kelto countered quietly.

"Wait a minute," I sputtered. "Are you

saying Myron Bell was the Emissary of Sate at Battle Harbor?"

Kelto nodded. There were tears in his eyes.

PART 10

Have you ever wondered how many kinds of revelations there are?

Some revelations astound us, while others merely confirm a cherished bias.

There are revelations that alter the course of our lives and in some cases even redefine history.

There are revelations that shape love and hate and revelations that are of no consequence.

I feel reasonably certain that if I took the time to page back through Wages's "Rules to Live By" I would somewhere rediscover that old adage that goes something like, "If it's all neat and tidy and you can wrap a pretty bow around it, the contents are likely to be spoiled." In other words, old E.G. had been sucker-punched, snookered and bamboozled.

I reflected back on that old man's cherublike face with its too warm smile beaming out over a gilt-edged Bible, the rickety old wheelchair, his wistful study of the turgid waters of the misty strait—and recast that image in light of Kelto's revelation.

E.G. Wages had bought it, hook, line and sinker.

Why else would the church take a man still in his prime and relegate him to an obscure cell in an obscure house in an obscure village in an obscure corner of the world? Why wouldn't the mother church try to capitalize on his message? Why, indeed, wouldn't that church send him forth? Why wouldn't this soulful message have the most universal of all appeals?

The answer, of course, is obvious.

The church had learned the real truth about Myron Bell.

Somewhere, somehow, some way, they had discovered that one of their own, one of their chosen, one of their annointed was in reality a disciple of darkness, an Emissary of the demon Sate.

What better way to conceal the embarrassment?

What better way to bury the fact?

What better way to close the pages on

what had to be one of the church's darkest hours?

Hide him.

Consider the liability if the truth were ever uncovered.

Kelto was telling the truth. Somehow I knew that. He was right on the money; all the components were there. The trusted, integral part of the community, driving the school bus to the remote retreat site, the mysterious mechanical failure, the sending of the younger group ahead by themselves, the convenience of three distracting boys—one, two, three—not obvious but very logical, very clever.

And who were the earlier ones? Was it the little nun who had so carefully assembled the Lute orphans for the coming of Sate on that remote Choker Point smoke site? And is it now painfully evident why the Erickson woman was never found at Baffin Island? Finally, was it Marry Marry or Dawn at Owl's Head—or was it both?

Kelto's revelation told me everything I needed to know. Now the burden was as much mine as his.

As Madden shepherded us back into town in the crawling four-by-four, we worked through the logistics of an alternate approach to Kendall's sweep plan, but before we could do that, we had a lot of convincing to do. There was still a great deal about the Chambers Bay situation that Kendall didn't know anything about.

There was a lot to be said for Kendall's plan. The RCMP sweep was militarily efficient, and we had the right gear for it. The men had already been through the exercise twice, and they knew what to do. The downside risk was equally obvious. Kendall was needlessly exposing his men to another encounter with one or more of the creatures that had already proven to be more than any one man could handle.

The Wages plan, on the other hand, was the flip side of the coin—and, to be fair, its primary appeal was to long-shot lovers. Before Kendall would consent to my plan, though, he would have to be convinced we knew what we were talking about, and that wasn't going to be easy. All this was compounded by the fact that neither Madden nor I had any experience with caves, and there was no sure way of knowing for certain if our two-thumbed, three-fingered adversaries had gravitated to the underground network for their Chambers Bay sanctuary.

I was basing a great deal of my hypothesis on the belief that there was a system of subterranean tunnels and passageways in, around and under Chambers Bay. It is a known fact that caves exist throughout North America and that they are almost always found in and around the Great Lakes area. At this point I was willing to wager that Sate's crew was down there somewhere.

On the other hand, if I accepted Madden's premise that the creatures numbered more than one, then I had to be willing to tackle a host of other unanswered questions. How many are there? And what was their role in all of this? And Kelto's repeated reference to an equinoctial awakening was raising other questions.

At that moment, I had only one objective —to get Kendall to delay his planned sweep until he had the chance to hear Kelto's story and in turn listen to the plan Madden and I had developed to check out the caves.

There was one other disturbing dimension to the Chambers Bay situation that up to this point hadn't been given a great deal of consideration. If Kelto was right about the Emissary being someone who was moving freely in the mainstream of all this, then the so-called Emissary was in a position to reveal our plan to the true believers.

So, while Jake inched us back to the village, I used the opportunity to whip out the trusty old three-by-fives and frantically make notes on the whole affair. Kelto and B.C. rode in the cramped back seat, both morose, both absorbed in their own thoughts. It was almost twelve-thirty, and I was getting concerned about being able to get to Kendall in time.

It didn't take long after we arrived at the schoolhouse to get the answer. Kendall had deployed his six man force and initiated the sweep at twelve o'clock sharp. The schoolhouse, the women, the children and everything else the Chambers Bay residents held near and dear had been entrusted to young Constable Gregory and a handful of grim-faced teenagers backed by a squad of stalwart and equally grim-looking young ladies. According to Ferris, Kendall's plan had been set in motion and was being implemented exactly as he had diagramed it.

I found Ferris entrenched in what had come to be known as the operations center, a pipe jammed in the corner of his mouth, a stethoscope around his neck and a squalling urchin, pants down, butt up, laid out on the table in front of him. The mother, who had just spied the needle Doc was preparing for her youth, looked even more apprehensive than the distraught youngster. Doc had already cornered B.C. and elicited her assistance.

Kendall had launched his sweep at high noon with a squad that included Constable Hawkins, Caleb Hall, Bert Johnson and three others. Doc informed us that the plan called for them to start from the marina and work their way west. Their arsenal included the tranquilizer guns and the trap blanket. While Madden listened to Ferris's disturbing report, his shoulders sagged and his craggy face settled into a concerned scowl.

"Why the hell couldn't he have waited one more hour?" Jake fumed. "One damn hour couldn't have made that much difference. He knew we were tryin' to get back before the deadline."

Young Gregory defended his superior. "He wanted to make sure they covered everything before they lost what little light they had left, sir."

Jake sighed, headed for the coffee and motioned for me to follow him over to the area maps Kendall had tacked to the wall behind the riser. He picked up a grease pencil and scrawled a big X over the location of the marina. "They started from this point and they're workin' in this direction." His ungainly fist made a sweeping gesture across the expanse of map. "Now, if they space themselves back thirty yards from the shoreline, they'll cover this area." He encapsulated the area with another big black greasy circle and then drew another at the approximate location of the Austin widow's home. "Hell, they won't come within a mile of apple trees from that inlet you showed me."

I nodded, turned and motioned to Kelto.

He joined us, and I started interrogating him about the inlet. "Starting at the ridge on the eastern boundary of the Carson property, show me where you start running into the caves."

Kelto's feminine, too white hand with pencil-thin fingers crept out of his jacket pocket and moved to the general area where Madden had drawn the second circle. "Here and here," he said cryptically, pointing to two different locations. "These in this area are quite high." He pointed to the western or far wall of the inlet. "The ones located on the eastern wall, below the old woman's house, are at about water level. It's a sheer drop, and there may even be water in some of them. I've checked out the ones on the western wall. I never could figure out how to get to the ones below the house."

Madden stepped back as I circled around the two men and studied the map. "Then that means the old house sits directly over the caves."

"It's very steep—twenty, maybe thirty feet down to the first caves. They're smaller. The bigger ones are right at the level of the water," Kelto said.

Madden studied the maps. "Is there any way to come into the inlet from the lake side?"

"The water comes in through an underground passage. I've looked at it. The entrance is above the surface on the lake side and below the surface in the inlet."

Again Madden's shoulders sagged. "Okay, Researcher," he groused, turning to me, "got any ideas?"

"Only one," I admitted, "the obvious one. Scale down from behind the house."

"You know how to do that?"

"Not me," I protested. "I don't do caves and I don't do scaling. I leave that to the younger, more adventurous types."

"It would be difficult," Kelto interrupted. "When you're standing on the west wall, you can't determine which ones only go back a few feet and which ones snake back in for some distance."

I decided it was time to do more than just voice a passing objection to Madden's fast-forming plan. "Wait a minute, Jake, I know what you're thinking. You're talking about lowering someone some thirty feet down a sheer wall into a foggy inlet and looking for a cave that may or may not contain flesh-eating things that we know bullets don't stop. Think about that before you push this any farther."

Madden, still studying the map, grunted.

"Besides," I added, "we're not certain they're even down there."

"But you think they are," he insisted.

He had me. At this point I was convinced of it. "Yes," I admitted.

Jake hoisted his bulky frame up over the edge of a nearby table and allowed the scowl to erode into a half-grin. He finished off his coffee and plunked the empty cup down on the table beside him. "I think they're down there, too," he admitted, "and since the three of us can't handle it alone, we wait for Kendall. Then we head for the caves.''

Old E.G. wasn't all that thrilled with the prospect of hurtling his already battered body over a sheer precipice and dangling by a thin nylon line over churning waters hidden by fog. Add to that the fact that I was convinced the caves were populated by pre-historic throwbacks that indiscriminately ate meat, alive as well as dead, and compound that by the fact that my Mauser had proven to be next to useless against them. It was easy to conclude that I wanted no part of Madden's little caper.

Story or no story, it sounded like a very bad idea.

Waiting for Kendall's triumphant return gave me a chance to catch a few fast winks, which I did. Curling my weary frame up on one of the bleachers and using my jacket for a pillow, I slipped almost immediately into one of my typical, none too rewarding efforts at sleep. Laced into my apprehensions about chasing some man-eater down some dark, damp cave was a bad dream about Gibby.

"Wake up, E.G., wake up." B.C. was shaking me by the shoulder.

"What?" I mumbled. It was a question born out of confusion. The confusion was in the distance—frenzied voices, people

milling about, shouts. I forced one eye open.
"What's going on?"

"They were attacked," B.C. shouted,
trying to get through to me.

The other eye opened. "Attacked? Who?"

"The sweep team," Brenda sobbed. She
pointed to the throng milling around a
harried-looking Doc Ferris.

From there on it was automatic. The legs
unhinged and I was upright, vaulting over
that last two rows of rickety old bleachers
and sprinting toward the mass of confusion.
Doc, Jake and Kelto were at the core of the
crowd, gathered around and hunched over
a trembling form. It was elbowing, shouting
and shoving, but I got in and got a look at
him. He was hysterical, a matted, fear-
ridden, terrorized human being with a
missing arm.

Doc was twisting the bloodstained tourni-
quet first one way, then another, trying to
stop the hemorrhage.

"What the hell happened?" Jake
screamed.

That's when I saw the second one. He
couldn't have been more than on the threshold of puberty. He was smeared with
blood, trembling, his breath coming in
spasmodic gulps. "It . . . it . . . it tore Luke's
arm . . . arm off."

"Who tore it off?" Madden was near
hysteria himself.

"The . . . the . . . the thing tore it off," the

boy sobbed.

Out of the corner of my eye, I saw the mangled boy slump to the floor. Gregory was shoving people aside, trying to give Ferris and his tragic charge more space. Doc was on the floor beside the youth. A pool of blood bridged the distance between them, and the boy began to scream. Suddenly there was a violent convulsion, and just that quickly, it was over. The crowd was suddenly quiet. Ferris sagged to his knees, head forward; he too began to sob.

It was Madden who had the presence of mind to guide the hysterical youngster away from his companion. Jake's muted voice was working in a strange way, trying on one hand to comfort the youngster and at the same time probing, still trying to discover what had happened.

"Benny, listen to me, you've got to get hold of yourself. I've got to know what happened."

The redhead looked up from the protective crook of Jake's huge arm with fear-ridden eyes. The words were being blocked out by desperate gulps of air. Ferris moved in and took the boy by the shoulder, shaking him. "Answer the Constable, Benny. You have to answer him. We've got to know."

"How many of them were there?" Jake kept digging.

The youngster hunched his trembling

shoulders and looked down at the floor.

"Was there more than one?" Doc pushed. The boy managed a single nod.

"More than two? More than three?" Benny nodded a second time.

"What happened to the rest of the sweep team?" Madden shouted.

"They . . . they . . . they took 'em," the boy gulped.

"Who? The sweep team? They took the sweep team?"

The boy managed another nod.

"You saw those damn things carry off Kendall and Johnson and Caleb and the others?" Doc repeated incredulously.

The boy tried to clarify his answer, but the effort came out garbled and broken.

Madden looked at me, then at a stunned B.C. "What the hell were you kids doin' out there in the first place?"

"When . . . when you didn't come back," Benny stuttered, "Sergeant Kendall figured . . . figured they got you and the . . . the others. He was . . . he was . . . goin' after you. Luke and me . . . decided to follow. We . . . we thought we . . . could help."

Ferris patiently guided the terrified youngster to a chair, set him down and took a seat facing him. "Look, Benny, I know you've been through a lot, but this is important. We have to know what happened. You keep saying 'they'. How many of them were there?"

The boy could manage little more than a shiver. He looked back with pleading eyes at his interrogator. Again, words failed him.

"Which way did they go?" Ferris asked quietly.

The boy pointed.

"That's west," Jake declared, looking back at me.

"Benny," Doc began again, his voice measured and calm, "we can't help if we don't know what happened. Now, I want you to take a deep breath and try to tell me everything that happened from the time you left here. Do you understand?"

The youngster choked back still another sob and somehow tucked his head down deeper between his narrow shoulders. It was as if he were trying to hide from the awful thing that he had witnessed.

"Benny, you've got to try," Doc urged.

Again the boy nodded.

Finally the first effort broke through the wall of fear. "We . . . we saw 'em leave." The voice was still fragile and hesitant. "Luke and me, we . . . we decided to follow. They . . . they headed straight for old man Hall's marina. We . . . we watched them spread out. Luke wanted to follow . . . but I was scared. We kept losin' them . . . in the fog. I never saw fog that thick. Luke . . . Luke called me a chicken. Then all of a sudden . . . we heard growlin' sounds . . .

lots of noise . . . like stuff breakin'. There was shots and screamin'."

"Did you see anything?" Doc interrupted.

"It was them," Benny blurted.

"Are you certain?"

"All of a sudden I heard one of the men cussin' and then he started to scream. Luke saw it. One of them . . . one of them things had Sergeant Kendall. Luke said he was all bloody. The thing was draggin' Sergeant Kendall by his head. Luke said it just stopped and tore Kendall's head off . . . like he was some sort of a doll or somethin'."

"What happened to the rest of the team?"

"Luke and me could hear them things growlin' and screamin' . . . screamin' like animals. We saw the bodies of Mr. Hazel and the two Click brothers . . . they was all torn apart."

"What about Caleb Hall and Bert Johnson?"

"We . . . didn't find their bodies . . . but we could hear all . . . all that noise in the fog up ahead of us."

"Which way were they headed?" Jake was double-checking.

Benny shrugged his shoulders again. "There was so much fog. I . . . I . . . kinda lost track."

"What happened to Luke?"

Benny's eyes suddenly clouded with terror again. Another wave of tears began streaming down his dirt-smudged face.

Ferris put his gnarled old hand on Jake's shoulder. "Give him a minute," the doctor said softly.

"I started . . . started runnin' back toward town . . . and all of a sudden like, Luke was yellin' to let go. When I turned around, this big black thing had Luke by the arm. He . . . he took one of them weird-lookin' paws and put one against Luke's head and held onto Luke's arm with the other. It . . . it just ripped his arm right out of the socket . . . like it was a chicken wing."

In the background I heard Brenda shudder; she turned away and began to cry. Madden put his arm around her.

"Then . . . then the thing shoved Luke away and . . . and squatted down and started eatin' Luke's arm. . . ." The words trailed off, and Benny stared silently into our faces.

Jake didn't waste any time. We huddled briefly, and the decision was made to implement the still somewhat sketchy Madden-Wages plan. He was convinced it was pointless to go back to the spot where the two boys had witnessed the Kendall atrocity. He had bought my theory, and he was determined now to find access to the caves.

Ferris seemed to be evolving as one of the few rational voices in the rapidly developing scenario. He listened carefully while Madden roared through the hastily constructed plan, questioning where appropriate, confirming when he thought we were on the right track.

Madden considered time to be our biggest enemy. The longer the creatures had Johnson and Hall, the less likely we were to find either of them alive. I didn't tell him that as far as I was concerned, the moment the two men became captives their chances of survival were next to nothing.

Gregory was dispatched to Caleb's marina with instructions to round up a specific list of supplies—heavy nylon rope to be used for scaling, cotton rope, pulleys, tackle and four one-gallon containers of gasoline. B.C. was hustled off to Palmer's market for flashlight batteries, empty milk bottles, work gloves and matches. My assignment was a little more complicated. I had to gain access to Clayton's Hardware, locate some kerosene lanterns, heavy duty snaps, two utility tool belts and anything else that looked as though it might come in handy in exploring caves. All of this left Jake with the task of rounding up additional ammunition—a flare pistol, two more revolvers and the department's two 40-channel hand held units with boom mikes.

That left the big man with one final chore—determining who was going with him, that is, besides Gregory and yours truly. In retrospect, the decision to take Kelto shouldn't have been any surprise. He was probably the only one who really knew anything concrete about the apelike disciples of Sate. The four of us, given the nature of most caves, were probably all that could be really effective, but I would have felt a helluva lot better if the entire Seventh Fleet had been thrown in for our back-up.

It was at that point that B.C. announced she was going with us. I started to protest, but Madden was quick to accept her offer.

It was a little before four when we loaded the last of the supplies in Madden's four-by-four and headed back for the Widow Austin's place. Outside the steamy windows of Madden's truck was a gray world that I was growing to hate.

It took us all of 30 minutes to get out to the old house and get the supplies transported from the road up to the porch. While Madden and Gregory went around to the rear of the house to assess the inlet, I captured B.C. and cajoled her into helping me search the house one last time. With any luck at all, I figured we could find some other way of getting to the caves besides scaling over that ledge and risking a drop into a pit we knew nothing about. All I wanted was a few minutes to see what we could find.

Elaborate hypotheses are the bane of academics. I wasn't one, but I'd been hanging around too many salty old scholars for too long a time. In plain and simple terms, I reasoned there had to be an entrance to the caves through the Widow Austin's house. Somewhere in that ramshackle old structure there had to be an entrance. It was the only thing that made sense in this scenario of insanity.

My reasoning went something like this. It was one thing for the apelike creatures to use an inlet entrance. After all, they had already demonstrated both the strength and agility to handle just about any kind of obstacle. On the other hand, the Emissary, if he was what Kelto suspected him of being, one of the locals, would have the same trouble negotiating the inlet cave entrances that we were going to have. It just made sense that the Emissary and the rest of the true believers had an access that was a little more suited to mere mortals.

My conclusion to this rather simple-minded hypothesis was that somewhere there was an entrance to the labyrinth and that entrance was somewhere in the old lady's house. The trick was going to be finding the damn thing—and fast.

It boiled down to a race. If I could find what I was looking for before Big Jake was ready to go over the side and dangle on the end of a thin nylon line, the risk of scaling down into the pit could be at least partially minimized.

Brenda and I launched our search in the old woman's cluttered living room. Glenna Austin was still holding her silent, if lifeless sentinel, and B.C. thoughtfully draped a dusty old throw over the woman's rigid body. Not that it made all that much difference, but for some reason I was a little more comfortable poking through her belongings just knowing that those dull black eyes weren't fixed on my every move.

There were four rooms on the main floor —a sitting room, a kitchen, a bedroom, a pantrylike affair that was piled high with an assortment of rubble, debris and just plain dirt. Our hurried and clumsy approach to the search didn't even give the rats time to hide. Twice B.C. screamed when she uncovered nests of squealing, yellow-eyed creatures that chattered ominously when we invaded their shadowy domain.

The flooring under all of the rooms was badly warped and sounded hollow. There was the oppressive stench of mildew and decay in each of the rooms. At the far end of the kitchen, there was a narrow, coarse, boarded set of near vertical stairs that ascended into a loft whose access door had been nailed shut.

We spent a good 20 minutes tapping walls, moving rickety old pieces of furniture and found absolutely nothing—at least nothing that resembled a trap door that would lead us down to the network of caves that I knew had to be laced through the hill under the old house. As a last resort, we kicked aside the debris in the makeshift pantry and inspected it. All to no avail. In the end, B.C. stood in the middle of the tiny room with a look of "what's next?" on her troubled face.

I went back into the sitting room and stared at the shrouded figure of Glenna Austin. "Damn it, B.C., I'd have bet my last dime we would have found a trap door somewhere in all this mess. Nothing else makes sense. There has to be one."

"If this whole thing was being directed by Alfred Hitchcock, he'd have the old lady's rocking chair sitting on it," B.C. sighed, "or something like that."

Bingo!

A little light came on. The night I barged into Glenna's happy home only to find the crusty old girl waving a shotgun under my flaring nostrils, the rocking chair had been on the opposite side of the room. I had felt something was different about the room, and now I realized what it was. Why would the old girl move her rocker? After all, it was fairly obvious Glenna Austin wasn't a member of the homemaker of the month club.

There was only one way to find out.

"Help me move her," I snapped.

"What on earth for?" Brenda protested.

"Because that rocking chair sitting on top

of that threadbare braided oval rug is sitting directly on top of the trap door that leads down to the caves."

"You've been watching too many late shows," B.C. said, sneering.

"Never mind; help me move her."

Between the two of us, we managed, with an admirable degree of dignity, to scoot Glenna and her chair over a few feet and clear the rug. I jerked back the rug, and B.C. let out with an annoying little giggle.

"I have to admit," she said nervously, "I wish it had been there."

"Damn, it's got to be here," I protested. "It can't be that complicated. It's a simple house."

The uneasy smile faded from B.C.'s face. "Madden may be right. Maybe the only way into those caves is back there in the side walls of that inlet."

I sighed, picked up my flashlight, went out the front door and around to the rear of the old house. Madden and Gregory had completed most of the rigging. The requisitioned gear had been brought around to the back, and Kelto had carefully repacked the more critical items into two bulky backpacks.

Madden's plan had been further refined. He would go down first and find the cave that led back into the side of the hill, then Officer Gregory would follow. Kelto and yours truly would go down on the second wave. B.C. would come last.

While Madden tested the lines, I gave the old house one long, last E.G. Wages visual search. It was a drill in futility. The fog and darkness were doing their best to conceal whatever minor concession the old place was willing to make.

Madden was systematically laced into the makeshift harness. Brenda helped Gregory loop the lines through the D rings and snapped the gear at both locations on the tool belt. The lines were laced back through the fore and aft pulleys, and the knotted end, along with the gloves, were handed to me.

"You're the dead man on the first descent," Gregory said evenly.

"Can't you find something else to call it?" I said dryly.

Gregory looked at me with a blank expression. Another futile attempt at dark humor for naught.

I wrapped the line around my waist twice, knotted it, curled my hands into the leather gloves and backed away from the precipice. Madden was already lying on his stomach, inching his feet cautiously out over the edge.

Even in the chill gray darkness, their faces were easy to read. Madden and Gregory mirrored a kind of grim determination; Kelto was more a look of apprehension. B.C. was out-and-out scared.

Madden worked his bulk over the ledge and I could feel his weight snap up the line, then shiver into my hands. I took two steps back and dug in my heels to counterbalance his 260 or so pounds.

"Watch out for that old dry well," Kelto cautioned. "The boards laying over the top of it are almost rotted through."

Bingo, again!

If I hadn't had my hands full, I would have hugged the sullen little bastard.

"Jake, hold it!" I shouted.

Madden was suspended precariously over the yawning chasm with only his craggy face still peering back over the ledge at us.

"B.C., Kelto, somebody, kick the lid off that old dry well and see what's down there."

In less time than it takes to describe it, the trio had cleared away the dead leaves, pried the cover off and rammed the beam of Gregory's flashlight down the darkened hole. When the young officer looked up, his face was a death mask.

B. C. took one look, unable to put down the revolt in her stomach and looked away choking.

Madden somehow crawled back without my help, righted himself and joined me in peering down into the darkness. The ghostly yellow beam of light played down on the mutilated remains of Caleb Hall. He had been decapitated.

Just beyond him was the long sought opening, tunneling back away from the wall under and toward the house.

Jake's shoulders slumped, and he sagged to his knees. My suspicions, unfortunately, had been confirmed. We were already too late. If this was Caleb's fate, there wasn't much reason to hold out hope for Bert Johnson.

"Looks like you found your damn access," Madden muttered.

I nodded and looked around the tiny group. At the moment I wasn't sure they had anything left to give. The young constable still hadn't regained his equilibrium. Even Kelto was shaken; perhaps long buried fears had finally resurfaced. B.C. had crumbled. Only Madden still maintained the look of grim determination. If I read him right, the discovery of Caleb Hall had reduced him to rage.

"What do we do now?" Gregory managed.

Madden had the presence of mind to shut off the flashlight, and the ugliness of the scene was temporarily lessened. "Yeah, Researcher, it's your move now."

I had my own emotions to contend with. The situation had already far outstripped my ability to both comprehend and deal with it. The cost, in terms of human life, for the true believers to carry out their satanic mission was staggering. Only one thing seemed clear. It had to be stopped—here and now. Somehow we had to find a way to make certain that Chambers Bay was the final stop on Sate's terrifying journey through time. If we didn't, it would only get worse from here on in.

"Look," Madden said, reading the situation, "I don't have any choice. I've got to go down there and do what I can to put an end to this nightmare. I'll understand if any of you want to back out now."

"You can't get it done by yourself," I heard myself say.

Kelto was pacing back and forth. He had already shouldered one of the backpacks. "I'm coming with you," he said, almost mechanically.

Gregory reached down and picked up the other backpack. There was no way of knowing if the young man had even considered that he might have had an option. He had already lived too long with the old adage that the "Mounties always get their man."

Brenda looked at me, her face etched with tears. She was shivering. "I don't want you to go," she said, her voice barely above a whisper. "I'm afraid of what will happen down there."

"We don't have any choice," Madden said stoically.

"I don't think I can go any farther," she finally admitted. She reached out, took my hand and squeezed it.

Madden looked away. "Let's go," he said gruffly.

PART 11

Madden went first, and Gregory followed. Kelto went next, and I brought up the rear. We worked our way past the mutilated remains of Caleb Hall, through the opening and descended into the tunnel. I was worried about B.C., but I thought she had a better chance of getting out of this mess than we did.

We hadn't traveled more than 30 feet when we came to a small vaulted cavern some 30 feet across. Two tunnels led out of it, and Madden paused just long enough to fish out his compass.

As usual, Kelto's deep-set brooding eyes revealed little of the storms that were raging in his tortured soul. Our eyes locked, and I had the feeling that I knew what he was feeling.

"This is what you've waited for, isn't it?"

He nodded solemnly.

"What are we gonna find down there?" Madden asked.

"I only know what the troubled soul of Myron Bell revealed to me," Kelto whispered.

"More of them damn creatures?" Madden growled.

"Those creatures, as you call them, are all that remains of Korbac and his generals."

"They're what?" I exclaimed.

Madden and Gregory exchanged uneasy glances.

"I have already told you. It is the time of the equinoctial awakening. Sate will be among us at any time now."

"You mean there's something down here besides those damn things we've been shootin' full of holes?" Jake blustered.

"Those creatures and things you refer to are nothing more than Korbac's generals, the flesh-eaters. They, like their contrite leader, have gathered once again to make their appeal for release from atonement."

"Christ, how many of them are there?"

"Their number is legions. That is why I asked you not to become involved. As you have seen, every assault by nonbelievers only results in their proliferation."

"How's that possible?" Gregory asked numbly.

"They mate with those they do not destroy. Over the centuries they have multiplied."

"Holy shit," Madden muttered, "are you saying that nut and the Erickson woman, those three boys, those two girls from the commune have have evolved into those creatures now?"

"They have, and untold more like them. Now they are true believers; now they, like those they have mated with, must have Sate free them from their perpetual state of atonement."

Madden's troubled face was drawn and weary.

"What about Bell?" I protested. "If what you say is true, if he was an Emissary, why isn't he with Sate? Why is he sitting up there in some half-forgotten corner of the world reading the Bible?"

"Myron Bell is a soul in conflict, torn between two masters. Now he serves neither."

Little by little, the jigsaw pieces were coming together. Kelto's frequently confusing revelations had again peeled away one more shadow from the cloak of mystery that surrounded those who called themselves the true believers. Still, I had to decide just how much of it I was willing to accept.

Madden pushed himself away from the wall, turned and took several steps deeper into the cave.

As I started after him, I made a solemn commitment to myself. If I lived through this to write another journal, all, I repeat, all research was going to come from the pages of an encyclopedia. The days of "living it" were definitely over.

Gregory worked his way around Madden and took the lead. The walls of the dirt tunnel were caked with a putrid, greenish slime that bombarded the senses with an overpowering stench of mildew and rot. Huge gray rats, first disturbed by Gregory, had worked themselves into a frenzy by the time I sorted my way through their sordid little world. One, perched precariously on a narrow ledge at eye level, stared back defiantly as I passed. At the last minute I threw the beam of my flashlight in his angry red eyes to dissuade him from what I only guessed he might be thinking.

The floor of the cave was gradually sloping down. I had my compass out—we were heading east and north—and deducted we had already passed under the old woman's house and beyond.

At the first turn, a sharp angle to the right, Madden had stopped to wait for me. He was holding his fingers up in a silencing gesture. Gregory was just a few feet beyond him, transfixed.

I gingerly lowered myself down off of a small ledge until I was standing next to the big man. If anyone had bothered to ask me, I would have unashamedly informed them that old E.G. had just discovered a whole new dimension to his fears—claustrophobia. It was every bit as disturbing and irrational as my long harbored and openly acknowledged fears of heights and sharks.

The reason we were pausing was obvious. The cave ahead abruptly forked off in two directions. The one to the right took a sharp right turn some 20 feet from where we stood. The ceiling was lower, and it narrowed down to the extent that I wasn't at all certain it was big enough to accommodate either Jake or me.

To my way of thinking, the passageway to the left looked like it had far more potential.

We started disconnecting the life line and slipped it back through the D rings until Madden and I could operate independently from Gregory and Kelto. While we were going through that little exercise, I tried to get a better understanding of my surroundings. At the moment, we were in a chamber where two entirely separate forces of nature had been at work. We had the nearly smooth surface of basaltic material which indicated that the walls of the cave had been carved out by the surging waters of the great lake itself. Yet I was equally aware I had just emerged from an area that was mostly hacked out of dirt and limestone. All of this was going a long way toward proving my theory that the network of caves, caverns and tunnels was, in all likelihood, a reality.

It also stood to reason that we were now in enemy territory. This had to be the bivouac of the creatures, and the caves were their underground highway, the very thing that enabled them to move so handily from one region to another.

Gregory searched along the walls of the cave until he found a crack big enough to accommodate a stainless steel anchor pin. He inserted an O ring, connected his own nylon line, laced it through and inched his way sideways into the narrower cave. Within a matter of seconds he had disappeared into the shadows.

The other tunnel shot straight ahead, then began to slope down again. It was big enough to accommodate all three of us, walking straight in single file. It also served as a darkened universe of spiders, crayfish and a host of other scurrying creatures that shared a world devoid of light.

"Come on, Researcher," Jake grunted, "we've got work to do. You ready?"

"Ready," I lied.

* * *

What at first appeared to be a stand-up, no-nonsense cave rapidly deteriorated into a big man's nightmare. The gentle slope became a steep incline where the ceiling dropped to no more than 24 inches, forcing us to crawl on our hands and knees. At one juncture, the passage narrowed to the point that we had to strip off our utility belts and backpacks and inch them along in front of us as we crawled on our bellies.

At one point we had to come to a complete halt while Madden squeezed himself through a small opening and explored several feet of cave branching off to our right. All the while I was locked to the floor of the cave with no more than six inches of headroom. When Madden returned he had a quick exchange with Kelto, and a large, ghostly pink, eyeless spider meandered casually through the beam of my flashlight. The creature, about the size of a softball, abruptly changed directions, stumbled over my fingers, conquered my arm, brushed my face and casually traversed the length of my aching body. I felt the little bastard every inch of the way.

A few feet further ahead, the decline grew steeper, and Jake again came to an abrupt stop. At almost the same time, I became aware of the sound of rushing water. A few feet ahead of that, we inched our way into a small cavern with a four foot ceiling and right in the middle of it a hole some 36 inches in diameter.

Jake curled himself into a kneeling position, poked his head down through the hole and spent several minutes assessing the situation. When he looked back up, a small part of the grimness had gone away. "Take a look, Researcher. I think we've found what we're looking for."

It didn't take me as long as Madden. I poked my head through the hole and feasted my eyes on a cathedral-like cavern bathed in a world of eerie half-light, a universe of majestic limestone structures above and below, and thundering through the middle of it, a black, turbulent underground river.

I came back up, caught my breath and looked at Madden. "I don't understand," I began cautiously. "Where's the light coming from?"

"There's torches placed at intervals all along the far wall. I think we've stumbled onto their main passageway." He propped himself back against the wall and began to reassemble his gear, checking the items in his backpack and his tool belt. "Damn," he muttered, "I think we finally caught up with 'em."

"Okay, now that we've found them, what's your plan?"

"We're gonna blow 'em to kingdom come. I don't think there's much hope of findin' old Bert alive down there. I just hope he didn't have to suffer much."

"We have to find them first," I reminded him.

"They're here, all right. I can smell the stinkin' bastards."

Jake lowered his backpack down through the hole, then shimmied gingerly down, lowering himself to the floor below. The drop was less than ten feet. He had no more than landed when he started signaling for me to follow.

I turned around to signal to Kelto.

He was gone.

A shudder ran down my spine, and I found myself scurrying frantically to get through the hole.

The news stunned Madden. "Where the hell could he have gone?" the big man blistered.

I stood there in the chilled dampness of the subterranean universe, wondering, like Jake Madden, what kind of terrifying world I had entered.

The world that surrounded me was right out of Jules Verne. The walls virtually shimmered with a palette of muted colors. We had entered an underground domain created by literally thousands of years of undisturbed, unhurried eroding waters. From some long-buried convolution in the back of my mind I recalled a seemingly unimportant (at the time) lab experiment— water absorbing tiny amounts of carbon dioxide and the ultimate formation of carbonic acid. It had, over time, created a world of massive pillars and exquisite hangings, curtains of stone and altars of maverick granite.

The torches had been placed at what seemed to be random intervals. It was obvious now how elaborate the preparations had been. I was overwhelmed with the feeling that I had been catapulted into another time and space, a universe where every known human reference becomes completely useless.

Suddenly the tranquility was shattered by a mechanical sound, a metallic click, a sound completely out of harmony with the bizarre underground world that confronted me. I recognized it immediately, but immediately was too late.

"I knew it was only a matter of time," the familiar voice whispered.

I spun in one direction, Madden in the other.

It was Bert Johnson. Behind him was a smiling, white-gowned Angie. Bert's hand was tightly clenched around a very ominous looking, very big revolver.

"Jesus, Bert, you scared the hell outta' me," Jake sputtered. "We've been lookin' for you. You okay?"

Johnson's stony face relaxed into a mocking half-smile. "Of course I'm all right, Jake. At long last I'm among my own."

Madden went slack-mouthed; his face

furrowed into a frown. "What the hell's goin' on? You're talkin' weird, Bert."

I dug my elbow into Madden's ample ribs. "I think Bert has just informed us that he is one of the true believers, maybe even our long sought after Emissary."

"Mr. Wages is quite clever," Bert volunteered.

Jake's eyes darted from Bert's gun up to his face and then over to me. The look of utter disbelief was etched into his craggy face. Words failed the big man.

"What about it, Bert?" I pushed. "Am I right? Are you the Emissary?"

Jake was still stunned. "I don't understand what's goin' on here."

"The pieces are falling into place," I continued. "Your old friend Bert here didn't bother to seek sanctuary in the old schoolhouse when you enforced the curfew because he knew there was no danger, and little Angie standing back there was equally safe. They knew exactly what was going on. They didn't need to be concerned."

The smile inched its way back into Bert's haggard face. "So far, so good, Mr. Wages. I'm sure Angela is equally impressed. What else have you figured out?"

"It's a pretty good guess that you're the one who killed Vernice and the old Austin woman, right?"

"Those of us who receive the calling are blessed, Mr. Wages. You surely understand that we are the chosen few among the many. And once a true believer has been chosen, there is no room for those with a wavering commitment. Vernice became involved with our local peace officer. We discussed it and found it to be a completely intolerable situation. As we grew near to the great moment of the equinoctial awakening, there was too much danger that she would reveal herself to our esteemed friend. We could not risk that. The course of action was clear. The holy Emissary gave me my instructions, and I followed them."

"And Glenna Austin?"

"She fulfilled her commitment," Bert said evenly, "but she was beginning to talk too much. In a way, Mr. Wages, you are responsible for her death. If you and your skinny companion had not been quite so nosy and stumbled into her home to discover the sarcophagus, she might have been allowed to live long enough to share in this momentous event with us. But she was revealing more and more, and it was a risk we could not take."

"You . . . you're the one who killed Vernice?" Jake repeated in a hollow voice. His usually gruff voice had deteriorated to a barely perceptible tremor.

"There is no place in the domain of the Ancient of Ancients for those who waver in their commitment to the great Sate," Bert pontificated.

"So what happens now?" I asked sarcastically. "What about us? Or should I assume that we're just two more minor inconveniences in your sordid little scenario?"

"Quite the contrary, Mr. Wages. Your stumbling in here like this is most fortuitous for you. Because you are an academic, you will have an opportunity to be a part of something that no other nonbeliever has ever been allowed to witness. You, perhaps more than all the others, will have some appreciation for what you are about to see. Your propensity for logic and your delight in the search for truth bids you well. As for my old colleague, Mr. Madden, he is not so fortunate. Our esteemed lawman, we fear, is not to be trusted. If we allow him to live much longer he could be disruptive to the proceedings."

"Yeah," Madden snarled. "Well, I think it's about time somebody put an end to this bullshit."

In the few short hours that I had known Jake Madden, he had proven to be a man of impulses. He acted on one now, but this one came at the wrong time and the wrong place. His hand darted for his .38, but it never cleared the holster. The unlikely-looking man with the unlikely-looking gun fired first, three times in succession.

The first shot caught Jake in the throat, the second in the chest, and the third blew away part of his craggy face as he plummeted backward. His body slammed against the wall of the cave, erupting geysers of thick black crimson. The series of violent explosions had punctuated the stillness, only to plunge us into an unreal, almost ghostly silence.

Angie watched in dispassionate silence. Bert did likewise. It was left up to me to experience the full range of terrifying emotions that accompany the witnessing of the violent and needless death of another human being. Tears welled up in my eyes, and my stomach revolted; I couldn't breathe. For a moment or two I thought I was going to suffocate. Then, gradually, all my chaotic emotions evolved into one—a realization that my own intellectual curiosity would be satiated only to suffer the same fate as Madden. I stared down at the twisted kaleidoscope of tissue and blood and hoped I had the strength to handle it like he did—no whimpers, no protest, no apology.

Finally, Johnson spoke. "Are you ready, Mr. Wages?"

I took one final look at the earthly remains of Jake Madden, still unable to cope with the helpless feeling of outrage. Through the pocket of my windbreaker I fingered the Mauser. One thought kept racing through my fevered mind: "Cool it." Madden was dead as the result of an irrational reaction. In that sense, I was one up on him. I was still alive, and if I wanted to stay that way, I had to have a plan. If I didn't, it could very well be that I wouldn't be around to make that final entry in the Wages Journal.

"Ready for what?" I managed, a little too surly.

"To witness what no other nonbeliever has been privileged to witness—the sabbat of the all-powerful, the rebirth of Sate." As Bert Johnson finished his invitation, his eyes drifted shut as though he had been transported into some kind of ethereal dimension.

It was only then that I realized that the man had shed his normal attire for a black, featureless, coarse robe with a simple single strand of gold rope at the collar. In the flickering light of the bank of torches, he looked pale and hollow, uncertain of his own destiny as well.

Angie stepped away from us as though she was in a trance. She moved around to the front and led the way.

"You will follow," Bert instructed. The ungainly pistol that had brought an abrupt and violent end to the life of Jake Madden was still clutched tightly in his hand.

Isolated fragments of a rapidly formulating plan for self-preservation were starting to materialize. I nonchalantly stooped over and picked up the backpack, hefted it over my left shoulder and started to follow.

The whole thing was ludicrous. I was moving through the bowels of the earth, blindly following a man and woman wearing the garb of an ancient satanic cult that believed their long dead lord and master was about to reawaken. The grotesque limestone formations gave the illusion of being in some kind of unreal stone and glass mortuary. Enormous stalactites stabbed down from a shimmering vaulted ceiling that looked like fragmented crystal. The floor was sporadically tortured with a similar outgrowth, this time up, raping the tunnel with an evil intent.

Angie, gliding along several feet in front of me, turned right and disappeared through a small opening.

No matter what I anticipated, regardless of what I had conjured up, everything paled in light of the spectacle that suddenly confronted me.

We had emerged into an enormous cavern, a magnificent hall bathed in the eerie orange-blue light of countless flaming torches. The natural grandeur of the place selected for Sate's reawakening was overwhelming. The ceiling was laced with a montage of stone and ice curtains, the walls were shimmering with chips of lime green and pale pink, and the granite floor in the center of the room was polished to a mirror-like smoothness by the ravages of the eons.

In the center of the enormous room was a natural stone altar; atop it sat a black, brooding sepulcher, the top half constructed of beveled glass and the bottom of a flat black depthless material that defied description.

The perimeter walls were sheer, nearly vertical, networked with a multitude of depressions. The creatures, the generals of Korbac, as Kelto had referred to them, languished like indescribable gargoyles waiting for the momentous event; their squinty, prehistoric burning yellow eyes were fixed on the centerpiece entombment.

"Behold the great Sate, Ancient of Ancients," Bert Johnson beatified.

His hand clamped down on my shoulder, forcing me to my knees, as if I was just one more supplicant of his devil god. It was uncomfortable, but it afforded me an opportunity to get a better fix on my surroundings.

The sepulcher was guarded by no less than eight hooded and shrouded true believers who knelt at the base of the altar. Each knelt with their heads devoutly bowed, hands folded. Next to each of them was a single candle and a sprig of pine in a crystal vase. Spread before them was an opened, large, leather bound journal—the Book of Commitment.

The room was filled with a monotone

dirge, a monosyllabic litany with a haunting, unnatural clarity; it was the chant of creatures cursed.

I had to get hold of myself. I was running out of time. If I was going to find a way of saving my highly cherished hide, a plan had to be developed and implemented fast. The whereabouts of both Gregory and Kelto were complete unknowns. There was no way of knowing what had happened to either them or Brenda; I could only hope against hope that each of them had found a way out.

It was an underground world without orientation. All my reference points were gone. East wasn't east, and down wasn't anything except an indication of the way the eroding waters had once flowed. Gregory and Kelto could be anywhere now—hopelessly lost, alive, dead, trapped. The possibilities were endless.

I was jolted out of my speculation by the single, loud, ominous thump of what sounded like an ancient drum. As the beat intensified, the battalion of prehistoric creatures became more restless.

Suddenly, one of the creatures stood up. He was larger than the rest and somehow different. A tissuelike glaze of proud flesh covered the upper half of his hideous, shapeless body. The beast lumbered from its hollow in the wall and staggered crookedly toward the altar. Along the way it made a pathetic attempt at communication with the other beasts—a series of blunted growls and distorted, almost childlike whimpers. With its ascension to each succeedingly higher step, it paused, pounding its chest triumphantly. Ultimately it reached the level of the sepulcher and began slowly to circle it. Each clumsy, half-stumbling step was accompanied by ritualistic gestures of battle—the thrust, the parry, the lunge, the retreat. Then, as if from nowhere, it produced a lance with a hook-shaped blade configurated on the end and thrust it menacingly at the eight shrouded figures kneeling around the base of the altar.

"What the hell's going on?" I snapped.

Bert Johnson eyed me with the contempt all true believers hold for all infidels. "Be quiet," he threatened.

The dull thump of the drum continued, now at decreasing intervals.

The dirge intensified.

The creatures milled about, openly restless yet somehow restrained in their three-sided cells.

The one at the altar worked himself into a frenzy. His warlike gestures became more and more aggressive, the thrusts at the shrouded ones now perilously close. Still, there was no movement.

"Damn it, Bert, what's going on?" The sound of my voice was all but drowned out by the increasing crescendo.

Creatures seemed to be emerging from out of nowhere, as if they were multiplying right before my eyes. Two of them, grunting, gesturing, performing some kind of grotesque and macabre dance, were dragging a protesting, kicking form toward the altar. It was young Gregory, his hands manacled, his face reduced to fleshy ribbons of torn tissue. He was pleading for them to stop.

They presented their beleaguered prize to the warlike creature at the altar. The end was swift, perhaps even merciful.

The thing lunged forward, and the barbed lance ripped savagely through the young officer's body. The dirge drowned out the officer's final screaming protest.

As the monster jerked the lance violently out of the lifeless body, the barb disgorged the useless entrails. The creatures were ecstatic.

The hollow beat of the drum continued. Through it all, the mournful dirge intensified.

My stomach had gone down under, trying to hide. Once again I couldn't breathe.

The supplicants were delighted with their barbaric presentation.

"My God, Bert, have you gone mad?" The question sounded stupid and pointless, but my senses were reeling.

Bert Johnson looked at me with glazed

eyes. "Korbac has again demonstrated his allegiance and has asked Sate to be released from the curse, granted dispensation from the bane of eternal atonement. The ritual was all for Sate, to show the Ancient of Ancients how he had defended the sacred sepulcher in the interval between the equinoctial awakenings."

"That thing . . . that grotesque, misshapen monster with the lance . . . is Korbac?"

Bert nodded solemnly and pointed to the sepulcher.

The beast's frenzied dance had ceased, and it cocked its bloated head to one side.

The dirge and drum stopped.

Silence.

The monster slowly approached the glass-topped sepulcher and peered in; its massive two-thumbed, three-fingered claws pressed down on the tomb's surface.

Suddenly the beast released an agonized wail of anguish. Its ugly head rolled back, the slitlike mouth opening to emit the terrifying sound. Then its head slumped forward, and it staggered back from the bizarre coffin in abject dejection.

"Sate has refused dispensation," Bert said solemnly.

Almost instantaneously, one of the beasts leaped from its granite cubicle, picked up the ceremonial lance and buried it savagely in Korbac's massive, scarred chest. Korbac slumped, staggered momentarily, righted himself and stoically withdrew the lance, all the while watching the black putrid fluids of his condemned body pump madly out onto the floor of the cave. Then it ceased.

One of the generals had tested Korbac, but the answer was clear. The curse continued.

Korbac, like his attacker, lumbered clumsily down the steps of the altar and back to his cubicle. Korbac buried his obscene face in his deformed paws and began to whimper.

The true believers were mesmerized.

Under most circumstances, I would have been as well, but another message was coming through loud and clear. There was a great more at stake here than the appeasement of a cult god. I didn't know exactly what the true believers had in mind for old Elliott, but whatever it was, I knew I was the only person inclined to put a stop to it.

The action wasn't well planned, nor was it all that subtle. Neither really matters, because I got away with it. While Bert and Angie were still caught up in the ritual that had just unfolded, I had slipped my trusty little Swiss army knife out of my pocket and used the butt end to crack one of the glass containers. Almost immediately the air was assailed by the pungent aroma of gasoline. Then I carefully extracted the other container and slipped it under my jacket.

For a moment I thought I had overdone

it. The pink, yellow fluid began to pool around us.

Suddenly the dirge began anew.

The drum beat was incessant.

Bert and Angie both bowed their heads again and, like the eight sentinels at the base of the altar, began to chant. This time the beasts did not join in with their mournful wail.

A clear, pure voice raised above all the rest, and I looked up, stunned. Polly was gliding toward the sepulcher; in her robed lap was a sterling silver tray. It was only then that the final piece of the puzzle tumbled into place. Polly was the Emissary.

At the base of the altar, she rose up out of her wheelchair and walked up the steps with her offering, placing it carefully on the lid of the coffin.

As Jake would have said, it had to end somewhere—and somewhere was here and now.

I bolted—not straight, but a zigzag pattern. I hadn't come all this way only to be denied one brief glance at the Ancient of Ancients. If anybody was ever going to live to say they had actually witnessed the disciple of evil, I had the best shot at it.

With one of the containers still spewing its high octane contents, I raced up the steps of the sepulcher. When I saw the suddenly alert Bert Johnson raise his gun, I heaved the leaking container straight at him. It shattered against the floor, spewing its contents all over him and Angie and just as quickly saturating the bank of torches illuminating the walls of the granite cubicles.

What I hadn't counted on was the size of the explosion.

The blast slammed me against the base of the altar, and I felt both legs fly out from under me. The ball of flame engulfed the cavern and raced up the walls of the cave, consuming the oxygen and blowing the timeless creatures from their stone cocoons like so many pieces of useless debris.

Bert Johnson was burned and bleeding, staggering toward me, screaming out Polly's name. He still clutched the oversized revolver. Angie was behind him on the floor, scorched, her gaping mouth belching out the last vestige of life.

Bert suddenly stopped, steadied himself and leveled the gun at me. It was his final gesture.

Bert fired, and I heaved the second container at the same time.

The ensuing explosion was louder, bigger and more devastating than the first. For one terrifying moment I was at ground zero. The cavern became a white hot world of blast furnace proportions. The tumbling, madly careening ball of flame swelled up until it consumed itself.

Bert Johnson was instantly incinerated. Choking, acrid gas and smoke filled the cavern, fanned by wild winds now roaring through the maze of connecting tunnels to fill the sudden vacuum.

Out of the corner of my eye I saw Polly. One moment she was there, the next she wasn't; only a charred, deformed, grotesque shape remained.

The walls began to rupture, spewing massive chunks of jagged granite and cascading a violent rain of rocks and debris down on the frenzied beasts.

My only refuge was the small space between the two stone supports for Sate's sepulcher. I buried my face in my arms, felt the searing heat and prayed.

There was a chain of explosions. Boulders and chunks and fragments of the subterranean world synthesized into a deadly rain of destruction.

And just as suddenly, it was over.

It was the ultimate irony. The sarcophagus of Sate, Ancient of Ancients, Force of the Consummate Evil, had been my protector.

The area was a choking world of dust and fog, the damp grayness rushing in to fill the void and mingling to form a mask, a cloud, a cloak. Then there was silence.

The carnage was indescribable.
Everything had been destroyed.
Slowly, almost frantically, I began to inch my way out from under the sepulcher and

claw my way through the rubble. The immensity of the situation was mind boggling.

I stood in a gray world void of detail and bathed in an eerie unreal silence. My numbed fingers fumbled along the length of the still intact utility belt looking for the flashlight until my fingers discovered it.

Praise the Lord, it worked.

The probing pale yellow beam ricocheted from one pile of rubble to the next. The scene was numbing. It resembled a battlefield. Charred remains of Korbac's army of generals were everywhere. The hooded true believers were now little more than piles of purposeless ashes. The still eviscerated mortal remains of the young officer Gregory were mercifully partially hidden by a jagged chunk of granite.

The final moments of Bert and Polly Johnson, along with the young woman called Angie, would forever remain a brooding secret. Little more than charred and twisted fragments of their once human forms remained.

I played the beam of light across the scene of devastation until my stomach revolted and the horrible realization of what I was witnessing stuck in my throat. As I slumped to my knees in the debris, I caught a barely perceptible movement out of the corner of my eye.

The beam of my flashlight snapped up

and captured it.

It was Kelto, his face shredded into meaty ribbons of tortured flesh. His arms were outstretched and draped between them was a shapeless tangle of rotted rags. He stared dumbly into the light.

"My God, Kelto," I blurted, "you're alive."

"Is that really you, Mr. Wages?" he sobbed.

It was then that I realized that his eyes were open, but there was no way for him to see. The blast had burned out his eyes.

"I have it," he stammered. "I have it right here in my hands."

I staggered through the rubble toward him.

"After the first explosion I came out of hiding and ran for the sepulcher. I managed to get it open. I grabbed Sate and held onto him." His tortured voice was almost ecstatic. Then the laughter faded away into agonized sobs. "Now I have him—have him right here in my arms—but now I can't see him. After all this time, I can't see him. Tell me, Mr. Wages, tell me—what does he look like? What does my tormentor look like?"

I shined the beam of my flashlight into the tangle of rotted rags.

It was a grotesque and macabre collection of human parts, a pile of rotted, foul-smelling human odds and ends, a putrid assemblage of what the true believers and Emissaries had surgically collected over the agonized years. It was the pathetic, sick attempts of the followers to give a man long since dead the attributes of life.

I looked up into Kelto's seared and useless eye sockets. Tears of frustration streamed down his anguished face.

"Tell me," he pleaded, "what does he look like?" Consummate agony had invaded his voice.

Then I realized, once again, every plot has one final twist, one final bit of bitter irony.

"You are a true believer, too, aren't you?"

Kelto sagged wearily to his knees in the debris. Racking sobs engulfed his frail body. The admission was barely audible. "I tried not to be," he quaked, "but as I walked in these very woods, plotting my revenge, the hatred began to dissipate. It was subtle at first, only a question, but then I realized why the beasts did not attack me. They somehow realized that I was an emerging vehicle of Sate, that without me and others like me there would be no release from their curse of atonement." His trembling voice trailed off. "You must tell me, what does he look like? How magnificent he must be. Imagine . . . in my arms, I shelter the Ancient of Ancients."

Those were the last words he uttered.

There was one last tortured breath, and then there was silence.

The cluttered tangle of decaying human

parts and mildewed rags trickled out of his arms and hands, spilling into the rubble and mingling with the dust.

For a moment I played the beam of light over Kelto's lifeless body and the barbarous collection of Sate's heathenish zealots.

Then I pulled myself together and began the long, arduous climb out.

PART 12
AN EPILOGUE

Cosmo's prickly sense of humor, coupled with his penchant for thoroughness in exploring every last detail, was beginning to get on my nerves. He had listened to the story of Chambers Bay, from start to finish, no less than five times. He was like an over-zealous lawyer, probing, poking, searching through the seemingly endless fragments, looking for something that would allow him to pronounce the whole affair just so much bullshit.

I knew the old curmudgeon too well.

"Okay," he harumphed, "then what happened?"

"I've told you a dozen times already," I moaned. Having to endure one of Cosmo's relentless interrogations is bad enough under any circumstances. But when you're flat on your back, staring up at the wild-haired old coot from a hospital bed, it's even worse than bad; it's downright devastating.

"So tell me again," he snarled.

"Like I said, Kelto was dead. I saw that stuff crumble out of his hands and decided there was nothing more I could do for him, so I started to crawl my way out of there. That must have been when I passed out."

"Then what?"

"I figure I must have been out for quite awhile, because when I came to, there was daylight streaming in on all that rubble."

Cosmo looked over at Lucy, precariously perched on the window sill, hastily scribbling notes.

"But you said this whole nightmare transpired in an underground cavern. How could you see daylight in an underground cavern?"

"Damn it, Cosmo, where have you been? Haven't you been listening? I told you the explosion turned out to be a lot bigger than any of us intended. It blew the top right out of that cavern, clean through to the surface. It was one helluva hole."

"It must have been a very large explosion," he repeated sarcastically.

"It was big," I sighed, "B-I-G, big." The fact that my voice elevated an octave or two tickled him, and a sneaky little smile worked at the corners of his mouth. He sauntered away from the side of the bed, took out his pipe and went through the whole maddening ritual. A cloud of billowy white encased his gnomelike face before he started in on me again.

"Then you came to and crawled out," he repeated, as though he had to remind me where I was in the stream of events.

"You got it," I snapped.

"Go on," he urged.

Time out. Let me draw you a somewhat clearer picture of my predicament. I am still battered, still bruised and still beaten. My face is a swollen montage of cuts, abrasions and tiny little sores where the good staff of the hospital have deemed fit to dig razorlike slivers of flint from my epidermis. There is an IV in my right arm, and my left arm, starting at the shoulder, is encased in miles of gauze and adhesive because of damage inflicted during my impromptu fireworks display. For four days I've had nothing but water and a paste the staff of this miserable hospital assures me is oatmeal. I am, to coin a phrase, not a happy person.

Now that you have that image securely tucked away, picture a bucolic old geezer with a crusty, somewhat impish manner, an individual devoid of the human response known as sympathy, browbeating a helpless patient—and you have some idea why I'm a trifle testy.

Add one grinning, gum-popping blonde graduate assistant who seemingly shares the old bastard's delight in my discomfort, and testy suddenly evolves into downright unpleasant.

There was, under the circumstances, nowhere for me to retreat, no place to hide and no sympathy. No cigarettes. No Black and White.

"Go on," he repeated.

"Go on where?" I grunted.

Cosmo gave me a glowering look. "It's quite obvious you were able to get out of your predicament, Elliott, so why don't you tell us about it?"

"Damn it, Cosmo, I already told you that story half a dozen times."

"Then once more won't hurt, will it?"

Lucy snickered.

Finally, I gave in. "In all honesty, I don't remember much detail. I do remember I was surprised at the degree of destruction and all those creatures buried under tons of rubble. They were just blown away."

"Go on," he insisted.

"Somehow I managed to crawl out of that tomb." My mind reluctantly began to pull back the curtain, and I started to relive the nightmare. I could again see myself standing amidst the carnage, living with the paradox of the lifting fog, listening to the ominous sound of an approaching storm, feeling the fresh breeze coming in off the lake and rushing down into the abysmal pit. Then my mind leapfrogged ahead to the devastation in the village itself when I realized that the collapsing caves had swallowed up most of the village in the chain of explosions. It was like I was suddenly catapulted into a surrealistic painting.

"You said the town itself was gone?"

"Most of it." I nodded. "There were just a few stunned villagers stumbling around in a daze. They said the earth just opened up and swallowed most of them."

The smile had faded from Lucy's now sober face.

"Did you tell the people what happened?"

"There wasn't anybody to tell."

This time Cosmo had no comeback.

"When the disaster teams finally got there, I told them there had been an explosion and that there were only a few survivors, most of whom had no idea what had happened."

"Did you tell them everything?"

"I told them nothing. If you arrived on the scene of a catastrophe like that and some half-crazed man started telling you about apelike creatures with two thumbs and three fingers that ate people, what would you do?"

"I'd lock him up so he wouldn't hurt himself," Cosmo acknowledged.

"Precisely. That's why I couldn't tell them what really happened at Chambers Bay."

"What about the woman?" Lucy asked. "You haven't told us about her."

The words had to snake around the lump in my throat. The price to bring an end to centuries of nightmare had come high. In a matter of a few short days I had developed a real fondness for the man called Jake Madden—and in the case of Brenda Cashman, it was something even more than that. It would be a long time before I forgot the woman-girl with the jeans with the hole in the knee. I closed my eyes and hoped against hope that the thought would somehow hurt a little less in the darkness.

"I suppose she suffered the same fate as the rest of them," I whispered.

Lucy drifted over to the side of my bed, shuffling through a fistful of scraps of paper. "I know you don't want to get into all of this now, but there are a lot of loose ends we need to take care of."

I nodded my understanding, but for the moment, as far as I was concerned, the world outside that hospital door could go straight to hell on a unicycle. It was going to be a while before E.G. Wages gave the matters of the living a high priority.

Lucy was more pragmatic. "I called Milt and told him the Z was blown up in an accident. He wanted some details, so I made some up. He'll send you a check in the next couple of days."

"No hurry," I said, somewhat ascerbically.

Lucy was undaunted. "I called the Dean. He'll rearrange your lecture schedule." She finished and graced me with a cherubic grin. "Now you're supposed to say 'nicely done, good and faithful graduate assistant'."

"Nicely done," I muttered. Under the layers of gauze I was appreciating all her efforts. "Don't know what I'd do without you," I managed.

Lucy's smile intensified. Suddenly she glanced at her watch, and the smile curdled into a frown. "Oh, good grief," she sputtered, "I was supposed to be in Doctor Carlson's office twenty minutes ago." She picked up her jacket, blew me a kiss and started for the door. "Don't wait up on me," she said grinning.

Cosmo waited for the door to close then propped his slightly stooped frame up against the wall next to the bed. "Man to man, Elliott, how do you feel? I mean inside, where it counts."

In all the years I had known Cosmo Leach, I had never known the man to be so solicitous. So I took it for an honest question and decided it deserved something more than the standard flip repartee that tended to dominate our mentor-student conversations.

It seemed appropriate to preface my confession with a sigh. "It's gonna hurt for a while," I admitted. "I feel especially bad about Brenda Cashman. I knew from the start that I shouldn't have taken her with me. If I'd have followed through on all of this like a sane man instead of dragging her out to Chambers Bay with me, she'd still be alive. Maybe I'll get smart one of these days and take your advice. Get myself a little hideaway on some pristine little pond and spend the rest of my days contemplating my inverted navel."

"So that's what's at the bottom of all this," Cosmo grunted. "A woman! It had to be more than you were telling us. You've been through worse."

I nodded.

Still, Cosmo lingered, and I knew from experience that there was even more on his mind, maybe something he hadn't told me. Finally he harumphed and pushed himself away from the wall. "Even if you're not ready for this, I still think you should know." He walked solemnly to the door, opened it and spoke to someone standing in the hall. "Would you come in now?"

A shadow fell across the bed first, and the doorway was suddenly filled with a young, round woman with coal black hair and a full face half-hidden by large, horn-rimmed glasses. The face was dominated by a look of concern. She entered the room tentatively, carrying a small brown paper-wrapped package.

"You have company, Elliott," Cosmo informed me. "I suggest you sit up and act like a gentleman."

"Hi," the young woman said nervously.

"Do I know you?" I stammered, suddenly fearing that one of Korbac's grunting, foul-smelling generals had permanently altered one of my memory cells.

She didn't answer.

Cosmo stepped forward. "Elliott," he began cautiously, "I want you to meet the real Brenda Cashman."

The words raced repeatedly through several reference files in the E.G. Wages bank of cerebral clutter and kept sending back the same messages: "Does not compute." It took me a while before I managed to get the words out. "Did you say Brenda Cashman?"

The young woman grinned and nodded.

"When Lucy couldn't get through to you in Chambers Bay, she called me," Cosmo explained. "That's when I learned that you took Brenda with you. I, in turn, called an associate of mine in Ann Arbor. I had him do some checking. Within a matter of hours Brenda returned my call. You see, Elliott, it didn't hang together. The Brenda Cashman I knew wasn't the kind to go flitting around the countryside on the kind of insane jaunts you take."

Still grinning, the young woman confirmed Cosmo's assessment.

"But if you're Brenda Cashman," I sputtered, "who was . . . ?"

"Her name was Adair Lindley. Like the real Brenda Cashman here, she was a doctoral candidate at the U of M, not to mention Brenda's roommate."

"I still don't understand," I protested.

The real Brenda Cashman was eager to clear up the confusion. "I really did discover the similarities in the events that traced all the way back to Choker Point on Baffin Island. I discussed it several times with Adair. We always discussed our research. She was interested, but no more than usual. Then one day I discovered all my research notes on the incidents were gone. She pretended to help me look for them, and we finally decided I had lost them somewhere on the campus. About two weeks later, she disappeared—no note, no nothing. Up to that point we always told each other where we were going. Now that I think back about it, she was a little strange at times but a really nice girl. I really liked her. All the while she was gone I figured she'd come waltzing in one day and tell me what she had been up to."

I was too stunned to say anything.

The real Brenda Cashman wasn't through. "So when Doctor Leach and I talked, it got me to thinking. I started snooping around."

"This is what I wanted you to see," Cosmo harumphed.

Brenda began to peel away the wrapping of her tightly held package. When she finished, she reached in and emerged with a small coarse brown figurine of a grotesquely shaped creature with a bloated belly. It was a replica of the sarcophagus of Sate. She held it out for my inspection. "It was sitting on the top shelf of her closet next to a small vase with a sprig of pine and a single tapered candle."

All of a sudden it was difficult to breathe. Brenda's hand again darted into the package and again emerged, this time with a crumpled piece of paper. "Cosmo thinks you should see this."

I read:

ADAIR LINDLEY—
YOU AMONG THE MANY ARE CHOSEN. PREPARE YOURSELF FOR THE COMING OF THE ANCIENT OF ANCIENTS. THE EQUINOCTIAL AWAKENING OF THE YEAR '87 WILL NOT GO WELL. LEARN FROM THIS. AS EMISSARY OF THE NEXT FULL CYCLE, YOU AND YOU ALONE CAN ASSURE ATONEMENT.

I let the piece of paper flutter down on

my bed.

Suddenly it all made sense. I found nothing because there was nothing to find. They had not perished in the explosion after all. They had simply moved on to begin a new cycle. The cycle was destined to be repeated—somewhere, sometime.

BLACK DEATH
by R. Karl Largent

THE PLAGUE

It rose from the grave of a long-forgotten ceme-tery—virulent, malignant, brutally infectious.

THE VICTIMS

The people of Half Moon Bay began to die, their bodies twisted in agonizing pain, their skin rup-tured and torn, their blood turned to a thick, viscous ooze. Once they contracted the disease, death was near—but it could not come quickly enough to ease their exquisite suffering. There was no antidote, no cure, for the . . .

BLACK DEATH

What God created in six days, the plague could destroy in seven. And time was running out . . .

____2591-4 $3.95US/$4.95CAN